WHO LET THE GODS OUT?

WHO
LET THE
GODS
OUT?

Maz Evans

Chicken House

SCHOLASTIC INC. / NEW YORK

First published in the United Kingdom in 2017 by Chicken House, 2 Palmer Street, Frome, Somerset BA11 1DS.

The publisher does not have any control over and does not assume any responsibility for author or third-party websites or their content.

Library of Congress Cataloging-in-Publication Data available

ISBN 978-1-338-06556-5

10 9 8 7 6 5 4 3 2 1   17 18 19 20 21

Printed in the U.S.A.   23

First edition, April 2017

Book design by Mary Claire Cruz

For Ian
Who thinks like Athene
Loves like Aphrodite
And marries like Zeus

You are a God amongst men.

LYING LOW

It began on a Friday, as strange things often do. This particular Friday turned out to be stranger than most, although it had started normally enough. Elliot Hooper got up at 7:30 a.m. as normal, made his mom breakfast at 8:15 a.m. as normal, went to school at 8:55 a.m. as normal, and was in the headmaster's office by 9:30 a.m., which was, in fact, slightly later than normal.

"Oh, Elliot," sighed Graham Sopweed, headmaster of Brysmore Grammar School. "What are we going to do with you?"

Elliot scratched his shaggy blond head. He figured that "excuse me from school forever and make me Lord High Emperor of the Universe" wouldn't be deemed an acceptable answer, so he said nothing.

"You seem rather . . . distracted lately," said Mr. Sopweed to fill the silence. "Is everything okay? Is anything wrong at school? Or at home?"

Elliot avoided his headmaster's concerned stare. School was . . . well, it was school. Annoying, boring, pointless. Nothing new there. But home? That was a different story . . .

"I'm fine," he said after a lengthy pause. "Thank you, sir."

"Oh, Elliot." Mr. Sopweed sighed again, nervously flicking his floppy gray fringe. "You know you can call me Graham. Let's all use the names our mothers gave us."

There were many more creative names for Brysmore's headmaster than the one his mother gave him, but the politest by far was Call Me Graham.

A shout outside nearly made the jumpy headmaster fall off his chair. Elliot couldn't help but feel sorry for Call Me Graham. There were many theories at school as to why he was such a bag of nerves, not all of them started by Elliot. Some said it was because his wife had left him. Others said it was because she hadn't. Elliot's favorite was that Call Me Graham was actually a serial killer on the run. He could imagine the appeals on the news: *So be on your guard against Graham Sopweed, the Cardigan-Clad Killer, and be sure to call this number if he's bored someone you know to death . . .*

"The . . . the . . . the thing is, Elliot, everyone at Brysmore wants to help you to achieve your fullest potential," Call Me Graham went on.

"Mmm. Not everyone, sir," muttered Elliot.

"Whatever do you mean?" squealed Call Me Graham, nearly pulling a button off his cardigan. "Everyone at Brysmore is committed to encouraging, nurturing, and inspiring every pupil in our care. We're always here for a friendly word, helpful advice, or to make sure we know—"

"WHERE IS THAT SNIVELING RUNT OF A PATHETIC EXCUSE FOR A BOY?!"

The office door blasted open with a furious roar, making Call Me Graham scream like a kitten on a roller coaster.

Elliot was all too familiar with that loathsome voice.

"Ah—hello," whimpered Call Me Graham. "As you can see, I am just having a little chat with Elliot . . ."

"Hooper," sneered the new arrival, lurching up behind Elliot's chair and polluting his airspace with weapons-grade body odor.

There was only one person who could make Elliot's surname sound like a dirty word. It was Mr. Boil, head of history, Brysmore's deputy headmaster and, unless there was a schoolmaster somewhere on the planet who minced his students into sausages, the world's worst teacher.

Boil was a stumpy, piggy little man who was the only person Elliot knew with fat eyes. He squashed them behind a pair of thick, bottle-lensed glasses and glared at his pupils like most people look at used cat litter, as if he had a permanently nasty smell under his nose. (In fairness, he did— his own.)

His few remaining strands of dark, greasy hair were pasted over the top of his head, held in place by hope alone. To the naked eye, Mr. Boil had three chins, but who knew how many more were lurking beneath his shirt, which always smelled like three-week-old vegetable soup? He truly hated everyone, but reserved a special revulsion for Elliot, who had been getting up his pudgy nose for the past year.

"Sir?" asked Elliot, innocently.

"Don't you 'sir' me, Hooper," growled Boil, bringing his sweaty face inches from Elliot's own. "What you did in my assembly was disgraceful, disrespectful, and downright disgusting!"

"Yes, we were just getting on to that . . ." stammered Graham.

"He disgraced the Brysmore name!" roared Boil. "He shamed himself! He shamed the school! He ruined my brilliant PowerPoint presentation on Napoleon's favorite socks! He—"

"He fell asleep," said Call Me Graham quietly, looking at Elliot's pale face and dark-rimmed eyes. "Let's try to keep a little perspective, Mr. Boil. This isn't the first time this has happened lately, Elliot. Why are you so tired?"

"Pah!" spat Boil. "Out all hours terrorizing old ladies, I expect! Or playing violent computer games until dawn! Or putting my underpants up the school flagpole! Again!"

Elliot tried not to smirk at the memory of his all-time favorite prank—which Boil knew but could never prove—that Elliot was responsible for last year. But pranks were long gone. These days Elliot couldn't afford any more trouble.

"Hooper!" shouted Boil. "The headmaster asked you a question! Don't be so disrespectful . . . !"

"It's quite all right," whispered Call Me Graham, "Elliot can take all the time he—"

"SHUT UP, GRAHAM!" shouted Boil over his shoulder, his chubby eyes not leaving Elliot's face. "And look at the state of you! When was the last time that shirt saw an iron? A tramp would turn his nose up at those shoes. And if I've told you once about that pocket watch—jewelry is forbidden at Brysmore . . . Well—come on, then! Let's hear your pathetic excuse!"

"Yes, talk to us, Elliot. Perhaps we can help," said Graham kindly. "You're only twelve, after all. We don't expect you to get everything right."

Elliot's fingers instinctively tightened around the old watch in his pocket. For a moment, he considered telling the truth. Perhaps his headmaster could help him? Elliot certainly didn't know what to do. Maybe if he just explained about . . .

But as soon as the thought formed in his head, he silently crushed it. Elliot had to keep what was happening at home a secret. Telling anyone was far too risky.

"Mr. Boil's right, sir," said Elliot, the lie jamming in his throat. "I keep staying up late playing computer games. It's all my own fault."

"You see!" wobbled Boil triumphantly, punching the air with an arm the size of a fatty leg of lamb and knocking Call Me Graham backward off his chair. "I knew it!"

"Do you have nothing to say in your defense, Elliot?" asked Call Me Graham from the floor. "Anything else we should know?"

"No, sir," Elliot mumbled.

"I tell you what he needs to know," sneered Boil with a grin that could curdle custard. "He's failing at this school. His grades have dropped across the board. And if he doesn't get eighty-five percent in all the end-of-term exams, he's out of Brysmore for good. You've got my mock history test on Monday, Hooper. That should give you a much-needed kick up the—"

"Thank you, Mr. B-Boil," stuttered Call Me Graham.

Elliot's heart sank at the reminder of the exams he was sure to fail. He tried to find time to study at home, he really did.

"Please, Elliot," said Call Me Graham. "Let us help you."

As he looked into the kindly eyes of his cowardly headmaster, Elliot once again considered telling the truth about home, about Mom. He didn't know how much longer he could carry on like this. It was getting to be too much.

"I . . . it's just . . . sometimes . . ." he began, searching for impossible words.

"Detention!" bellowed Boil, as he lumbered jubilantly out of the office. "Hooper—see me after school!"

2

HOME IS WHERE THE FARM IS

At 4:30 p.m., when Elliot had arranged all the books in the history department into alphabetical order for Boil's detention, he finally made it outside into the darkening but still very welcome evening air. The crowds of proud parents eager to drive their children home had long since left, but no one had been there for Elliot earlier and no one was there for him now. No one ever was. With a quick backward glance, Elliot dived off the driveway, hopped over the school fence into the fields beyond, and started the long walk home.

The stroll back to Home Farm was Elliot's favorite part of his day. Or it was on dry days—when it was pouring with rain he didn't feel the love for the mile-long hike. But today was one of those mild early-winter evenings that made him content simply to wander through the fields as the stars assembled above.

He raised his head to feel the fresh air on his face, but his peace was interrupted by a gaggle of Brysmore girls walking in the opposite direction, pointing and staring at Elliot before retreating behind their hands in giggling fits.

Had Elliot listened to these, or any of the other silly girls at school, he would have known that he was considered one of the better-looking boys at Brysmore. But he didn't listen to what anyone said and he didn't care what anyone thought. He went through his school life—most of his life, in fact—on his own. There was a time when he'd enjoyed hanging out with his mates and might have been considered quite popular. But things had changed. Right now he didn't have time for friends. And besides, friends had parents. And parents asked too many questions.

Elliot arrived at Home Farm just as the stars started to rule the night sky. They were especially bright tonight, and cast their dreamy glow over the ancient stone circle of Stonehenge, which was just visible from his front gate. The mysterious stones looked magical in the glistening light, and Elliot drank in his favorite view. He lifted the rope that held the rotting gate in place and dragged his tired feet up the path. He and Mom had laid those stones together, and every crooked step reminded Elliot of them flinging mud at each other in fits of giggles as they worked.

The farm had been his family's home for generations. He could see the holes where fallen tiles made the roof look like a mouth missing some teeth, the dirty windows that blocked more light than they let in, and the peeling red paint on a door that could barely keep out a draft, let alone a burglar. And Elliot loved every crumbling brick.

He put his key in the lock—a pointless exercise for a door that could be knocked in by a strong cough—but before he could push it open, a terrible screech erupted behind him.

"Coo-eeee! Have you got a sec, poppet?"

There were so many irritating words in that sentence, but none as irritating as their speaker. Elliot slapped on a fake grin and turned around.

"Hello, Mrs. Porshley-Plum," he called in his least sincere voice.

"Hello, pickle!" Patricia Porshley-Plum shrieked in return, using one of the countless stupid nicknames she used in place of anyone's real name. "Have you got a seccy?"

"I'll have to be quick—I need to—"

"Gre-eat!" squealed Patricia as she approached the house, tottering slightly as the heels on her shoes struggled with both the uneven path and the ample backside they were supporting. "Shall we go in for a cup of tea?"

"I'd love to," Elliot lied as he shut the door behind him, "but Mom's got another stomach bug."

"Oh, no, sugarplum!" Mrs. Porshley-Plum pouted dramatically, her dark-pink lipstick making her mouth look like a monkey's bottom. "Perhaps I should come in and see her?"

"It's contagious," said Elliot quickly, running out of imaginary illnesses to keep his mother safe from this annoying neighbor. "And squishy. And smelly. Seriously. Stay away."

"I see," said Patricia, her narrow eyes scanning every inch of her young neighbor, as if she could spot the lie on his shirt. Patricia's mouth always smiled, but her eyes never did. She straightened her tweed jacket over her generous hips. "Well, when she's feeling better, we must have That Chat," she added with a ridiculous wink.

Patricia had been trying to have That Chat with Elliot's mom, Josie, for a while. At Nan's funeral the previous year, she had whispered to Josie at the graveside about her new property-development business and how the farm was sitting on a valuable piece of land.

When the doctor came to Grandad's bedside six months later, Mrs. Porshley-Plum popped by the next day and made an offer for the farm to "get him into a decent nursing home."

The morning that Elliot and Josie laid Grandad to rest, Patricia Porshley-Plum called to say that if they fancied moving on, now that the two of them were completely alone in the world, she'd happily take the farm off their hands for a quick sale.

"Patricia Horse's-Bum will never get her hands on this family's home!" Josie had raged that night. "She can keep her plastic houses for her plastic people! This is a real family home for a real family and if she thinks she can flash her cash and move us out then she can stick her checkbook right up her—."

Elliot smiled at the memory of his mom's rude suggestion. But she was right. This was their home and Elliot needed to protect it. He just didn't have a clue how.

"I'd better go and see to Mom—lovely to see you, Mrs. Horse's . . . Mrs. Porshley-Plum," he said.

"And you, sweet-cheeks," trilled Patricia. "Get Momsy to call me—aaargh!"

Maybe it was the crooked paving stones, the ridiculous heels, or because her nose was stuck so far in the air she couldn't see where she was going, but Patricia Porshley-Plum crashed down on the path like a newborn foal on roller skates, spilling herself and the contents of her handbag all over it.

"Let me help you," Elliot offered. "I'll get these for you." He picked up the mysterious items that fill a lady's handbag and replaced nearly all of them. "Here you go," he said, giving the overflowing bag back to the world's most irritating neighbor.

"Thank you. I'll see you soon," said Patricia, her eyes smiling even less than usual as she turned and staggered down the rest of the path, finally leaving Elliot to make it into his house.

Once his front door had closed on the world, Elliot took a moment to rest against it. Home. At last.

He dropped his schoolbag next to the pile of mail on the mat and picked up the letters. All were reminders about unpaid bills. As if he needed reminding.

"Mom?" he called softly in case she was enjoying a nap. "I'm home."

He peered around the door into the cozy living room, but Mom wasn't in her usual battered armchair by the fireplace. Elliot checked the kitchen, Mom's bedroom, and tentatively knocked on all the bathroom doors, but there was no reply to his gentle calls.

With a dark fear rising through his veins, Elliot started to look more frantically, flinging open doors and running through rooms.

"Mom!" he shouted. "Mom—where are you?"

He desperately searched every corner of the farmhouse, even looking under the beds. Racing past the kitchen for a third time, Elliot's stomach tightened into a familiar knot. The back door was ajar. His heart plummeted.

It had happened again. Mom had disappeared.

A STAR IS BORN

"Virgo! Virgo! Wake up!"

"*Brrlpmpmgh*—pencil sharpeners!" burbled Virgo, her long silver hair flopping over her face as she woke with a start in the middle of the Zodiac Council meeting.

"Whatever are you babbling about, child?" grumbled Pisces, the large fish whose turn it was to chair the council in November. "So have you done it?"

Virgo tucked her hair neatly behind her ears and fidgeted slightly in her sumptuous red chair—sofa, really—one of twelve that surrounded the circular golden table, which was elaborately engraved with every councillor's zodiac sign.

She had only been half listening as the other eleven members of the council (twelve if you counted the Gemini twins separately) discussed whether to renew Dionysus's liquor license, and if the Cyclopes were entitled to half-price eye care. Her mind had started to wander, as it frequently did these days, to what life might be like outside Elysium, her heavenly home above the Earth's clouds.

This was absolutely *not* because there was anything wrong. Not at all! Virgo's life, like her, was completely perfect.

Administering the immortal community was, after all, an immense privilege—the Zodiac Council had been appointed by Zeus himself when he and the other Olympians retired. Now it was responsible for organizing every aspect of immortal life, from government to garage sales.

But however scintillating it was to ensure that sea nymphs had regulation swimming goggles, or that chimeras' smoke alarms were tested quarterly, Virgo found herself wondering if there wasn't something . . . else? Nearly two thousand years in the same job looked excellent on the résumé, but it was possibly getting slightly . . . less than fascinating. Immortal life was a gift, a miracle, a blessing. It just went on a bit.

"Virgo!" shouted Pisces, snapping her out of her daydream. "So have you done it?"

Virgo tried to look as if she'd been listening, but realized that either answer could be wrong. Deciding that no response was better than the incorrect one—Virgo was *never* incorrect—she shrugged a bemused apology.

"For goodness' sake, child, pay attention!" snapped Pisces, a frustrated bubble escaping his pink lips. "The Muses need that stationery order right away! It's no use being the source of all creativity if you can't find a paper clip!"

"Yes—absolutely right—of course," said Virgo, picking up her golden quill and scratching "paper clips" on a piece of parchment. A job. Excellent. That should keep her busy for . . .

She looked out of the council chamber's glass pyramid at another perfect day in her perfect home above the clouds. She knew how lucky she was—after all, who wouldn't want to live in paradise? It was, well, perfect. Once the council's business was done for the day—perhaps she'd fly a unicorn over the marshmallow meadows? Or swim with the dolphins in the warm waters of Honey River? Or possibly ride the roller coasters at Wonderland? Or maybe not—she'd done all of those things yesterday. Or was it the day before? Or last week maybe? Virgo couldn't remember, and there was no one to remind her. But that was fine. Her life *was* completely perfect. And if she'd had any friends to talk to, she would have told them exactly that.

"So if we're happy to agree that Pan can do another stadium tour—so long as he stops by eleven p.m. so he doesn't upset the Furies—then I think that's everything . . ." said Pisces. "Ah. No. One more thing. Prisoner Forty-Two."

A chorus of moans rang around the chamber as Pisces produced a small golden flask.

Virgo's ears pricked up. She'd always liked the sound of this job. It required a Zodiac Councillor to deliver a dose of ambrosia to an immortal prisoner on Earth. It was particularly unpopular among the council, none of whom wanted to leave the warmth and comfort of Elysium to visit the cold and dirty mortal realm. But as the youngest councillor, Virgo had never yet been allowed to go. Her mind started to buzz with excitement as she shot her hand up.

"Any volunteers?" Pisces asked.

Virgo waved her hand in the air, letting out a strained grunt as she tried not to shout out.

"Anyone?" said Pisces, somehow oblivious to Virgo nearly exploding right in front of him. "Anyone at all?"

At that moment, every other pair of eyes in the chamber had somewhere else to look. Whether it was something fascinating they had written down, something out of the window, or an imaginary speck of dust (of course no such thing existed in Elysium) on their purple robes, not one of them met the fish's glassy gaze.

Virgo stretched her left arm as high as it could reach, supporting it with her right to get some extra height.

"There must be someone," sighed Pisces.

"Me! Me! Let me!" Virgo blurted out. "I mean . . . I could perform this task proficiently."

The laughter of her colleagues echoed perfectly around the chamber.

"Don't be ridiculous," snorted Aries, the golden ram. "You're only a child."

"I'm one thousand nine hundred and sixty-four!" Virgo challenged, to an outpouring of "Aw, bless your heart" from her colleagues.

"No," declared Pisces finally. "This is an important job for an *experienced* councillor. You stick to your paper clips."

"But I—"

"Enough!" snapped Pisces. "My decision is final."

Virgo accepted this perfectly wise and fair decision without question. Curiously, at exactly that same moment, her golden quill snapped in her hands.

"Well, then, if we have no other offers, I volunteer Taurus," said Pisces to the bull, who was crocheting a scarf with his horn.

"Me?" whined Taurus. "It can't be my turn again. Capricorn's never done it."

"Oh, yes I have," snorted the indignant half-goat Capricorn, spitting out the pencil she had been chewing. "I had to do it in the middle of a plague. The place stank. If anyone's been shirking, it's Pincer-Pants over there."

"Put a sock in it, you old goat!" yelled Cancer the crab. "I went during the Norman Conquest—I caught so many arrows in my shell I looked like a hedgehog! What about Castor and Pollux? Just because they're one constellation shouldn't mean they get only one turn."

"Get lost," huffed the Gemini twins simultaneously and, before long, as so often happened at council meetings, an earsplitting fight had broken out around the golden table.

"Take that, you big drip," yelled Scorpio as he hurled Libra's scales at Aquarius, who threw his water jug at Aries, accidentally hitting Cancer and earning himself a very personal nip from her pincers.

"Shut it, Goldilocks!" shouted Sagittarius the centaur, who fired a banana from his bow, splattering squashed fruit all over Leo's flowing mane.

Virgo surveyed the unfolding carnage with a sigh.

And then something strange happened.

Virgo was perfectly aware that she had the perfect life in the perfect home. But at that precise moment, she knew that it was the perfect time to leave.

Dodging the flying insults, fruit, and body parts, she quietly picked up the golden flask, slipped it into her purple robes, and backed out of the council chamber.

The moment Virgo's feet touched the cloud outside, she began to run, picking up superhuman speed with every step. As soon as she reached the edge of the clouds, she threw her arms wide open, which immediately transformed her into her starry Virgo constellation. She felt the exhilarating rush and familiar warmth radiating through her as her body melted into a million glimmering stars from the feet up, and she whooshed into the air before plunging down through the clouds into the realm of Earth.

This was as far as she'd ever been from home. There was still time to turn back—perhaps this was a mistake? But then, Virgo reasoned, she never made mistakes. She was perfect. So this must be the right thing to do.

She blasted into the Earth's night sky, feeling gloriously happy and free. She'd heard so much about this realm, and as she looked down she could see that, yes—it *was* extraordinary.

One minute she was flying over dense jungle pulsing with every species of creature imaginable; the next, vast deserts with no life in sight for thousands of miles. Some parts were filled with tall buildings and moving lights, others with nothing but empty and desolate wastelands. Strange scents filled her lungs—fresh green grass, salty ocean air, frozen mountain dew. She circled the Earth countless times, noticing different details every time she went from day to night—from the wonderful to the worrying to the downright weird. The diversity was endless. Everything was just so . . . new. Not perfect, like her home—just different.

Indeed, Virgo was so excited by this journey of discovery that it took her a while to realize she was missing one useful piece of information.

She had no idea where she was supposed to go.

Virgo racked her brain for any details she'd gleaned from other councillors. Leo had once mentioned that Prisoner Forty-Two was held on a small island in the north, peopled with an eccentric breed of mortals who liked to drink tea and stand in lines. And Taurus had said that the spot was marked by a stone circle. But up high in the darkness, she couldn't make anything out.

She decided to drop a little to get a closer look, and soon she could distinguish the tiny mortals scuttling around like ants below. What would it be like to meet one? she wondered. But, no—that was against the rules. And Virgo always obeyed the rules. Well. Nearly always.

Finally, after she'd spent hours rocketing around the night sky, the stone circle leapt out at her in the darkness.

How considerate of the mortals to light it up for us, she thought happily, and started to make her descent.

This was all going to work out perfectly. She'd be back in Elysium for supper. What could possibly go wrong?

4

MOM'S THE WORD

Elliot didn't know what to do. He couldn't find Mom anywhere and it was now completely dark. He considered calling the police. But if they found Mom before he did . . . Where could she have gone this time?

He ran into the kitchen for the tenth time, trying to keep the sickening panic at bay. He would find her. He always did.

In that moment of reason, he finally noticed her pink gardening gloves on the kitchen table. He grabbed his coat—and Mom's—and headed out to the fields.

As he ran across the farm, he could just discern a tiny figure in the darkness up ahead. He breathed a sigh of relief. There was Mom, kneeling on the grass, happily planting vegetables in the empty field.

On his approach, he could hear her chatting away to the empty space, occasionally breaking into a cheery song. He remembered a time when Mom had seemed so much bigger than him, when one of her hugs could smother him in a warm embrace of rose-scented love, lit up by her wicked laugh.

"I blew into England on a breeze," she would giggle in an accent that wasn't familiar and wasn't strange. "I am a child of the world!"

It made her seem almost magical. But these days she seemed so small, so fragile, so . . . old. Elliot wished he'd asked her more about her life while he'd had the chance.

Elliot hurried over to where Mom was busily digging and slipped her coat gently over her shoulders. She turned around and her face shone in a hundred places, as it always did when she saw him. She pushed her messy brown hair out of her face and reached up to give her boy a hug.

"So how was your day?" She smiled.

"Really great," Elliot lied. "Top of the class in history."

"You're so clever, Elly," she laughed, rubbing some soil on his nose.

"Must take after you, Mom. So what are you plant—"

He stopped as he realized what his mother was doing. A packet of unopened carrot seeds lay by her side and she was putting the final loving touches to planting a row of clothespins. Elliot's heart plummeted. She was doing it again.

"Come on, Mom, it's cold. Let's get you inside."

Elliot helped her up and gently guided her back toward the house. He settled her in the living room, lit the fire, and went to the kitchen to prepare their supper.

Elliot couldn't pinpoint exactly when Mom started acting strangely. She'd always been strange, but in a good way— dancing around stores or doing handstands in the street. But something had changed. The last year had passed in such a blur of worrying about Nan and Grandad when they were ill, then grieving for them when they died, that he hadn't really noticed Mom's odd behavior until a few months ago.

It began with small things—she'd lose something she'd had two minutes ago, or she couldn't remember the name of a person or a place. At first, Elliot thought these were the normal short circuits of a stressed and tired mind. But the memory lapses soon became more serious—forgetting there was food in the oven or leaving the bath running. Then one day, Elliot came home from school and Mom was nowhere to be found. He ran down the path to the village and found her in the middle of the road in her nightgown, lost and confused with no idea where she lived. He couldn't ignore it any longer—Mom needed his help.

By doing all the shopping, cooking, and housework, Elliot had convinced himself that everything was going to be okay. But deep down he knew that Mom needed a doctor. Her mind was unwell. And it was getting worse.

But it wasn't that simple. What if a doctor said Mom was too ill to look after him? What if they took her away? What would happen to him then?

Elliot had no other family. He didn't even know if his dad was alive. Elliot and his mother had always lived with his grandparents, and Elliot knew only two things about his father: he'd given Elliot his pocket watch as a baby, and he wasn't there now. Elliot never knew where he had gone, nor why, and whenever he asked, Mom would get upset and say he was too young to understand.

"Now's not the time," she'd say, holding his face in her hands. "One day I'll explain everything."

Elliot wasn't sure now if that day would ever come. Besides, his mother and grandparents had made him happier than any dad could have. His dad obviously didn't care about him, so he wasn't going to care back. Elliot quickly checked his pocket to make sure the watch hadn't fallen out when he'd run outside.

No, it was better this way. Mom had looked after him all his life and now it was his turn to look after her. If he could just keep everyone else's noses out, they'd be fine. Really.

Elliot opened the kitchen cupboard, even though he knew exactly what it contained. A box of tea bags, some stale cookies, three small cans of beans, and half a loaf of bread. He looked in the chipped cookie jar that guarded their weekly spending money and counted the remaining £3.76 inside. He put the twenty pounds he had "borrowed" from Mrs. Porshley-Plum's handbag into the jar and added an IOU to all the other notes reminding him that he needed to pay someone back. He'd had to "borrow" a lot of money lately. There were a lot of IOUs in the jar.

Nan and Grandad had never trusted banks and the farm used to provide most of their food, so they kept their life savings in a box under the bed. Elliot was careful to use as little of the money as he could, but he knew it was running out and there were only so many vegetables he and Mom could grow. Over time, the farmworkers had left and the animals were sold—all except Bessie, the lame cow Elliot had raised from a calf, who lived in the derelict cowshed across the paddock.

Elliot's early-morning paper route brought in a bit of money, but there was barely enough for the basics, let alone the expensive things he needed for school. He remembered Mr. Boil's moan about his uniform and made a mental note to sew some buttons on his only shirt and polish the shoes that had been too tight since Easter.

"Beans on toast all right for dinner, Mom?" he called through to the living room.

"Lovely, baby, haven't had that for a while," she replied cheerfully.

Mom's forgetfulness worried Elliot a lot. But if it stopped her from remembering that beans on toast had been their supper every night for the past three weeks, perhaps it wasn't all bad.

He made their meal and they snuggled in front of their small black-and-white TV to watch a cooking competition Mom enjoyed on Friday nights. She used to be an amazing cook and Elliot laughed as she colorfully insulted the contestants' efforts.

"I wouldn't serve that with a tennis racket," she yelled at one woman's attempt at a Baked Alaska.

But by nine o'clock, Mom was falling asleep in her chair—she slept a lot these days. Elliot gently woke her and helped her upstairs. He laid her nightgown out on the bed, left the room while she changed, then came back to say good night.

"Do you have everything you need?" he asked as he always did when he tucked the sheets around her.

"Do I have you?" she asked with a sleepy smile.

"Always," whispered Elliot.

"Then what more could I want?" whispered Josie as she pulled him into a hug. "Good night, my little miracle."

He stayed for a few moments until Mom fell asleep, then crept quietly out of the room and shut the door.

Elliot returned to the empty living room, cleared away the supper things, and sank down into the comfy armchair. He clicked open the gold cover of his pocket watch, observing the exposed cogs as they ticked the seconds away. He didn't feel like going to bed, so he flicked the TV on again. The elderly set could only receive four channels—three if it was windy—and when he came across a documentary, he remembered Mr. Boil's test on Monday. For a moment, Elliot considered studying the unopened history book on the coffee table, then saw the mountain of bills and letters next to it. Each one was more threatening than the last. Water, gas, electricity—the list went on and on.

And there, right at the bottom of the pile, was the Really Scary Letter.

The Really Scary Letter had arrived three weeks ago and had cost Elliot more sleep than all the others put together. There were no Really Scary Letters mentioned when Mom had seen the ad on the TV promising instant loans if you owned a house. In fact the letter that arrived with the check to pay for Grandad's funeral—and the bit extra they'd suggested Mom borrow on top—was as friendly as the man on the commercial, who seemed very happy about the "hassle-free instant cash" and "affordable monthly repayments."

But the monthly repayments weren't that affordable after all. And the cash hadn't been hassle-free. And the man wasn't very friendly when you couldn't pay his money back.

Dear Mrs. Hooper, Elliot read for the millionth time. *We act on behalf of EasyDough! Ltd. Your failure to make payments in accordance with your loan obligation of £20,000 has resulted in proceedings to recover possession of Home Farm, Little Motbury, Wiltshire. If the outstanding payment reaches us by one calendar month from the date of this letter, no further action will be taken. If you do not take the action required, your home will be repossessed on Friday, November 19 . . .*

The letter waffled on for another two pages, but Elliot understood what it meant in plain English. Unless he found twenty thousand pounds in exactly one week, he and Mom were going to lose their home. And then where would they go? They had nowhere and no one. Mom was confused enough in the home she'd known all her adult life. There was no way she'd cope with somewhere new.

Elliot picked up another letter from the electricity company. *We regret to inform you that due to nonpayment of your outstanding balance, your service will be terminated on—*

The rest was lost as the house was suddenly plunged into darkness.

Elliot pulled out the flashlight, candles, and matches he kept nearby for every time the electricity was cut off and did some rough sums on the back of his math homework. He could pay the electricity bill tomorrow—thank you, Mrs. Porshley-Plum—but that would leave them less than five pounds for food next week. But next week would have to take care of itself. Elliot quietly vowed that if he were ever rich, he'd never eat a baked bean again.

Elliot looked out of the window into the night sky. With no light pollution from the house, the stars sparkled in the cloudless darkness. He smiled as he remembered how he and Mom used to climb onto the cowshed roof to look at the constellations. Tonight he could see the V-shape of Pisces, which ruled the sky in November. At other times of the year, he could recognize the circle that formed Aquarius, the kite shape of Scorpio, or triangular Libra. But there wouldn't be any other constellations out tonight . . . although . . . He was sure that rectangle of stars was Virgo—but that didn't make any sense. What was it doing in the sky at this time of year? And . . . why was it moving?

An airplane suddenly roared overhead. Had it . . . hit the Virgo constellation? It looked like it. And was Virgo . . . ?

He scoffed at his impossible notion. Stars couldn't fall out of the sky.

Elliot stared into the darkness as the stars hurtled through the sky. They weren't shooting stars—more like . . . tumbling stars. They were definitely dropping. He peered into the night. He was right—the stars were falling, and every second they came nearer, they gathered speed and size. The stars were out of control . . . What were they going to hit?

His question was quickly answered by an almighty bang a few yards from his window.

The stars had come crashing to the ground. Right in the middle of his cowshed.

5

STRANGERS IN THE NIGHT

Virgo didn't come down to Earth with a bump—more of a damp, loud splat.

For a moment, she lay absolutely still, trying to figure out exactly what had just happened. Everything had been going perfectly until that giant metal bird came out of nowhere and knocked her into a tailspin. Hitting the ground had re-formed her into her bodily shape—surely such a great fall should have shattered her into a million pieces? But in the darkness she thought she could feel her arms and she thought she could move her legs. Indeed, the fact that she was thinking at all was a positive sign, so she risked some small movements. She slowly wiggled her legs until her feet met with a solid floor. Greatly encouraged, Virgo groped around to see what had broken her fall. She felt the immediate area around her body, but every time she put a hand down, it simply disappeared into the squelchy substance upon which she had landed.

She let out a tired sigh and lay back in the mush. There was a slight possibility that this was not going perfectly.

Once the shock of being in one piece had passed, Virgo's

nostrils were hit by a truly disgusting stench. She realized it was coming from her squishy landing place and her floundering around had spread it all over her long silver hair and purple robes. With a great heave, she pulled herself to her feet. She closed her eyes, pressed her hands together, and opened her palms slightly to summon her star-glow.

She found herself in a large, dark cavern that seemed to contain nothing but straw. The only other light came from the hole her dramatic entrance had made in the roof and that, at first sight, appeared to be her only way out again. As her eyes grew accustomed to the dark, she could make out another figure—to her great relief, she recognized the form as a female Bovinor, the same species as Taurus on the Zodiac Council. This was good news—Bovinors were renowned for their wisdom and Virgo knew that she was in safe hooves. She decided to make her acquaintance, remembering that Taurus was a stickler for good manners.

"Greetings, Lady Bovinor. My apologies for the abrupt arrival," whispered Virgo, bending into a respectful curtsy.

The creature didn't return her polite greeting, which Virgo tried not to find extremely rude.

"Forgive me interrupting you," she continued, "but could you tell me where I might find Prisoner Forty-Two?"

Once again, there was no reply—and to add insult to injury, the Bovinor simply sniffed her udders and released a wholly unimpressed moo.

"I'm so sorry, your ladyship, I'm unfamiliar with your accent," said Virgo more curtly, crouching down to try to catch her eye. "Would you mind telling me where I am?"

The Bovinor seemed quite determined to contribute nothing to the exchange, although she did release a loud, wet noise from her backside that Virgo couldn't translate. It certainly smelled like the conversation was over.

"Well, er, thanks for your time," she said, discreetly covering her nose as she backed away.

This was no good—she needed some guidance. Wiping her hands carefully on her hair, Virgo reverently pulled out her copy of *What's What*, the immortal guidebook she always kept in her robes. *What's What* was a known authority on every subject and invaluable in any situation. She opened the two ends of the rolled parchment and spoke clearly into it.

"Mortals," she said to the scroll, which immediately filled the empty page with scratched words from an invisible quill.

Mortals, she read by the light of her own star-glow. *Category: Human. Realm: Earth. Powers: Various; sometimes too many, sometimes not enough. Mortals are the result of a failed experiment by the Olympians to create a perfect race. After several unsuccessful attempts to improve on the prototype, mortals were kept as entertaining pets for the Gods, but soon bred out of control. Mortals are very complex and all major studies have proved inconclusive as to their use. But it has been observed that most respond well to food and discount coupons* . . . "Hmmm. Interesting."

Virgo was about to do more research into her whereabouts when a loud creak interrupted the silence of the cavern. There was a door. And it was opening . . .

Not only that, she was completely unarmed. She clapped her hands to snap off her glow, retreated to the smelly mush and grabbed the nearest thing at hand to await her attacker.

"Bessie?" Elliot whispered as he shone a flashlight into the pitch-black cowshed. "Bessie, are you okay?"

A low moo reassured Elliot that his cow was unscathed by the star-ball. Thank goodness. He looked around as well as the feeble light from his flashlight would let him. Nothing was on fire, and apart from a huge hole in the roof, no other damage appeared to have been done. What could it have been? A meteorite? Space junk? The contents of an airplane toilet? It didn't matter now. He could go to bed—everything else would keep until the morning.

But a sudden rustle in the straw made his heart pound.

"Hello?" he whispered. "Who's there?"

"Don't move, mortal!" threatened a piercing voice, cutting through the silence of the shed like a thunderbolt.

Elliot stopped in his tracks, his ragged breathing betraying his thumping heartbeat. He shakily aimed the weak beam of light from his flashlight at the figure in the gloom.

Standing in the large pile of cow dung in the corner of the shed was a girl, no older than himself, dressed in a purple toga costume with a long silver wig. Her big round eyes were as dark as the night outside and although she was doing her best to twist her delicate features into a ferocious stare, she just looked like a china doll on a bad hair day. She was pointing a large yellow rubber glove threateningly in Elliot's direction.

"I'm not afraid to use this," she warned.

"I've seen where the vet puts that glove," said Elliot to this strange, angry girl. "Trust me, I'm not coming anywhere near you."

The girl inched closer to Elliot, not taking her eyes from his.

"Where am I?" she demanded.

"In the cowshed," Elliot replied.

"Hmmm—Kowsh Ed," said the girl. "I've not heard of this region of Earth—are the inhabitants friendly?"

"When they're not being threatened by a trick-or-treater covered in cow poo," said Elliot.

The girl picked up a handful of Bessie's cow feed and threw it enthusiastically at Elliot's feet.

"Help yourself." She smiled.

Elliot sensed that he was supposed to be pleased with this gesture. The girl appeared confused when he didn't respond. She moved a little closer and placed her right hand on her left shoulder in some kind of greeting.

"I am Virgo, Constellation of the Zodiac Council and Guardian of the Stationery Cupboard. And you are?"

Elliot eyed her suspiciously. "I'm Elliot. What the heck are you doing in my shed?"

"Looking for Prisoner Forty-Two, Mr. What-The-Heck-Are-You-Doing-In-My-Shed. Is he here?"

"Is who here?"

"Pri-son-er For-ty-Two," Virgo spelled out, as if she were talking to a deaf baboon. "Where is he?"

"Oh, Prisoner Forty-Two," said Elliot sarcastically. "Walk down the road to the nearest Yeti and take a left at the Boogeyman. Prisoner Forty-Two lives two doors down."

"Don't be absurd," snorted Virgo. "Everyone knows that the Boogeyman lives in Belgium. But it's not your fault; I've heard how simple you mortals are. If you don't know where the prisoner is, I'll just have to find him myself. Farewell."

Virgo marched past Elliot and out of the barn.

Elliot instinctively knew that getting involved with this girl would be trouble. He knew he should just go back to the house and worry about how he was going to pay for the roof on top of all the other debts. But more than anything, he knew he couldn't let a young girl with some sort of head injury from the star-ball hitting his shed go wandering around the lonely Wiltshire countryside on a cold, dark night.

He threw some more feed into Bessie's trough and ran after the girl as she ambled aimlessly across the paddock.

"Hey!" he called after her. "Zodiac girl!"

"Virgo," said the stranger grandly.

"Yeah, you," Elliot said. "Look, it's really late and it's really dark—come back to my house and you can call your parents. You can't walk around here all night, you'll freeze to death."

The strange girl stopped, clearly considering his proposal.

"I have no parents, child, nor can I do anything to death," she said. "I am immortal. But there is a surprising degree of intelligence in what you say. You're not as stupid as I was led to believe."

"You're too kind," said Elliot, thinking about his warm, comfy bed.

"I am unlikely to find Prisoner Forty-Two tonight, and you will make an excellent case study. I am keen to learn more about mortals. You sound very curious. Is it true that when you become unwell, you can generate green slime from your nostrils?"

"You've never had a cold?" said Elliot, wiping his nose on his sleeve.

"I'm never ill," said Virgo haughtily. "I am perfect."

"And I'm the queen of Sheba," sighed Elliot. "Please. Will you just come inside?"

Someone else with problems. Just what he needed.

"Very well, Your Majesty," the girl finally conceded. "Show me to your dwelling."

Back in the farmhouse, the stranger was soon sitting in front of the cozy fire in the candlelit living room. Elliot had given Virgo a pair of his old cargo pants, a T-shirt, and sneakers to replace the robes that had nearly made him puke as he put them in the garbage, and offered her the bathroom to remove the worst of the dung from her hair. He had made them both a cup of tea on the gas stove and had spent the last half hour trying to obtain any information that might explain where she came from.

It was not going well.

"So let me get this straight." He sighed for the umpteenth time. "You're an immortal Constellation who lives in Ilium?"

"Elysium," corrected Virgo.

"Right, there," said Elliot, "and you traveled to Earth from the sky in the big star-ball?"

"Constellation," said Virgo, who seemed fascinated by how soggy she could make her cookie before it plopped into her tea. "Constellation travel is one of the most sophisticated transport systems in the immortal world."

"So sophisticated it landed you in a pile of cow poo?"

"That was unfortunate," snapped Virgo. "I haven't visited the realm of Earth before and got a little lost in all the pollution you mortals have created. Your atmosphere is filthy."

"And why do you have to find this Prisoner Fifty-Six?"

"Prisoner Forty-Two," corrected Virgo, handing him the golden flask. "Because I need to give him this."

"Nice," said Elliot, pushing away the dark thought of how

much money he could get for such an expensive trinket. He started to unscrew the lid.

"Don't open that!" shrieked Virgo, snatching the flask back. "It's full of ambrosia."

"Am-what-now?" said Elliot.

"Ambrosia," huffed Virgo. "Immortal elixir. It keeps us young. I must say, your basic education has been very poor."

"Says the girl with her pants on the wrong way around," said Elliot as Virgo shrugged stubbornly and tried unsuccessfully to put her hands in her backward pockets. "And when you've given it to him, you'll just turn back into stars and whiz back up to Elision?"

"Elysium," Virgo repeated impatiently.

"Yes, there. And you're, like, a million years old?"

"Actually," said Virgo huffily, as the last of her cookie fell into her tea, "I'm one thousand nine hundred and sixty-four. But don't be fooled by my youth. I'm very advanced for my age."

Elliot knew some people were funny about their ages— his math teacher, Mrs. Goodwinge, had been thirty-eight for the past five birthdays—but this was ridiculous.

"Are you sure I can't call your parents?" He sighed yet again.

"How many times, child—I don't have parents! I am a Constellation of the Zodiac Council, sent here to deliver ambrosia to an immortal prisoner. But if that's too much for your feeble mortal brain to comprehend," she said matter-of-factly, rising to leave, "then I'll be on my way."

Elliot didn't know what to do. He really couldn't let this deluded girl leave on her own, but if she wouldn't let him call anyone . . . it was better if she stayed tonight. At least that way she was safe and tomorrow he could take her to the police station in Little Motbury and find her some help.

"No, don't go," he grumbled. "It's late, we both need some sleep. There are loads of rooms here; I'll find you a bed."

"Thank you, Elliot, but immortals rarely sleep."

"Of course," said Elliot, too tired to argue with this silly girl anymore. "Well, if you change your mind, there's a quilt on the sofa and you can sleep under that. Promise me you won't run off in the night?"

"I swear it on the Styx," she said solemnly.

"Marvelous," said an exhausted Elliot as he climbed the stairs to bed. "I'll see you in the morning."

"Sleep well, mortal child," said Virgo.

"Stay awake, loony star girl," yawned Elliot.

6

THE SWIMMING LESSON

Despite his tiredness, Elliot had a lousy night's sleep. The thought of Virgo—or whatever the weirdo called herself—stealing the family silver kept him tossing and turning for half the night. The fact that he'd already sold all the family silver helped him to sleep for the other half, but the new day had barely broken before Elliot was pulling on his clothes and heading downstairs.

He expected to find Virgo snoring beneath the patchwork quilt that hid the holes in the sofa. But as he reached the bottom of the stairs, she was wide awake in front of the TV. The sofa didn't appear to have been disturbed, but nor did Virgo show any signs of having been awake all night.

"Morning," said Elliot cautiously.

"Good morning, Elliot," said Virgo, scowling at the television. "I hope you enjoyed a better night than I did."

Elliot was about to launch into a tirade about how no, actually, a delusional stranger breaking into his cowshed had rather disturbed his evening. But something more important struck him. Virgo was watching television. They had electricity.

"What, how?" he mumbled sleepily, trying to find words that had yet to wake up.

"I must say, even your hospitality puts your fellow mortals to shame," Virgo began, clearly relishing the chance for a moan. "The little people who live in this box are incredibly rude."

Elliot glanced at the soap opera Virgo was watching as he pondered how the power had been miraculously restored to his home.

"I have been trying to make conversation with them all night," she huffed. "But I have been completely ignored. I didn't mind so much earlier when some of them had to go and fight werewolves—these things happen—but these people are downright stupid. Take this woman," she said, pointing to a well-known soap actress. "I tried to advise her against running away with this man, but would she listen? Now she's trapped in a car with someone who killed his own mother only twenty minutes ago. And he ran over the neighbor's dog. And pretended to be his own sister. Now, when do we leave to find Prisoner Forty-Two?"

"When did the lights come back on?" he asked.

"Oh, I rerouted your electricity through your neighbor's system. I had to do some considerable research on electrical circuitry in *What's What*, but it was worth it. This place was darker than a cupboard in a labyrinth."

Elliot stared at Virgo through his puffy red eyes. The weirdo was also an electrician. Interesting. And he only had one neighbor—Patricia Porshley-Plum. So Virgo had "borrowed" electricity from Mrs. Horse's-Bum without paying for it. Surely that wasn't right. Elliot knew what he had to do.

"Show me how?" he asked Virgo.

"Elly?" His mom was standing at the doorway, rubbing her drowsy eyes. "Who is this?"

Elliot's tired mind failed to construct a quick lie.

"Virgo, Constellation of the Zodiac Council," said Virgo, raising her right hand to her left shoulder. "I didn't realize mortals lived in packs, like gorgons. Pleasure to meet you, adult female mortal."

"I'm Josie, Elliot's mom," said Josie with a warm smile. "Elliot didn't say we were expecting company."

"He couldn't have," said Virgo. "I'm afraid I—"

"Arrived very late," Elliot interrupted. "It was a bit of a surprise. I'll run you a bath, Mom—why don't you go and relax? Virgo's just leaving."

"Oh, that's a shame," said Josie. "Well, nice to meet you. Hope to see you again."

"That is highly unlikely, Josie-Mom," said Virgo. "I will soon return to my realm of Elysium, where no mortal has ever set foot."

"Oh, well. Safe journey," said Josie kindly, as Elliot gently guided her toward the stairs.

Half an hour later when Mom was safely out of the bath, Elliot gave Virgo her flask and a piece of toast, and bundled her out of the door in an old hoodie.

"I won't be long, Mom," he shouted. "Stay here and don't let anyone in."

"Yes, boss," laughed Josie, happily reading a magazine at the kitchen table. "See you later, gorgeous."

"Look! There it is!" exclaimed Virgo as she spotted Stonehenge from the front gate. "If we cut across that field, we'll be there in no time."

"Er—this way's quicker," mumbled Elliot, not intending to take Virgo anywhere but the Little Motbury police station.

Elliot and Virgo walked in silence down the track that led to the nearby village. The river Avon babbled peacefully alongside.

"I appreciate your assistance in taking me to Prisoner Forty-Two," said Virgo. "As soon as I've delivered this, I will leave you to your imperfect mortal life."

"Whatever," muttered Elliot, who was counting the seconds until this freak was off his hands. He wasn't a morning person at the best of times and his sleepless night had made him grumpier than usual.

After they had been walking for a few minutes, Virgo spoke up.

"I have a suspicion, young Elliot, that you don't entirely believe me," she ventured, eyeing her toast.

"No. Really?" Elliot said as he chewed on his, wishing he had peanut butter. Or butter.

"It's true," she said, using the untouched toast to brush her hair. "I appreciate it must be confusing for your tiny mortal brain, but I really am an immortal Constellation, sent to administer this ambrosia."

"Actually, I don't care!" snapped Elliot, stopping to face her. "I don't care that you think you're an immortal tea lady! I don't care that you think you're a walking fireworks display! I don't care if the Easter Bunny forgot your birthday and the Tooth Fairy cancels your lunch plans! I have real problems in the real world and this whole weird fantasy of yours is really getting old!"

Virgo considered his outburst.

"Well, that's up to you," she said eventually. "Although I'm sorry the Tooth Fairy bothered you with our social arrangements. She can be thoughtless like that."

"Oh, for—" Elliot yelled as he stormed away.

Virgo ran to catch up with him. "But I can prove to you that I am an immortal," she mused, looking around. "I'd transform, but it's in my contract that council members can't reveal their constellations to mortals . . ."

"How convenient."

"So I just have to find a way not to die."

"Don't try too hard."

"Aha!" said Virgo, spotting the river. "If I were a mere mortal, I could stay underwater for—what—thirty seconds maybe?"

"Something like that," said Elliot, stopping but with his arms folded.

"Well, then," nodded Virgo, and she turned toward the riverbank and waded, fully clothed, into the Avon.

With a guilty prickle in his guts, Elliot realized this had gone far enough. "Look, you don't have to prove anything," he said, snapping out of his bad mood. "Don't be stupid . . ."

"Urgh, it's cold and the water is just revolting," moaned Virgo, striding on regardless. "You mortals need to take better care of your realm. After all, it won't all be here forever and then you'll be right in the *glug, glug, glug*—"

The remainder of Virgo's complaint was lost as her silver head disappeared into the river, which swallowed her up with a gentle suck.

"She even talks underwater," Elliot said to the empty space beside him, glancing at his pocket watch. No need to worry. Virgo hadn't even paused for breath—she'd be out of there in no time.

Twenty seconds. Elliot looked around for the telltale bubbles that would betray Virgo's hiding place. Nothing. Not even a ripple. She was stubborn, that was for sure.

Forty-five seconds. Fair enough, the girl could hold her breath. She'd come bursting out of that river with an almighty gasp any second now. Any second at all. Absolutely any second now. Elliot took off his jacket to warm her when she'd finished her silly stunt. Virgo might be a pain in the butt, but he didn't want her to catch pneumonia.

One minute and fifteen seconds. Elliot's heartbeat quickened. He'd been so busy getting cross with Virgo, it suddenly occurred to him that maybe she actually believed all this craziness. What if she really did think she was immortal and was floating unconscious down the river while he stood there like an idiot? He could be responsible for the life of a seriously unwell young girl. What would he tell her parents? What would he tell the police?

Two minutes. Elliot was now in a full-blown panic. He'd stood by and let this poor sick girl drown herself just because he'd had a crummy night's sleep. He was going to prison and rightly so. He was a horrible human being. There was nothing else for it. He had to go in after her.

Elliot kicked off his shoes, dropped his watch on the grass, and ripped off his T-shirt. He was about to lose his jeans, but looking at the mist rising from the cold water, he quickly thought better of it. With a deep breath for air—and another for courage—Elliot plunged into the freezing river. The water bit him with a thousand icy teeth.

"Virgo!" he yelled, thrashing around. "Virgo! Where are you?! I believe you! Come out!"

Once, twice, three times he dived beneath the murky surface, but he couldn't see or feel Virgo anywhere. He stood breathless in the middle of the river, desperately looking for any sign of the girl he'd left to drown. He threw his hands into the water in despair. She was gone. And it was all his fault.

"Let's hope you're immortal," called Virgo as she suddenly popped up from the water behind him and calmly walked out onto the bank, picking up Elliot's discarded T-shirt to dry her soaking hair. "Or you're going to freeze to death in there."

Elliot didn't understand. This was impossible. She'd been underwater for nearly five minutes.

"What? How? You should be—" he spluttered.

"Well, here we go again," sighed Virgo. "Hello. I'm Virgo. I'm an immortal. Shall we move on?"

She helped a shivering Elliot out of the river. He took her hand gingerly, as if she had suddenly turned into Bigfoot. Virgo handed him his soggy T-shirt, which he put on in a stunned stupor. He trembled in a confused, freezing puddle.

"Hold my hands," the young Constellation instructed, and Elliot obeyed her in a daze. "I shouldn't really, but I think this is an exception . . ."

With Elliot's hands in hers, Virgo pulled her palms gently apart. At her touch, a million tiny stars crept from every inch of her body, curling into the air in wisps of light. These golden strands reached around them both with a warm, starry glow. Elliot felt the gentle heat seep into his soaking clothes and beyond, penetrating his skin and warming him from the core of his body. In seconds, he was dry.

"Better?" asked Virgo.

"Better," answered Elliot, staring at her as if for the first time. He couldn't believe it. She was telling the truth. Virgo really was immortal.

"Now, can you please take me to the stone circle?" said Virgo, looking over the countryside.

"Stonehenge?" asked Elliot.

"Is that a prison?" asked Virgo.

Elliot thought of the countless tedious school trips he'd endured at the ancient attraction.

"That's the one," he said. "It's about a mile this way."

"Excellent," said Virgo. "This is going to get me a promotion for sure. I'll probably be asked to make more of these trips. You might be seeing plenty more of me."

"Fantastic," said Elliot, his mind still reeling from the morning's unexpected turn of events.

Virgo strode off across the field, forcing Elliot to run to keep up with her this time.

"So are there more . . . like you?" he asked.

"Immortals, you mean?" asked Virgo. "Of course. Thousands. That's why the Zodiac Council exists—we support them all."

"So you're like . . . a government?"

"Not at all!" scoffed Virgo. "A government! For immortals! The very idea . . . No. Nothing like that. We just tell them all what to do and punish them if they don't do it."

She halted as she stepped in a ginormous cow pat. "What is this stuff? It's everywhere in this realm . . ."

"Do any immortals live here? On Earth?" said Elliot, looking around as if he might bump into one at any moment.

"Of course," said Virgo nonchalantly. "You probably encounter them all the time."

Elliot thought about some of the strange inhabitants of his tiny village. This actually made a lot of sense.

"You can identify us by this," said Virgo, pulling a necklace out from her T-shirt.

Elliot examined it closely. On a golden chain hung a small pendant, about the size of a grape. Exquisitely carved in crystal was a heart inside an elaborate flame.

"This is my kardia," Virgo explained. "All immortals wear them."

"Let me see," said Elliot, reaching out to get a better look. Virgo snatched the necklace away in horror.

"Don't touch it!" she gasped. "A kardia is the essence of immortal life! Without it, we become mortal! Being stripped of your kardia is the most severe punishment in the immortal world! Without a kardia, an immortal could die! An immortal could be killed! An immortal could be . . . an accountant!"

"Okay, okay—chill out. Your kardia's a big deal. I get it," said Elliot, stuffing his hands into his pockets.

"I'm pleased to hear it," said Virgo more calmly. "Kardia also help immortals to identify each other and declare our category."

"Category?" asked Elliot.

"Yes, there are five: Deities, Constellations, Elementals,

Neutrals, and Daemons. Every category is made up of different classes and each has a different kardia. For instance, all Deities' kardia are precious metals, but they are bronze for Heroes, silver for Gods, and gold for Olympians. Elementals' kardia belong to their element—a troll is an Earth Elemental, so their kardia are stone. Constellations' kardia are crystal and Neutrals' are glass."

"So Deities and Constellations are better than Elementals and Neutrals?"

"We wouldn't express it like that," said Virgo grandly.

"You would if you had a stone kardia," Elliot pointed out. "What about the Daemons?"

"Oh, them—they don't exist anymore," she said as she stepped in more cow dung. "Is this substance some kind of decoration . . . ?"

"Don't exist? But you said Daemons were immortals?"

"Not without their kardia. Mighty Zeus stripped the Daemons of their onyx kardia and destroyed them all before he retired. Horrible creatures apparently—loved to torture mortals with their powers—illness, death, old age, that kind of thing . . ."

"So who is this Prisoner Forty-Two? And why is he at Stonehenge?" asked Elliot.

"No idea," said Virgo breezily. "And he's under it."

"What did he do?"

"I don't know. Something wrong, obviously. When Zeus appointed the Zodiac Council after his retirement, he left instructions that he'd imprisoned a dangerous immortal on Earth and we were to deliver ambrosia to the stone circle every two hundred and fifty years," explained Virgo, pausing to sniff her dung-covered shoe and wrinkling her nose. "This has a distinctive aroma. Is this what mortals use for perfume?"

"No. But you can if you like," said Elliot. "How long has the prisoner been there?"

"Not sure exactly. It was before my time. Zeus retired two thousand years ago. I'm only . . ."

"One thousand nine hundred and sixty-four. You said." Elliot pulled up as a realization hit him. "So this dude has been imprisoned for two thousand years and it's never occurred to you to ask why he's there?" he asked. "Don't you think that's wrong?"

"I have been told what I'm supposed to think."

"Shouldn't you make up your own mind?"

"Don't worry about matters that your suboptimal mortal intellect can't understand," she said haughtily, her sneakers squelching across the field.

"I understand justice," said Elliot a little too loudly.

"Our systems are perfect. They have worked for two thousand years."

"Doing something wrong for a long time doesn't make you perfect," said Elliot. "It makes you really wrong."

"I don't expect you to understand," said Virgo airily. "But these are our rules."

"Your rules suck," said Elliot.

"Suck what?" asked Virgo.

"Your rules are stupid," Elliot sounded out.

"How dare you!" huffed Virgo. "They are not and I will follow them."

"And do you always follow the rules?" asked Elliot.

Virgo paused. "Yes," she answered eventually. Elliot immediately recognized a fellow liar.

"Ah—perhaps they are some form of mortal delicacy?" said Virgo, leaning down to the cow poop. "Not to my taste, but I'm willing to try . . ."

"No!" shouted Elliot, holding Virgo back before she tucked in to the cow pat. "Just leave that stuff alone, all right? So why are you taking him that flask? Why not just leave him there to rot?"

"All immortals are entitled to ambrosia, even prisoners," said Virgo. "We need it to stay young. Otherwise we'd just get older and start falling to bits without dying. That is every immortal's worst fear. Not to mention a litter hazard. Ambrosia is a basic right."

"So is freedom," said Elliot. "You're just going to give this guy a drink and then leave?"

"No," replied Virgo. "I'm going to throw the flask into his prison and return to Elysium. The rules strictly forbid any contact whatsoever with the prisoner."

"That's cruel."

"Those are the rules. And we're here."

Elliot had been so caught up in Virgo's story, he hadn't noticed that they had already reached the outer boundaries of Stonehenge. He had never understood the excitement about some prehistoric lumps of rock, but now that he knew they were an immortal prison, they seemed a lot more attractive.

With the busy summer season over and the sun only just peering through the stones, Stonehenge was eerily quiet. The only people present were Cyril, a lone guide who was on hand to answer any potential questions from any potential visitors, and two security guards enthusiastically arguing over the sports pages of a paper.

Virgo turned to Elliot and placed her left hand on her right shoulder by way of farewell.

"Well, thank you, Elliot the Mortal, for your begrudging hospitality and cantankerous company. It has been curious knowing you and I wish you well in your uneventful mortal life."

And with that, Virgo hopped over the barrier and strode toward a huge stone, set apart from the stone circle, which Elliot recalled was called the Heel Stone.

"Wait!" he hissed. "You can't do that . . ."

But it was too late. Elliot watched agog as Virgo merrily walked across the hallowed ground and stopped by the Heel Stone, as yet undetected by Cyril, who was looking in the opposite direction and picking his nose. Virgo crawled around the base of the stone, searching for something in the grass.

"Elliot!" she hollered, causing Elliot to wince and Cyril to spin around. "Would you mind giving me a hand?"

It took Cyril a moment to comprehend the full horror of the scene before him, as a silver-haired girl stood up and kicked the sacred Heel Stone of Stonehenge.

"Hey!" he yelled, reaching for his whistle. "Stop right there, you hooligan!"

He blew three sharp blasts, summoning the two burly, if portly, security guards from the parking lot, who ran straight at Elliot.

There was no way he could get in trouble with the police. If they took him home to Mom, they might report her to the authorities. With Cyril approaching from the other direction, he had no choice but to run toward Virgo at the Heel Stone.

Oblivious to the fuss around her, Virgo was yanking up tufts of grass at the stone's base, tearing the soil around the sacred stone and throwing it carelessly over her shoulder before she finally seemed to find what she was looking for. As Elliot skidded to a halt, he could see a small golden handle and an ancient-looking red keypad buried beneath the overgrowth.

"Oh, crud!" snapped Virgo. "I don't have the passcode."

"Then make one up!" shouted Elliot. "We need to get out of here!"

"I bet it's the one Aries uses on the cookie tin—he uses the same four digits for everything, it's very insecure . . ."

"Will you hurry up!" yelled Elliot, glancing over his shoulder at the fast-approaching guards, as Virgo pressed the keypad.

"I knew it!" she chirped as the keypad turned green. "It's always 2483: Capricorn's horns, Gemini's arms, Scorpio's legs, Libra's IQ. That golden ram is just asking to be fleeced."

"What the—?"

Cyril pulled up in shock. Virgo had turned the handle and was lifting the enormous rock as if it were made of papier-mâché.

Elliot saw he had no other escape. As she raised it above her head, he launched himself at Virgo and bundled them both into the hole beneath the stone.

It was a blind, frantic leap into the unknown—and Elliot's flying feet only just made it through the gap as the almighty Heel Stone came crashing down and locked them into the darkness below.

7

PRISONER FORTY-WHO?

Elliot's mom always said that when one door closes, another one opens. Unfortunately, Josie's wisdom didn't apply on this occasion.

When Elliot threw himself and Virgo into the hole, he'd had no time to worry about what lay beneath the Heel Stone. He quickly found that it wasn't a hole at all—it was a set of stone steps, and he tumbled down every hard one.

Two things prevented him from fracturing every bone in his body. Firstly, there were only five steps. Secondly, his fall was broken by a soft landing.

"What have you done?" whispered the soft landing angrily, throwing Elliot off her.

Elliot spat out a mouthful of dirt.

"Saved us getting clobbered by the security guards you summoned, Genius Girl," Elliot retorted, hauling his bruised body upright.

"We have to leave!" Virgo whispered.

They both pushed at the Heel Stone above their heads. It was immovable. They were trapped.

"I can't be here. It's against the rules. I'm supposed to drop the flask and go."

"Looks like the rules will have to deal with it."

Virgo gently pulled her palms apart to illuminate the cave. They were on a narrow ledge at the top of a winding iron staircase, which spiraled down into the endless gloom below. It was surrounded by a stone circle, which Elliot realized was a continuation of the stones above the ground.

"Right," said Virgo shakily. "The most important thing is not to panic. I never panic. Never, never, never. I absolutely never, ever, ever panic. It's completely vital that I . . ."

"Stop panicking," hissed Elliot.

"All right!" said Virgo. "I'll go down and see if there's another exit. But you have to stay here."

Elliot never had liked being told what to do. Particularly when that involved standing alone in a pitch-black cave from which he might never escape. He swallowed back his fear.

"Not a chance—I'm coming with you," he whispered back.

"No, you're not! You can't be here!"

"Well, I *am* here. So get over it."

Virgo growled with frustration, but Elliot mustered as determined a look as he was able.

"Fine," Virgo conceded. "But stay close. And don't . . . do anything."

Guided by Virgo's faint glow, Elliot edged down the stairs behind the Constellation. Their breathing was the only sound to disturb the heavy air, the huge stones looming higher above them with every step that drew them farther into the darkness.

They reached the bottom stair and looked nervously at each other before tentatively placing their feet on the cold floor. They scanned the cave with faltering movements, afraid of what their eyes might find.

"Is that a . . . ?" asked Virgo, summoning more stars with her hands. A small stream ran noiselessly along the back wall. But apart from the odd spider scuttling across the floor, the cave appeared to be completely empty.

"There's no one here," said Elliot at normal volume, taking a bolder step into the cave. "You've been conned."

"That's not possible," said Virgo, walking toward a dark spot beneath the staircase. "It just doesn't make any—"

"HELP ME!" screamed a terrified voice. A spectral figure launched itself at Virgo, knocking her to the ground and extinguishing her glow.

The cave was plunged into total darkness.

"Virgo?" cried Elliot. "Where are you?"

The silence that greeted his question may have lasted seconds or hours, but was even more petrifying than the scream before it. Elliot had only caught a flash of Virgo's attacker out of the corner of his eye. Where was it? And was it coming for him?

"Virgo!" Elliot shouted. "Virgo! Are you here?"

A weak glow pierced the darkness as Virgo illuminated once more. She was on the floor, dazed and rubbing her head.

"I'm here," she croaked. "And that hurt."

Elliot ran over and helped her to her feet.

"What was that?" he asked, whipping his head around to see if it was still there.

"I don't know," said Virgo, looking more urgently about the cave. "But we need to—"

A faint sobbing silenced them both. Virgo slowly dropped her hand from her head and pulled her palms farther apart to light up the darkness. Elliot peered nervously into the gloom.

In rusty iron chains, fastened to a rock beneath the staircase, was the most pitiful man—if you could even call him that—Elliot had ever seen. This figure was beyond old—ancient, in fact—with the remnants of a black robe clinging to his skeletal frame. What was left of his gray hair stuck to his skull, which was buried in his emaciated limbs. He was huddled, shivering on the cold floor, wrapping his arms around himself for warmth and comfort.

"Prisoner Forty-Two?" asked Virgo uncertainly.

The man lifted his head from his knees, fresh tears streaming down the thousand tiny crevices that lined his face. His eyes met Elliot's squarely, with a look of longing and desperation that made the boy's heart ache.

"Is that what they call me?" he rasped. "I don't know who I am anymore."

"I've brought you ambrosia," said Virgo, extending the golden flask with shaking hands.

"Thank you," said the prisoner. "I'm sorry for scaring you. You are the first immortal I've seen in millennia." His gaze switched to Elliot. "And the first mortal . . ."

"How do we get out of here?" asked Virgo, who seemed unable to meet his pleading eyes.

"I will tell you. But first—please, could I have some water?" he asked, gesturing to a rusting metal cup at his feet.

"I am forbidden," said Virgo quietly. "The rules state—"

"Why are you here?" asked Elliot.

The man gave a weak, pitiful laugh. "The same reason anyone hides anything, child." He smiled sadly. "Because they don't want it to be found."

Elliot looked over at the stream. Virgo caught his glance and shook her head.

"Elliot—you can't," she warned. "The rules state—"

"Your rules," said Elliot, picking up the cup. "Not mine."

He walked to the stream and filled the cup to the brim with icy water. He returned to the prisoner and placed the cup at his feet.

"You are kind, child," the man said, raising the cup to his lips. He shakily drained it, spilling as much water as he managed to drink.

"You've had your water," said Virgo nervously. "Now show us the way out."

"Behind that boulder," said Prisoner Forty-Two, pointing

to a huge rock on the far side of the cave. "There is a tunnel that leads outside. It's how he left."

"He?" asked Elliot.

"Zeus," said the man mournfully. "He chained me here and left me to rot."

Virgo ran to the boulder and tried to push it. It was immense—and it wasn't budging.

"I can't move it," she said. "There must be another way."

"There is none," the prisoner declared, looking straight at Elliot. "But I can move it. Simply free me from my chains."

"Out of the question," said Virgo, the panic rising in her voice again. "We'll stay here. The council will come eventually."

"In another two hundred and fifty years," said the prisoner. "You and I can afford to wait. I don't think our mortal friend has the time."

"You think you can move that boulder?" asked Elliot. "No offense, but you don't look like you work out much."

The prisoner laughed his sad laugh again. "I am stronger than I look. If you free me, I swear on the Styx you will leave this cave."

"How are you going to do that?" asked Elliot.

"I have many powers," said the man, his eyes boring straight into Elliot's soul. "Powers that the Gods don't understand. Powers that the Gods fear. That's why I'm here. I can do what the Gods cannot."

"Elliot, don't listen to—" Virgo started.

"I understand mortals," the prisoner continued with greater strength, the intensity of his stare making Elliot feel as though he was invading his mind, trespassing among his thoughts, intruding on his feelings. "I know their dearest hopes; I understand their deepest fears. I understand wanting something so badly your heart might burst with longing. I understand loving someone so deeply the thought of losing them is worse than death. You know how that feels, don't you, Elliot?"

Elliot froze. How did he . . . ?

"Elliot—come away from him," said Virgo. "Come and help—"

"Free me from these chains!" pleaded the man desperately, holding his manacles out toward Elliot. "We have both been wronged. But I can help you, Elliot. I can give you what you want most in the world. Just the touch of your hand. A mortal touch. That's all I need to free me. I'm begging you. Help me. Let me help you. Let me help your mother . . ."

"You can . . . ?"

"Elliot! Elliot, don't listen to him," said Virgo, leaving the boulder and breaking into a run toward him.

Elliot drew a halting breath. If this man could read his mind, perhaps he could heal his mom's? The idea of Mom back to her old self, back to the happy, healthy woman that he loved and needed, overwhelmed him. The months of hiding his fears as he watched her slip away from herself started to well up from the pit of his stomach, and Elliot had to force them back down his throat before they burst out of his mouth. This man could cure Mom. That was what Elliot wanted most in the world. That was all he wanted.

He raised his fingers toward the chains, but Virgo was at his side.

"No—don't," she said, grabbing his arm.

Elliot shook her off as his right foot overtook his left, bringing him closer to the thick iron shackles.

"Elliot, you can't," Virgo insisted, standing in front of him. "The rules clearly state—"

Elliot stopped and looked into Virgo's terrified face.

"Her rules," said the man's voice in the cave, or maybe in Elliot's own head. "Not yours, Elliot . . ."

There was an eternal pause as Elliot looked from the silver-haired Constellation in front of him to the wretched man behind her.

"I'm sorry," said Elliot. "I have no choice."

Elliot shoved Virgo to one side and made a frantic dive toward the prisoner. But Virgo was quick. She grabbed Elliot by the ankles, pulling him to the floor just before his fingertips could reach the chains.

"No! You—don't—know—what—you're—doing . . ." she panted.

But Elliot was possessed with the strength of someone a moment away from the thing they wanted most in the world. He gave one almighty kick to free himself from Virgo's grip, hauled himself to his knees, and threw himself toward the chains held in Prisoner Forty-Two's outstretched, bony fingers.

And this time, he made it.

Elliot clasped his fist around the shackles between the prisoner's wrists. Immediately, plumes of black smoke rose from the chains that were securing the man to the rock, melting the links away like sand. The sound of maniacal laughing from deep within the Earth filled the cave, making an overwhelming din.

"He's free!" The laughter reverberated around the cave. *"He's free!"*

"Wha-what's happening?" Elliot shouted to Virgo.

Virgo yanked out her *What's What*.

"Prisoner Forty-Two . . . er . . . chains . . . er . . . SOS!" she yelled at the parchment.

Sorry, I didn't get that, scrawled the invisible quill.

"I said—" Virgo began again, but her voice was drowned out as the ecstatic clamor from below the ground reached a deafening crescendo.

The prisoner rose to his feet and threw his head back with a victorious roar. When he brought it forward again, he was no longer the ancient, gray-haired scrap of a man Elliot had so pitied. He started to grow taller, stronger, younger. Limp black hair slithered down his long, angular face, meeting a razor-thin beard that brought his chin into a piercing point. The shredded black robe began to mend until it swathed his body like a shadow. His dark, lifeless eyes seared into Elliot's skull. And around his throat hung a jet-black onyx heart inside a flame. The kardia of a Daemon.

The world stopped for a moment. The prisoner was the first to shatter the silence as he dusted himself down and admired his restored form.

"Thank you, Elliot," he said as he towered over the boy on the floor. "That's so much better. Those chains stopped me from feeling . . . quite myself."

"Wh-who are you?" stammered Elliot.

"How remiss of me," drawled the man. "My apologies. Two millennia underground have dulled my manners. Allow me to introduce myself. My name is Thanatos. Daemon of Death. King of the Daemons."

"Nonsense," scoffed Virgo. "There are no Daemons left. Mighty Zeus destroyed them all."

Thanatos held out his onyx kardia for Virgo to survey. "I think I'm in a rather better position to judge that than you." He glowered. "And I know far more about 'Mighty Zeus' than you could imagine . . ."

"I did what you asked," said Elliot. "You have to help my mom."

"Not necessarily," said Thanatos, stepping over him and grabbing a handful of Virgo's silver hair, yanking her clean off the floor.

"Yes, you do!" said Elliot frantically. "You said—"

"Ah—there's the thing," said Thanatos, carrying Virgo across the cave, oblivious to her kicking and screaming. He reached the boulder and moved it aside as effortlessly as if it were made of spun sugar, stabbing daylight into the darkness. "I said it. I never swore it. Vast difference."

"You lied—" shouted Elliot, holding back angry tears. He charged at Thanatos, determined to knock the cheating Daemon into the middle of next week. But at the last moment, Thanatos deftly sidestepped the attack, sending Elliot crashing into the cave wall.

"And as for you, my dear," said Thanatos gleefully, shaking Virgo by the hair, his eyes burning with delight, "it's time you went back to the Zodiac Council where you belong. Now, which piece of you shall I send first?"

Elliot pulled his winded body upright. "Are you going to kill her?" he asked, unable to look at Virgo's tortured face.

"Gracious no—she's only a child. I'm not a savage," said Thanatos, wrapping his fist more tightly around the hair. "But I'm going to really enjoy not killing her."

The Daemon walked slowly toward Elliot, dragging Virgo on the floor behind him as if she were a garbage bag, and towered over Elliot's bruised body.

"I'm very grateful to you, Elliot," he began. "And as a token of my gratitude, I'll spare you seeing what I'm about to do to your girlfriend."

"You're letting me go?" said Elliot, looking at Virgo, lying in a heap on the floor.

"Absolutely. I swore that you would leave this cave. Besides, I have no further use for you. You may go."

Elliot knew that outside lay safety. But his feet wouldn't move.

"What about her?" he said, gesturing toward Virgo.

"You didn't care much for her a few moments ago," said Thanatos. "I suggest this would be a terrible time to start."

Elliot locked eyes with Virgo and saw her pain and her determination.

"Just leave," she said unsteadily. "This doesn't concern you."

"Ah—finally," trilled Thanatos. "Some advice worth listening to. Good-bye, Elliot. Tell no one what you've seen. Or you'll be seeing me again."

Elliot took a few slow steps toward the tunnel. Virgo wasn't going to die, he told himself. But there were worse things than dying. He told himself that too. He looked back. The Death Daemon waved his fingers in dismissal.

"Run along now. There's a good boy."

Elliot sighed. There was nothing he could do for Virgo. She wouldn't die. But he could. And who would take care of Mom if he did?

He looked toward the daylight as Thanatos dangled his prey again.

"Now then, my dear. Where were we?"

Elliot tried to block out Virgo's screams as he reached the narrow opening. He crouched down to crawl through the tunnel, to where the sunlight was shining on an empty field—probably on the other side of Stonehenge. The coast was clear. Elliot could go back to his life and no one would ever know.

Except for him. He would know everything.

Elliot looked behind him again. Thanatos was shaking Virgo like a puppet on a string, delighting in her screams.

A golden glint caught his eye. The sunlight was gleaming on something on the floor. It was the flask containing Thanatos's ambrosia. It must have fallen out of Virgo's pocket when she tried to move the boulder.

Elliot picked it up. He knew what he had to do.

"Thanatos," he yelled into the cave. "Your ambrosia's here."

"It'll keep," the Daemon shouted back. "I expect I'm going to work up quite a thirst. I'll drink it when I'm done."

Taking a deep breath, Elliot went back into the cave.

"Not necessarily," he said, opening the flask and tipping it so the silver liquid teetered on the brink of the rim. "Let her go."

Thanatos looked murderously at Elliot.

"Don't be foolish," he seethed. "You've made a powerful ally today, boy. Don't turn me into an enemy. This will be the last time I ask you. Put. It. Down."

"And this will be the last time I ask you. Let. Her. Go."

"I mean it, Elliot!"

"So do I," said Elliot, allowing a drop of the sacred liquid to spill onto the ground, where it immediately evaporated in a golden wisp.

The two adversaries stood motionless with their bargaining chips, Thanatos holding Virgo, Elliot holding the flask.

"I'll put her down when you give me the flask," offered Thanatos.

"No. You first," said Elliot.

"I said that I will put her down."

"Swear it," said Elliot, his latest lesson in Daemon negotiations fresh in his mind. "And that you won't throw her, give her back in pieces, or damage her in any way," he added, quickly running through the most likely loopholes. He spilled another drop to underline his point.

"Fine," said Thanatos, seeing the ambrosia float into nothing. "I swear it on the Styx."

Elliot screwed the top back on the flask. "Let's each let go in one . . . two . . . three!"

"Elliot—duck!" screamed Virgo as she and the flask simultaneously flew through the air.

And this time, Elliot listened. For no sooner had the flask landed in Thanatos's hand than his fist swung out, blasting a hole in the rock where Elliot's head had been moments previously.

"You stupid boy," drawled Thanatos, standing before him. "I showed you mercy. I spared your life. A mistake I will not make again."

"You swore I'd leave the cave," said Elliot quickly.

"I did," said Thanatos, drawing his fist back. "But I never swore you'd do so alive. For the second and final time, Elliot—good-bye."

Had Elliot ever wondered what it would be like to have his body obliterated by the supernatural strength of an immortal Death Daemon, he couldn't have imagined the soul-wrenching pain he was about to suffer.

But two things prevented him from finding out.

As Thanatos launched his fist to smash Elliot, an invisible force violently repelled the Daemon, sending him tumbling onto the cave floor. Elliot didn't understand—he hadn't even touched him.

Then, before Thanatos could take another shot, Virgo threw her arms wide open, transformed into her constellation, whipped Elliot up into her warm glow, and whooshed him down the tunnel to safety in a shower of golden light.

8

PATRICIA HORSE'S-BUM

Patricia Porshley-Plum always got what she wanted. When Patricia was eight, she'd wanted a puppy. Her father, who had inherited his vast wealth from his great-aunt, told her she needed to learn the value of a hard day's work. So Patricia took all of Daddy's designer suits to a flea market and sold them for ten pounds. Her father—a man who admired an enterprising spirit—happily bought her Bonnie the puppy.

When Patricia was thirteen, she'd wanted a pony. Her father, who phoned from the golf course to point out that we can't always have what we want, told her to contribute half herself. So Patricia sold Bonnie, pushed Daddy's red Ferrari off a cliff, and instructed him how to spend the insurance money if he wanted to keep his Bentley. Her father—a man who wasn't sure about red anyway—nervously bought her Princess the pony.

When Patricia was twenty, she'd wanted a car. Her father, who'd retired at thirty-five, tried to tell her to get a job. But as his daughter produced a box of matches and a gas can in the drawing room, her father—a man who now feared for his life—simply handed over his credit card.

Now that Patricia was forty-something (but knew she could pass for thirty-seven), she wanted Home Farm. That vile farmhouse needed to be squished and the shed bulldozed, but it sat on a valuable piece of land that was ripe for development. Patricia could build dozens of overpriced houses on the plot and make a fortune. If only she could make Josie Hooper see sense. But that repugnant boy Elliot wouldn't let her near his mother and Patricia was running out of patience. Patricia Porshley-Plum was not getting what she wanted. And this was unacceptable.

Like anyone who has too much, Patricia had no sympathy for those who didn't have enough. She loathed poor people. Patricia treated poverty like most people treat a nasty stomach bug—a horribly catching affliction that necessitated plenty of hand washing. Besides, poor people only had themselves to blame. If you couldn't look after your money, you didn't deserve it. Which left plenty for her. And those ghastly Hoopers were poorer than unemployed church mice.

What made the situation even more intolerable was the fact that Patricia knew something fishy was going on. She didn't believe Elliot's excuses for one tax-efficient minute and she was determined to get her hands on Home Farm. And that twenty pounds the little sneak had stolen. Patricia Porshley-Plum might have deluded herself that she could pass for thirty-seven, but she wasn't stupid. Something was up. She just needed to find out what.

Most normal people would have given up long ago—she had been told many times that Home Farm wasn't for sale, and that should have been the end of it. But Patricia Porshley-Plum wasn't most people. And she wasn't especially normal. Giving up hadn't won her the Pony Princess Rider of the Year—although giving all the other competitors food poisoning had helped—and she wasn't about to give up now. Patricia Porshley-Plum had waited long enough.

So when Patricia saw Elliot leave Home Farm early that Saturday with a silver-haired girl—young people were so ridiculous with their hairstyles nowadays; a nice soft perm had done her perfectly well for years—she decided it was time to make her move.

"When opportunity knocks, answer the door" were her father's last words before he died. Or at least she assumed he was dead—she hadn't seen him since the day she claimed he'd gone crazy, stuck him in a home, and took all his money. There was no time like the present, especially since her electricity seemed to be playing up that morning. Patricia Porshley-Plum decided that today was the perfect opportunity to get what she wanted.

Armed with a homemade Victoria sponge cake—well, the label said that someone had made it at their home—the moment Elliot was out of sight, Patricia made her way up that stupid path to Home Farm. As she knocked gently on the door, she imagined destroying the path with a pickax.

"Why, hello! Josie-kins! It's Patricia!" she chirped like a canary on cotton candy. "Fancy a cup of tea?"

The door opened a fraction and Josie Hooper's delicate face peeked out.

"Hello, pumpkin!" gushed Patricia with her least sincere smile. "Shall we have some cakey?"

The mind is a complex machine and, although Josie's day-to-day memory had been getting worse, her long-term memory was as clear as a spring morning. So despite Elliot's warnings never to answer the door, Josie thought nothing of admitting her long-standing neighbor, like Grandma inviting the Big Bad Wolf in for a granny sandwich.

"Hello, Mrs. Horse's-Bum," she said cheerily. "Do come in."

Even without the insult, Patricia thought Josie looked dreadful. She hadn't seen her for months, but really, the woman was aging horribly. That's what happened when you didn't spend money on expensive beauty creams that were packed with dynoflavinemperorclotheazines to keep the skin firm. And Josie wasn't even dressed! Shuffling around in her robe—had the woman no shame? Of course not. She was poor. Poor people were so very, very lazy.

Patricia entered the cozy sanctuary of Home Farm. As she looked around the cherished home, stuffed with joyful mementos of all the Hoopers who had lived there, she happily pictured the day her bulldozers would flatten it to the ground. She might even take the first swing herself.

"Can I get you a cup of tea?" Josie asked kindly, ushering her guest through to the kitchen.

"How lovely, dear," said Patricia, offering Josie the sponge cake.

"Thank you," said Josie as her neighbor sat warily at the kitchen table, wishing she could run an antibacterial wipe over the seat. Or that her house cleaner could do it for her. "Would you like a cup of tea?"

"Er . . . yes—thank you again," laughed Patricia. "Just as it comes. Milk in first, only three dunks of the bag, two-and-a half sugars stirred counterclockwise, and a small teaspoon. Silver if you have one, but I'm not fussy."

"Right," said Josie, looking confused as she put the kettle on. "Thank you for the cake. Elly will be so pleased."

"Isn't he quite the . . . young man," said Patricia through clenched jaws as she sprayed her palms with hand sanitizer under the table.

"Oh, he's wonderful," beamed Josie. "He takes such good care of me. He's my gift."

"Let's hope you kept the receipt," muttered Patricia as she looked out over the neglected fields. She could see it now. Rows upon rows of identical houses where these pointless acres now stood. "Dairy Mews"—that's what she'd call her development. The idiots who bought her soulless houses liked a bit of character. Patricia felt richer just looking out of the window.

"Do you take sugar?" asked Josie, assembling the tea on a tray.

"Yes, please, two and a half," said Patricia trying to keep the irritation from her voice. Not only was the woman poor and lazy, she was clearly stupid as well.

Josie set the tea tray down and Patricia took in the chipped and mismatched crockery.

"I was so sorry about your father-in-law, poppet. He was such a . . . character." Patricia grimaced, knowing perfectly well that he'd invented the Horse's-Bum nickname that followed her around the village like one of those frightful charity collectors.

"Thank you," said Josie, quietly pouring the tea. "It's been a difficult year."

Patricia reluctantly accepted the stained cup, making a mental note of a wilting plant that would be grateful for the drink when Josie's back was turned.

"Shall we have some cake?" she said breezily, steeling herself at the prospect of another piece of Hooper crockery.

"You brought cake?" said Josie cheerfully. "How lovely— Elly will be so pleased."

Under Patricia's curious gaze, Josie stood up to fetch the cake she had put down moments earlier. Patricia had never spent much time with Josie before—why on earth would she? But she didn't remember her being this slow.

"May I use your facilities?" she asked.

"Of course," said Josie, rummaging around in a cutlery drawer for the big knives that Elliot had hidden. "The toilet's just down the hall on the right."

Patricia shuddered at the offensive word. Just because they existed, it didn't mean that "toilets" needed to be mentioned out loud. Just like "famine victims." Or "affordable houses."

She left the kitchen and immediately headed for the front room. Patricia had no intention of going to the unmentionable in this house—heaven only knows what she'd catch from the unmentionable seat. No, she wanted to find out what was really going on at Home Farm.

She peered around the homely room, which was cluttered with photographs of happier times. In a faded golden frame were Wilfred and Audrey Hooper on their wedding day. A chipped wooden frame displayed a euphoric Josie cradling the newborn Elliot. On one wall were yearly photographs of Elliot, showing the baby growing into a boy—although Patricia observed that the most recent school photo was two years old. Patricia turned her nose up at this pointless tat. All the walls in Patricia's own home were painted in "Essence of Penguin's Belly Button" and hung with expensive paintings by artists who were so exclusive that no one had ever heard of them.

Papers littered every surface and, checking that Josie was still fiddling with the cutlery drawer, Patricia turned some of them over. They were all final reminders and they came from everywhere imaginable—gas, electricity, and water suppliers, phone companies, the local government—and on top of them all was the Really Scary Letter.

Poking her sizable nose around the corner once more, she picked up the letter by its corner and began to read. Patricia Porshley-Plum's shriveled heart danced a tango as she scanned the letter threatening Elliot and Josie's beloved family home. She held the letter from EasyDough! Ltd. like most people hold a winning lottery ticket. A lazy mother and that idiot child couldn't possibly find twenty thousand pounds by next Friday. But nor could Patricia allow Home Farm to fall into someone else's hands once those tiresome Hoopers had been thrown out onto the street and the farm repossessed. Home Farm was going to be hers.

Putting the letter back where she found it, Patricia skipped around to the unmentionable, took a deep breath, and flushed it with her hand inside her sleeve. That blouse would have to be burned. But it had been worth it. Now Josie would have no choice but to sell her Home Farm—and for a fraction of its value.

She swaggered back into the kitchen with a smile that could carve an ice sculpture. But Josie wasn't there. Patricia peered out of the open back door to see Elliot's mother in the vegetable garden pulling up weeds.

"Er—muffinpops? Your tea's getting cold," she trilled.

Josie looked up from her work and smiled warmly at her neighbor as she rose to her feet and brushed the soil off her robe.

"Oh, hello, Mrs. Porshley-Plum—how nice of you to drop by. Would you like some tea?"

Patricia leaned against the door frame. The penny finally dropped.

Josie Hooper wasn't being lazy or stupid or slow. She was seriously unwell. This usually bright young woman had the mind of an old lady. So that's why Elliot had been keeping her tucked away. Patricia realized that she was dealing with someone who wasn't capable of making a sound judgment on her own. Josie now needed an adolescent boy to take care of her, to make important decisions, to keep her safe from harm. The woman was utterly defenseless. There was no way Patricia could buy Home Farm for a bargain price now.

It would be so much cheaper to steal it.

"A cup of tea would be lovely, sweetie pie," said Patricia with a smile that almost reached her eyes. "And then after that, I thought the two of us might have a little outing . . ."

9

BAD COUNCIL

Elliot had always dreamt of flying in an airplane. As his family couldn't afford a vacation abroad, he had wondered what it would be like to view the world from thousands of feet up in the air.

But after five minutes of flying by constellation, Elliot swore his feet would never leave the ground again.

He knew Virgo had saved his life. But now Elliot worried he was in danger of losing it again as his body spun wildly, climbing ever higher in the blinding glare of Virgo's constellation. He felt like a sock in a dryer. A sock that was about to throw up its breakfast.

Just as Elliot lost all sense of which end was up, his flight came to an abrupt halt.

"What you are trying to—?" he began, before being dumped on a pile of surprisingly firm cloud as Virgo's constellation flowed elegantly down to re-form as her physical self. "Ow! You didn't have to drop me."

"You're lucky I didn't drop you halfway across the Aegean Sea," said Virgo, running her fingers through her long silver hair. "You're heavier than you look. And you're welcome, by the way."

"You too," Elliot replied, trying dizzily to stand. "Where are we?"

"This is Elysium," Virgo announced grandly. "Welcome to my home."

His vision still a little blurred from the flight, Elliot took a moment to adjust to the sunlit scene. But when he did, he saw he was in the most perfectly beautiful place. The bright sunshine beamed down on the cloud meadow in which they stood, which was filled with fruit trees straining under laden branches. In the distance one way, Elliot could make out a flawless glass pyramid that sparkled on the horizon like a huge diamond. In the other direction, a river babbled along the edge of the clouds, dropping into a waterfall that shimmered with refracted rainbow light.

"Wow," whispered Elliot as he took in the paradise before him. So there really were other worlds. He found the thought strangely comforting.

"I'd better get to the council chamber," said Virgo, gesturing toward the pyramid. "They need to know what you did."

"What I did!" Elliot exclaimed indignantly. "I saved your stupid shiny head!"

"Which wouldn't have been in danger if you hadn't set the prisoner free. I told you not to."

Elliot knew that there was an excellent answer to that point. He just didn't have it right then.

"Stay here," Virgo commanded.

"You can't tell me what to do," said Elliot defiantly.

"No mortal has ever been to Elysium," said Virgo. "I need to handle this delicate situation with my expert tact and diplomacy. So stay here or I'll pick you up in my constellation and drop you on your curiously stubborn head."

"What will they do?" Elliot conceded.

"Something incredible," Virgo said breezily. "The Zodiac Council has been supporting the immortal community for two thousand years. This probably happens all the time. They'll have a contingency plan. It'll all be perfectly fine."

"YOU DID WHAT?" Pisces shrieked over the commotion in the chamber as the Zodiac Council erupted in outrage.

"Well, it was all a bit of an accident," Virgo began, every eye in the room making her feel only six hundred years old. "You see, Elliot wasn't supposed to be in the prison."

"*You* weren't supposed to be in the prison!" snapped Cancer. "You were supposed to be ordering paper clips!"

"I know, but—" Virgo couldn't quite find the words. She was finding it unusually difficult to make herself sound completely right. This wasn't going as perfectly as she'd hoped.

"You are a young, inexperienced councillor!" yelled Aries, his curled horns unfurling in fury. "In one day, you've disobeyed express orders not to visit Earth, released Prisoner Forty-Two, and missed the final stationery order deadline this month! Explain yourself!"

As Virgo tried to justify what had happened since she'd left Elysium, she spotted Elliot sneaking into the chamber and hiding behind a marble pillar. She had told him to wait outside. Was the mortal child incapable of following any rules?

"Whatever happened," she started uncertainly, "I felt that the most sensible course of action was to return here immediately and file a full report. I used my initiative."

"Shame you didn't use your brain," shouted Scorpio, accidentally squashing a banana into Leo's eye with his pincers.

"Well, there's only one thing for it," said Pisces. "We have to follow protocol."

There was a long pause as the council silently approved the decision.

"Deny all knowledge," shouted Aquarius, raising his jug in salute.

"Precisely," agreed Pisces. "Our official line is that we know nothing of Prisoner Forty-Two's escape."

"Excellent," said Libra, weighing two muffins on her scales. "And I move that we deny all knowledge of denying all knowledge."

"Seconded," said Sagittarius, firing a pencil at a dartboard. "This council knows nothing."

"Agreed," barked Leo. "After all, we have a reputation to uphold as the council that knows nothing about anything."

"Sounds like an excellent course of action," said Virgo, relieved that the situation was back under control. "I'm sure it's of no consequence. After all, how dangerous can this Thanatos be? Oooh—chocolate muffins . . ."

The air was nearly sucked out of the chamber as the councillors gasped as one.

"What did you say?" boomed Taurus.

"I said 'chocolate muffins,' although I really must cut down . . ." said Virgo. "Now, about our paper-clip supplier . . ."

"Thanatos?" said Capricorn, her horns pricked in anticipation. "Where did you hear that?"

"Oh, it was nothing—just the prisoner's name," sighed Virgo, thumbing a stationery catalog. "He is obviously suboptimal. Claims to be the king of the Daemons! More like king of the Dodos . . ."

"You must be mistaken," said Pisces dismissively. "Clearly your incompetence extends to your hearing."

Virgo knew she should leave well enough alone. She had escaped serious reprimand and the whole matter could now be put behind her.

But being right was far more important.

"So, Pisces—pardon me, but my hearing is perfect," she ventured. "The prisoner clearly stated his name was Thanatos."

"That is impossible," said the Gemini twins condescendingly.

"Why?" said Virgo.

"Because, child," said Pisces, "Thanatos has been dead for over two thousand years."

"He seemed thoroughly alive this morning," said Virgo. "Who is he?"

"Haven't you studied our history?" asked Aquarius.

"Er . . . yes, of course," said Virgo, finding it strange to say something that wasn't actually true.

Elliot's head poked around the pillar. Virgo mouthed to him to move out of sight, but he replied with a mortal hand gesture she didn't entirely understand.

"Thanatos *was* . . . whatever are you doing, child?" asked Pisces, noticing Virgo's strange head movements as she communicated with Elliot.

"Um, nothing. Just some . . . exercises," she replied, noting it was slightly easier to say something untrue this time.

"As I was saying—Thanatos *was* the king of the Daemons," explained Pisces. "You know that, at least?"

"Of course I do," said Virgo, embracing this curious new skill. She had no idea what Pisces was talking about—in all her years on the Zodiac Council, she'd barely been allowed to finish a sentence, let alone ask a question. For the first time, she realized this could be an advantage.

"That's right, it's all coming back now," she said. "Thanatos—"

"Was the son of Erebus, Daemon of Darkness," said Capricorn. "When Zeus became king of the Gods, he made his best friend, Erebus, the king of the Daemons."

"Absolutely. Erebus," said Virgo authoritatively. "Wasn't he the one who—?"

"Repaid Zeus's kindness by trying to overthrow him," snorted Taurus. "Erebus wanted to rule the world himself. But he was no match for the king of the Gods. Zeus took his kardia and slew him in noble combat."

"Of course," said Virgo. "But then—"

"Thanatos took his father's place as Daemon King. Years later, he too craved Zeus's power, so he challenged him," said Sagittarius. "But like father, like son; he was unequal to the task. Zeus killed him too."

"Absolutely!" said Virgo. "And so—"

"The only trace that remains of Thanatos is his Chaos Stones," said Leo.

"Indeed," said Virgo, "after all, the Chaos Stones—"

"Control the elements," bleated Aries. "Earth, Air, Water, and Fire. They were a gift from Chaos herself, Erebus's mother. But Thanatos abused the power of the stones, using them to terrorize the mortals with earthquakes, hurricanes, floods, and infernos. Thanatos was determined to enslave mortalkind and rule the world."

"But Zeus won the Chaos Stones when he defeated Thanatos and used them to rid the realms of all the Daemons before he retired. Took their kardia and exterminated the lot. And good riddance," explained Pisces. "So you see, child—it is simply not possible for Thanatos to be Prisoner Forty-Two."

"Er—hang on a minute," said Elliot, emerging from behind the pillar to the astonishment of everyone but Virgo.

"Elliot!" spat Virgo. "I told you to stay outside!"

"Elliot?" asked Libra. "This is the mortal child?"

"Yes, I was going to—"

"You've brought a mortal to Elysium!" roared Leo. "Are you out of your mind?"

"No, you see, Thanatos . . . Prisoner Forty-Two . . . was about to kill him, so I rescued him in my constellation," said Virgo proudly.

"Haven't you read your contract?" cried Capricorn incredulously. "Council members aren't allowed to reveal their constellations to a mortal . . ."

"I told you so," huffed Virgo to Elliot.

"No mortal has ever set foot in Elysium!" shouted Cancer.

"Well, it looks like I picked a good time to start," said Elliot, exchanging curious looks with Pisces. "Didn't you just say that Thanatos wanted to enslave mortalkind?"

"We know nothing about that," said Libra dismissively.

"You just said he did!"

"No, she didn't," said Capricorn. "She didn't say anything."

"So you're denying that the chubby golden sheep over there . . ."

"How dare you!" snorted Aries. "I'm a ram."

"Apologies," said Elliot. "So you're denying that the chubby golden ram over there just said that there might be a Death Daemon on the loose who could attack mortals with earthquakes, hurricanes, floods, and infernos?"

"No—technically he'd need his Chaos Stones back, and *then* he could attack mortals with earthquakes, hurricanes, floods, and infernos," said one Gemini twin, earning a slap from the other. "Not that we have any knowledge of that."

"So you look after the immortal community, but when something serious happens, you're not going to do anything?"

"We are a council," explained Taurus. "It's not our job to actually do anything. We just have to file the correct paperwork."

"Thanatos is dead. And even if he weren't, it's not up to us to wage war on vengeful Death Daemons," added Pisces. "Not that there are any of those. And if there were, we'd know nothing about them."

"So this is your perfect system?" Elliot said to Virgo, who had sunk under the table with embarrassment. "This makes you so much better than mortals?"

All eyes turned to Virgo. Or to the top of her head. Elliot had a point. She needed to stand her ground.

"The child is right," she finally squeaked from beneath the table. "If this Prisoner Forty-Two is Thanatos and if he is as dangerous as you say he is, shouldn't we at least try to recapture him?"

"If Thanatos is as dangerous as we say he is, perhaps you

shouldn't have let him go in the first place!" shouted Libra. "Not that he is. Dangerous. Or even exists. I know nothing about it."

"Well, on behalf of all mortals, you've been a huge help," said Elliot, turning to leave. "So if you could beam me back to my jeopardized mortal life, I'd be very grateful. How do I get out of here?"

"Virgo can show you the way. She's just leaving," said Pisces.

"I am?" asked Virgo, poking back up over the table.

"Yes, you are," said Leo. "You're absolutely right. This is your mess and you need to clean it up, before word gets out that an immortal prisoner is on the loose. Not that he is. Restore the mortal child to his home and do not return to Elysium until Prisoner Forty-Two is safely back in his prison. Not that he's out of it."

"How am I going to do that?" said Virgo.

"Your problem," Pisces pronounced. "Virgo of the Zodiac Council and Guardian of the Stationery Cupboard, you are to return to Earth and sort out the situation you have created. But not before ordering some more printer ink. To ensure you cannot risk any further exposure of the immortal world, the council hereby forbids you from using *any* of your Constellation powers on pain of suspension."

"What!" shrieked Virgo. "You'd suspend me from the council?"

"No, child," said Pisces grimly. "We'd suspend you from immortality. You could lose your kardia for this."

"But . . . but . . . You can't do that! I won't let you!" yelled Virgo, clutching the necklace at her throat.

"Er . . . yes, we can, and yes, you will," said Cancer, pulling a huge leather-bound volume from the bookshelf with her pincers. "Here it is."

Cancer handed the volume to Virgo.

"What's this?" asked Elliot.

"The Sacred Code," said Virgo grimly. "Our rules."

"During the reign of the Olympians, certain immortal behaviors were getting a little . . . excessive," said Aquarius.

"When the Zodiac Council took charge we decided to impose a little order. We made all immortals swear on the Styx that they would abide by the laws of the Sacred Code," explained Sagittarius. "Including Virgo."

Elliot peered over Virgo's shoulder to read the first page, which was covered in pencil notations, Post-it Notes, and rude pictures in the margins:

The Sacred Code
12,349th Edition*

I) All immortals have the right to ambrosia

b) Immortals cannot break mortal laws

7) Immortals cannot herd giraffes on a Tuesday

xic) Immortals cannot keep mortal money

F2) Immortals cannot wear socks with sandals

39.4) Immortals cannot break an oath

xy) Immortals cannot push cotton buds too far into their ears

*All rules subject to change with any or no notice

"Turn to page four thousand three hundred and twenty-nine," said Cancer smugly.

Virgo leafed through thousands more pages of rules and read aloud:

"'Rule 985 take-away-the-first-number-you-thought-of: The Zodiac Council reserves the right to confiscate the kardia from any immortal who behaves like a proper doughnut.'"

"You see?" said Pisces. "So there you have it. Virgo, your task is clear. Recapture the prisoner *without* using your Constellation powers. Or you will lose your immortality. Forever."

10

PLAIN SAILING

Elliot expected something incredibly dramatic to happen when Virgo was banned from her powers. He waited for the sparks to fly, for her body to be beamed up in a ray of light before being cast to the ground, a broken shadow of her starry self.

But in fact, she only had to sign a few forms and hand over the keys to the stationery cupboard.

Elliot didn't know what to say as they walked away across the clouds.

"I'm sorry you're in trouble," he finally offered.

"The council has spoken," said Virgo sadly. "And the council is always right."

"A right bunch of—"

"It's my fault. If I had obeyed the rules, none of this would have happened. Everything was perfect before."

"So why did you leave?"

"Because I . . . I wanted to experience a different perfect, that's all. I never thought it would come to this."

"Look, I'm sorry about your problems and I'm glad you saved my life and everything, but I really need to get home to

Mom. Let's get into your whizzy star-ball thing and get back to the farm."

"There is no whizzy star-ball thing now," Virgo sighed. "You heard them—I can't use my Constellation powers or they'll take my kardia and I'll become a pathetic, simple, pointless mortal. Just like you."

"Sounds terrible," said Elliot.

They came to the beautiful river that lapped gently at the banks of the clouds. Virgo pursed her lips to whistle, but all that came out of her mouth was a shower of spit.

"Eugh—gross!" grumbled Elliot, wiping it off with his T-shirt. "What are you doing?"

"Hailing public transport. Urgh."

"Here, let me."

Elliot put his thumb and forefinger into his mouth and let out a perfect whistle. He and Mom had spent hours practicing it, along with loads of other useful tricks, including pick-pocketing, semaphore, starting a fire, and burping the alphabet.

"Try again," said Virgo impatiently. "This is so archaic."

But before Elliot could give another blast, he was knocked flying by a huge wave that suddenly burst out of the river. As he spluttered and choked, Elliot mopped the wet hair from his eyes to see what had caused this unexpected tsunami.

"At last," said Virgo, who was completely dry. "It's here."

Rocked by its own waves in the middle of the river was a long wooden boat. At the prow was a carving of a ferocious lion, and at the stern, a serpent's winding tail. A pair of wooden oars balanced the boat on the river and a black sail hung from the tall mast, concealing the identity of the sailor.

"Hello, Charon," yelled Virgo. "Room for two?"

The black sail was drawn aside, and Elliot tried not to stare at the individual before him. The man, if that's what he was, was deathly white, almost transparent. His stringy yellow hair hung limply down to his chin and a pair of pale-gray eyes stared out of their dark sockets. His short figure was swathed in a rough brown robe, his dirty, veiny hands jutting from the sleeves. Charon raised his finger and pointed straight at Elliot's heart.

"Come hither, mortal," he said in a shaky, high-pitched voice, "if you dare to ride the Ship of Death."

Elliot decided that he didn't dare at all.

"Don't be ridiculous, Charon," snapped Virgo.

"Whatever do you mean, Lady Virgo?" trembled Charon, shifting awkwardly in the boat.

"You sound like you've sat on a mouse. Use your real voice, for goodness' sake."

"All right, darlin', you got me," chortled Charon several octaves lower. "Sorry, mate, don't normally come north of the river—the tourists love all that stuff. Hop in." Elliot waited for Charon to whip off his disguise, but it appeared that the boatman was unfortunate enough to really look that way. He tentatively walked up the gangplank as Charon assumed his position at the oars.

"Welcome aboard, mate," said Charon with something that was presumably a smile. "I'm Charon, proprietor of Quick Styx Cabs. *You won't wait an eternity for us.* Made that up meself."

"Well done," said Elliot uncertainly, taking his place on a narrow bench next to a particularly pungent sandwich.

"We need to get back to Elliot's farm. It's . . ." Virgo looked to Elliot for instructions. "You tell him. Charon can find anyone or anything."

"Better than Google Maps," said Charon proudly, tapping his head. "I can get you anywhere."

"Home Farm, Little Motbury? Wiltshire? England? The Earth?" said Elliot, unsure how much detail an immortal cab driver needed.

"What river's it on?" asked Charon.

"Near the Avon," said Elliot.

"Right-o, we'll take the Severn—the Wye's murder this time of day. Hold on and off we go."

And with an almighty tug on the oars, Charon eased the boat away from the bank and started along the glistening water. It was a nice change of pace after a hectic morning, although Elliot was worried that Mom had been on her own for too long. He hadn't even made her lunch. And if she went looking for him . . .

"Excuse me, Charon—how long will it take, please?" he asked the oarsman.

"Two shakes of a sphinx's tail," Charon assured him, "We'll have you home for lunch."

"And, er, how exactly are we going to row through the sky?" asked Elliot casually.

"We're on the river Styx," said Virgo.

"The Styx?" said Elliot. "The thing you swear your oaths on?"

"Yes," said Virgo. "It's a sacred river. If you break an oath sworn on the Styx, you lose your kardia. Then you spend a year unable to speak or move and are denied any nectar or ambrosia. For the next nine years, no immortal can speak to you and then you are banished from immortal society to be a lonely and desolate outcast until you die."

"It's also a nightmare trying to get a library card," said Charon.

"The Styx is the boundary between Elysium and Earth," Virgo continued. "All the rivers on Earth run into it at some point just below the Earth's surface, making it a very convenient way for immortals to get around unnoticed."

"Think of the world like a dirty great onion," Charon chipped in. "Elysium is like the skin, circling all around it above the clouds. The next realm in is the Earth—you know all about that one. Inside that you have the Asphodel Fields, then the Underworld."

"Each realm is reached by crossing a river—they run like a corkscrew through the world and Charon is the only way to move between them," said Virgo.

"And not everyone can go everywhere," said Charon. "Apart from me. And Constellations, of course, Miss Virgo."

"All other immortals have restrictions," said Virgo smugly. "Gods aren't allowed into the Underworld. Elementals can't visit Elysium. Accessing a forbidden realm costs an immortal their kardia."

"Why can't everyone just go where they want?" asked Elliot.

"Don't be ridiculous," snorted Virgo. "Because then everyone would want to live in the best places."

"So?" said Elliot. "Why can't they?"

"Of course, it's all a conspiracy," said Charon.

"Oh, don't start, Charon," Virgo huffed. "Not everything is a conspiracy."

"That's what they want you to believe," whispered Charon, tapping the side of his nose. "But I'm in the know."

"I feel like I'm in Crazyville and you're the mayor, Charon," said Virgo with a shake of her silver head.

"No, I'm not," said the oarsman defensively. "Besides, that's six hundred and thirty-seven miles due west, straight through the Northern Lights and second left after Dorking. Nah, we've all been fed a big pile of centaur droppings over the years. Take the creation story—if you really think that Uranus . . ."

Elliot zoned Charon out and looked over at Virgo staring mournfully out of the boat.

"What are you going to do?" he asked her.

"You heard them. I have to recapture Prisoner Forty-Two."

"How?"

"I have no idea," said Virgo heavily.

". . . and Theseus slaying the Minotaur? Do me a favor," Charon scoffed. "That boy couldn't win a food fight . . ."

"Tell me something," Elliot began. "If Prisoner Forty-Two isn't a Daemon, why did he have their kardia?"

"Maybe it was just . . . dirty," muttered Virgo. "I don't know. You heard Pisces. There's no way that Prisoner Forty-Two could be Thanatos. He's dead."

"No, he's not," announced Charon suddenly.

"Why do you say that?" asked Elliot.

"He's making it up—have you not studied our history?" said Virgo grandly.

"My mom says history is only what the winners wrote down," said Elliot.

"Hold on a sec—we're at Earth Junction," said Charon, pulling over to the riverbank. "Got some more customers to pick up."

Until that moment, Elliot had thought that the strangest passengers he'd ever seen were on a London bus. He had read about some of the creatures he now saw: There were two young goblins sniggering as they blew bubble gum into a centaur's tail, while a half man, half goat—Elliot remembered this was a satyr—was annoying an elderly fairy by playing heavy-metal music on his panpipes.

"Do you mind?" the fairy huffed, pointing to a sign with crossed-out panpipes on the mast.

"Whatevs," muttered the satyr as he plugged some headphones into the pipes and returned to his thrash panpipe solo.

"Urgh. Elementals . . ." Virgo tutted disapprovingly under her breath.

The boat pulled away from the shore and Charon regained his easy rhythm with the oars.

"So. Thanatos," he went on plainly. "He's alive all right. Must be."

"What are you talking about?" said a weary Virgo.

"Now listen, I'm as neutral as a magnolia living room in Switzerland. I don't play for any of the teams, see?"

Charon held out his kardia, which was made of glass.

"I get on fine with all sides—and none of their powers work on Neutrals, so I can do what I like," he said. "But if you believe that Zeus killed Thanatos, you're blinder than a Cyclops with an eye patch."

"And Charon, *you* are as full of poop as King Augeas's stables," Virgo scoffed.

"I don't know what happened," said Charon. "But I'd bet my eleventh toe it was something dodgy. Back in the day, I used to ferry the souls of the dead to the Underworld— mortals and immortals. Made a tidy living—the dead used to be buried with a coin in their mouth to pay my fare. No one does that anymore. I blame credit cards."

There was a kerfuffle at the back of the boat as the centaur put his hind legs on the seat next to the fairy.

"Do you *mind*?" she said haughtily, nodding toward another sign saying PLEASE KEEP YOUR HOOVES OFF THE SEATS.

"So where did you take Thanatos?" asked Elliot.

"That's my point," Charon insisted. "I didn't. I escorted every dead soul in those days—including Erebus after Zeus killed him. But I never saw Thanatos. And if he's flown the coop, he'll be heading straight for his Chaos Stones. He loves them like a dung beetle loves diarrhea."

"What are they like?" asked Elliot.

"Well . . . they're small black beetles that like dung," said Charon.

"The Chaos Stones," said Elliot.

"Oh, them," said Charon. "Boy, they're a sight. The four most beautiful jewels you'll see. The Fire Stone is a boundless sapphire, the Water Stone a deep-red ruby, the Air Stone a beautiful emerald, and the Earth Stone a brilliant diamond."

"Hang on," said Elliot, picturing the stones. "They're all the wrong colors?"

"Chaos—Thanatos's gran—who created the stones at the dawn of the universe, was an almighty Goddess with the power to produce day and night," explained Charon. "Unfortunately, the old dear was as color-blind as a shortsighted bat in sunglasses . . . If you control the stones, you control the elements—not to mention becoming as rich as King Midas. Before he invested all his wealth in seafront property in Atlantis."

Elliot's ears pricked up.

"Rich? How?" he asked, trying to sound casual.

"It's that Earth Stone," said Charon. "Think about it. If you control the Earth, you can find oil, gold, buried treasure—you'd be minted in a minute."

"And where are they now?" asked Elliot more keenly.

"Zeus must have them," said Charon. "Unless he lost them in one of his divorces."

A cell phone rang through the boat. The fairy carefully opened her handbag and gently pulled out the phone. She elegantly cleared her throat and answered the call.

"HELLO?" she yelled at the top of her lungs. "I CAN'T TALK NOW! I'M ON THE SHIP OF DEATH!"

"DO YOU MIND?" said all the other passengers in unison, drawing her attention to a sign showing a fairy shouting into a cell phone in a prohibited red circle.

Elliot's mind was whirring. A magical diamond that could make him instantly rich? A diamond that could help him pay off the debt and save his home? A diamond that was . . . a diamond. Now *that* was a diamond he needed to find.

"So Zeus is still alive?" Elliot asked.

"Of course he is, duh," sighed Virgo.

"And whoever this prisoner is, you're going to need some help catching him?"

"Pah—you offering?" said Virgo condescendingly.

"Maybe," said Elliot, a vision dancing in his head of the top-of-the-line game console he was going to buy with the treasure the Earth Stone would reveal. "But you also need someone with experience. Someone who knows Prisoner Forty-Two. Someone who has caught him before . . ."

Virgo looked as though she'd been hit by a thunderbolt.

"Oh, my Gods!" she gasped. "Zeus! He imprisoned him the first time! He can do it again! That's the best idea I've ever had!"

"Er . . . excuse me . . ." said Elliot.

"Charon—where can I find Zeus?" asked Virgo.

"Haven't seen him for a day or two—but Zeus doesn't blow his nose without his son Hermes bringing him the hankie," Charon put in. "This time of day, Hermes will be in that Café Hero in the Asphodel Fields having one of their high-powered coffees."

"Then let's go," beamed Virgo.

"Er—wait a minute—I need to get home," said Elliot.

"We're coming up to the junction with the Avon," said Charon. "Am I taking you home, or are we going to find Hermes?"

"Will it take long?" asked Elliot, weighing up leaving Mom alone against the prospect of finding the Earth Stone.

"Not at all," said Virgo, finally brightening up. "We'll have Thanatos back in prison by teatime. This is all going to work out perfectly."

"Well?" said Charon to Elliot.

"To the Asphodel Fields," said Elliot, reassuring himself that today was no different from leaving Mom on a school day. This was his best chance of saving Home Farm. "We've got some Gods to find."

The boat continued its descent along the Styx, the bright colors of the Earth starting to blur as if someone was rubbing them out with a giant eraser. The scenery faded slowly away until there was nothing but gray, foggy cloud. The boat sailed into a long, gloomy tunnel.

"Next stop," announced Charon as they came to a halt underground, "Acheron Junction. Exit here for the Asphodel Fields. Please ensure you take all personal belongings and limbs with you."

"Thanks," said Elliot as the other passengers jostled off the ship.

"No problem," said Charon. He looked down at the abacus at the front of the boat. "That'll be three thousand drachma," he said cheerily.

Virgo looked at Elliot, who looked blankly back.

"What?" he said.

"Well, I haven't got any money," she said. "I've never needed it before. You'll have to pay him."

"I'm sorry," said Elliot to Charon, rummaging around in his pocket and producing the three pounds seventy-six he'd stashed there earlier in the day and a random button. "This is all I have."

Charon's eyes became the size of saucers.

"Wow!" he whispered. "Can I? Can I really . . . ?"

"Of course," said Elliot, trying not to wince at the thought of losing his entire week's spending money. But as Charon withdrew his hand, Elliot saw that the boatman had only taken the button.

"Mortal treasure!" he said. "I collect this stuff—I've not seen a blue one before . . ."

"Are you sure?" said Elliot, uncomfortable at cheating the man who might just have solved all his financial worries.

"Oh, I'm not trying to rip you off, mate, that includes the tip," said Charon, still staring at his fare.

"Well, great—keep the change," said Elliot, bemused for the umpteenth time that day.

"And here," said Charon, fishing around in his pocket, producing a small piece of parchment. "Here's my card. If you ever need me, just drop this in the nearest water and I'll come and find you."

"See you, Charon," said Virgo as she and Elliot walked into the gloom.

"Ta-ra, kids," he said, pulling out a newspaper and the sandwich with something horrible wriggling inside it. "*Zodiac Council Pledges More Free Centaur Schools,*" he read on the front page. "Believe that, you'll believe anything . . ."

A short while later, a card floated down the river to announce a new job. Charon picked it out of the murky water.

"Well, I'll be . . ." he said, taking up the oars in his gnarled hands.

Charon rowed back along the Styx, this time taking the river Avon turning toward Stonehenge. A few moments later, he saw his passenger lurking in the cold fog that hung over the riverbank.

"Hello, Charon" came a drawling voice.

"Blimey," said Charon. "Your ears must have been burning—I was only just talking about you. Long time, no see."

"Too long," said Thanatos, taking his seat as the boat pulled away from the bank. "But I can promise you this—you'll be seeing a lot more of me from now on."

11

A TRIP DOWN MEMORY FLAME

"So what have I missed?" yawned Thanatos as the Ship of Death rowed through the melancholy depths of the Underworld along the river Lethe, the river of oblivion, passing forests of dead trees and vast expanses of barren fields.

"Oh, you know how it is—nothing really changes," said Charon. "I'm getting older, everything creaks a bit louder, bits keep falling off . . ."

"Nonsense," said Thanatos. "You don't look a day over four thousand."

"Too kind, guv'nor." Charon smiled.

They rowed past a building site on the riverbank, where a team of Penates were scuttling around a half-finished construction covered in scaffolding.

"What's this?" asked Thanatos disapprovingly.

"It's happening everywhere," said Charon. "You get a nice bit of riverside wasteland and someone snaps it up and builds apartments. That's going to be a luxury Underworld complex called 'Dun Livin.' These jokers are totally ruining the character of the area if you ask me . . ."

"Is that so?" said Thanatos, his eyes darkening. "Are we far from Tartarus?"

"I'll get you there faster than a satyr chasing a siren, guv'nor," said Charon cheerily. "In fact—I need to pop in anyhow. I've been diversifying my business model—branching out a bit. I've started a grocery delivery service—it's doing all right. I've got a drop to make in Tartarus as it happens. Be there in no time."

Ten minutes later, the boat pulled up alongside an infinite brass wall. Thanatos and Charon disembarked from the Ship of Death and made their way to a set of imposing ebony gates. The flaming letters across the top announced that this was the entrance to Tartarus.

ABANDON HOPE ALL YE WHO ENTER HERE! proclaimed a large sign. SECURITY CAMERAS ARE IN OPERATION IN THIS REALM!

Thanatos stood back as Charon slouched toward the security booth in front of the gates, where Cerberus, the three-headed hound, had one set of eyes on the gates, the second on a large sandwich, and the third on a small TV screen showing two harpies screaming over who stole the other's boyfriend.

"All right, mate," said Charon to the security guard. "How's the family?"

"Not bad," said Cerberus's middle head. "Wife's just had a new litter."

"Oh—congratulations! How many kids you got now, then?"

"Forty-seven boys and thirty-two girls," said Cerberus proudly. "Actually I think it's forty-six boys. One of them said his sister had put on weight. So she ate him."

"Kids do the funniest things," chortled Charon. "Got a delivery for one of your inmates—all right if I go through?"

"Help yourself," said Cerberus, buzzing the gates open before picking up the sandwich. "Oh, no—one harpy's just pulled the other one's wing! I know it's trash, but I love a good harpy fight . . ."

As the ebony gates creaked open, Charon and Thanatos proceeded into the fiery wasteland of Tartarus. They were in a vast, blazing valley where, on all sides, prisoners were performing everlasting punishments, moaning as they pursued their endlessly futile tasks.

"So what's the plan now you're out?" asked Charon. "Put your feet up? Take it easy? Find a new hobby?"

"I'm going to reclaim my Chaos Stones, take my revenge on Zeus, enslave the mortals, and rule the world," said Thanatos. "Although golf also sounds charming . . ."

"Important to keep busy," said Charon. "Well, how 'bout that—look who it is!"

Across the valley, a lone scrawny figure was struggling to push a huge boulder up a sheer hill.

"Sisyphus!" Thanatos cried. "How good to see you again!"

"Thanatoth?" said Sisyphus, raising a hand to wave, but quickly slapping it back as the boulder started rolling down the hill. "Well, thith ith a thurprithe. Lithen—no hard feelingth, I trutht?"

"Of course not," said Thanatos languidly. "The whole thing was hilarious. That time you tried to cheat your own death by tying me up and hiding me down here! Really, you are too funny. Oh, how I laughed."

"Thank heawenth!" said Sisyphus. "Thath very magnani-mouth of you. You know how it ith—you work yourthelf up into a thilly frenthy and then you jutht have to thay to your-thelf: 'Thithyphuth? Theriouthly? You are a thuch a thilly thauthage. Thanatoth won't give thith a thecond thought.'"

"Of course not," said Thanatos, gesturing to the boulder. "I'm not one to hold a grudge. Looks like you've nearly cracked that as well."

"Jutht one more push," said Sisyphus. "Thith ith the one. I can feel it in the pit of my thtomach."

"How many times have you tried to get that boulder up there now?" asked Charon.

"Thith will be . . . theventy-theven thouthand thix hundred and thixty-thix," said Sisyphus. "But thith time, I really thenth I'll be thuccthethful."

"Good for you," said Thanatos. "I'd shake your hand but . . . !"

"You thneaky thwine!" laughed Sisyphus with a heave, as Charon and Thanatos continued through the scorching inferno.

"This is the address," said Charon, reading his order form as they approached a large pool. "Tantalus. Number One, Pool of Despair."

"You're late," snapped Tantalus from the middle of the water, where he was chained to a post beneath a plum tree that was groaning with perfectly ripe fruit. "I specifically booked the one p.m. to two p.m. slot. It is 2:04."

"Sorry, mate," shrugged Charon, before adding under his breath, "didn't realize you had such a busy schedule . . ."

"Did you bring my order?" barked Tantalus.

"'Ere it is," said Charon, waggling the bag with a grin.

"At last!" whooped Tantalus. "I've done it! I've beaten the system! I will have food! I will have drink! I will have a refund—you're four minutes late!"

"Yeah . . . one little thing," said Charon, consulting his order form. "I've had to make an . . . item substitution."

"What do you mean, substitution?" snapped Tantalus. "I only ordered two things: water and fruit."

"Yeah—it was weird. I tried everywhere—Trader Plato's, Drachmo, Aesop & Perseus—every single shop was completely out of both. But I've brought you a replacement . . ."

Charon rummaged in the bag and proudly produced his shopping.

"Toilet paper," he announced. "You can never have enough."

"YOU IDIOT!" screamed Tantalus. "I haven't had anything to eat or drink for thousands of years! Every time I try to eat the fruit, it moves from my grasp! Every time I try to drink the water, it seeps away! I am mad with hunger and thirst, my skin is wrinkled like a prune on a pension, and YOU BRING ME TOILET PAPER!"

Charon hung his head. "It's quilted," he added hopefully.

"YOU TOTAL MORON!" Tantalus yelled. "I can't eat this!"

"Listen, pal," said Charon. "You served up your own son for dinner. I didn't have you down as a picky eater . . ."

"AAAAAAAAARGH!" yelled Tantalus, throwing his livid hands up in the air, sending the fruit-laden branches flying and the water slipping away. "I'M STARVING!"

"Now, now, now," smirked Thanatos, plucking the toilet paper from Charon's hand. "That's not very community-spirited of you, Tantalus. Just because you can't make use of this, it doesn't mean someone else shouldn't benefit. Hey, Sisyphus?"

"Yeth?" strained Sisyphus, his boulder teetering on the brow of the hill.

"Catch!" sneered Thanatos, tossing the roll straight at him.

Sisyphus instinctively snatched his hands away from the boulder to grab the gift.

"Wow—quilted, thankth!" said Sisyphus, before his face fell a mile. "Uh-oh . . ."

For a second, the boulder looked as though it might simply drop into a crevice on the hilltop. But as it wobbled precariously at the summit, it quickly became clear that gravity was going to win.

"YOU CAN'T BE THERIOUTH!" screamed Sisyphus, sprinting downhill as the boulder started to roll back down. "AAAAAARGH!"

The mighty rock came tumbling down the hill, picking up incredible speed and forcing Sisyphus to dive into Tantalus's pool to take cover. Tantalus howled with laughter as the boulder that had taken months to reach the summit rumbled back down in seconds, rolling up the other side of the valley and taking off like a skateboarder on a ramp.

"Oh, get thtuffed!" yelled Sisyphus, grabbing a huge handful of plums off the tree and cramming them greedily into his mouth.

Thanatos's thin lips curled into a satisfied smile.

"Whoops," he said carelessly, and headed onward. "Wait for me back at the boat, Charon."

Charon shrugged. "You're the boss," he said. "But remind me never to get on your bad side."

Thanatos strode on through the flaming valley until he came to the banks of a murky lake. In the middle there was a small island, surrounded by a river of fire. On the island stood a circular stone prison, from which a cacophony of shouting and argument was echoing around the valley.

"Comrades!" shouted Thanatos from the bank. "Can you hear my call?"

The din went quiet.

"Who is it?" a voice squeaked from within. "If you're one of those door-to-door vacuum cleaner salesmen, we've told you—we're not interested."

"It is I, your king—it is Thanatos," the Daemon cried across the water.

There was frantic whispering within the prison.

"Don't believe you," said the voice again. "Unless you're delivering pizza, get outta here."

"Is that you, Mendacium, Daemon of Lies?"

There was a brief pause.

"No," said the voice unconvincingly.

"I believe him," said Pistis, Daemon of Trust.

"I heard you were alive," whispered Ossa, Daemon of Rumor.

"It's true," said Thanatos. "And when I have reclaimed the Chaos Stones from the traitor, I will use them to free you too. We will fight! And this time . . . we will win!"

"No, we won't," moaned Penthos, Daemon of Misery.

"Let's do it!" said Alalal, Daemon of Battle Cries.

"I'm hungry," moaned Limon, Daemon of Famine.

"What's he talking about?" shouted Geras, Daemon of Old Age. "And who's got my teeth?"

"But first I must know this," Thanatos proclaimed. "Who betrayed me? Who put you here? Who escaped imprisonment?"

"It was Fuga, Daemon of Escape," said Mendacium.

"You liar!" Fuga shot back. "I'm still here. Ironically."

"Well, you didn't hear it from me . . ." said Ossa.

"Who?" barked Thanatos.

"It was Hypnos," said Ossa.

"My own brother?" said Thanatos incredulously. "My twin? Are you sure?"

"It was—that psycho sold you out," said Oblivio, Daemon of Forgetfulness. "Now what was the question?"

"It was Hypnos. I swear it," declared Aletheia, Daemon of Truth. "And that outfit looks terrible on you."

"I see," said Thanatos. "Be patient, my subjects. Victory will be ours."

"You will come back and get us?" asked Elpis, Daemon of Hope.

"It will be done. I will return with the Chaos Stones and free you all," shouted Thanatos. "I swear it on the Styx."

"Yeah, right," sighed Corus, Daemon of Disdain.

"Bungalow!" yelled Coalemus, Daemon of Stupidity.

"Ow! Who trod on my foot?" yelled Algea, the Daemon of Pain, and the arguing started up again.

Thanatos headed back across the barren wilderness of Tartarus to the Lethe, where Charon was waiting in his boat.

"Do you think you can find my brother?" Thanatos asked with a dark smile.

"Hypnos? Crikey, not seen that crazy kid for millennia. Must be up on Earth. I'll find him, don't you worry."

"Thank you," said Thanatos. "It's high time for a family reunion."

"Bet he'll be pleased to see you," said the ferryman.

"Oh, Charon," Thanatos laughed. "I very much doubt that."

12

THE GOD OF FASHION

"Where are we now?" Elliot asked Virgo, struggling to see anything through the nebulous gloom.

"The Asphodel Fields," Virgo announced, "the realm just beneath the Earth. When the Olympians ruled, it used to be where the souls of those who were neither particularly good nor particularly bad wandered for eternity. It was a bleak place, where those with unremarkable lives spent infinite hours roaming aimlessly with no particular purpose nor end in sight."

"So what is it now?" Elliot asked.

"A shopping center," said Virgo as they emerged into a brightly lit building.

At first, Elliot thought it looked like any normal shopping mall. Countless shops were arranged on several floors with a glass elevator running up the center. It was only when he noticed that many customers didn't require the elevator because they were able to fly, and that there were shops for wing repair, snake-hair blow-drys, or spare feet, that Elliot could see this was something different.

They passed a huge furniture shop where two giants were having a ferocious argument over whether they should buy some flat-packed furniture called a Wongledonk or a Fluberstink.

"I don't know what it is about that shop—it brings out the worst in everyone," muttered Virgo. "Mind you, Elementals have no idea how to behave in public . . ."

"You're a snob," said Elliot.

"I assume that this is a mortal word for someone whose head is screwed on correctly?"

"It's a mortal word for someone whose head is somewhere," muttered Elliot as they arrived outside Café Hero.

Inviting aromas floated out of the door as he and Virgo made their way inside the coffee shop, past a large bar steaming away with bubbling machines and surrounded by glass cases full of tempting cakes and pastries—and the occasional slimy insect with elaborate icing on top.

But a quick look at the inhabitants revealed that this was no ordinary café. The tables were filled with extraordinary creatures, from dragons to fairies to trolls to . . . he didn't even know what half of them were. To his left, a couple of elves were doing word searches over an espresso, while on his right, a unicorn fed her foal a giant blueberry muffin from the end of her horn.

The two members of staff had long necks supporting at least a dozen heads each and countless arms sprouting from their torsos. This allowed the server to take umpteen orders simultaneously and prepare them all at once, while the waiter could clear at least ten tables at a time, chatting merrily to several different customers. Elliot thought of Mavis in the Little Motbury tea rooms. He and Mom used to time how long it would take her to bring a cup of tea. Her personal best was twelve minutes and six seconds. She could learn a lot from this place.

"Hecatoncheires," Virgo explained, "hundred-handed ones. They run the most successful chain of coffeehouses in creation—they're springing up everywhere. Ah—Hermes."

Virgo pointed out a tall, tanned man standing between a vampire and a pixie in the long line for the counter. He was dressed from head to toe in designer labels, from his trendy T-shirt to his fashionable jeans. The outfit was topped off with a trilby hat and designer sneakers, both of which had small wings on the side.

"Hermes! Hermes!" yelled Virgo over the hustle and bustle, but Hermes carried on singing to himself and gently dancing on the spot.

"Great," huffed Virgo as she and Elliot worked their way down the line, narrowly missing a bite from a grumpy werewolf and apologizing to a Hydra for stepping on her tail. Having irritated most of the line, they reached the winged messenger and Virgo tapped him on the shoulder. Hermes turned around coolly and peered over the top of his designer shades.

"Virgo! Babe! SHUT UP!" he yelled warmly, waking a nearby stroller full of baby goblins. "Hold tight. I am, like, totally plugged into my iGod—The Sirens have released a new album and I can't switch it off. I'm not even joking. Hang on a sec."

Hermes fiddled around in the small leather satchel slung across his body and produced a golden screen, about the size of a paperback book, in a tortoiseshell case. He pulled two golden earphones out of his ears and hugged Virgo.

"How are you, darlin'?" He smiled. "Babe—it's been too long. Love what you're still doing with your hair, totes Golden Age. And oi oi! Who's this then? Finally giving a thousand years of spinsterhood the elbow, you cheeky mare?"

"You two know each other?" asked Elliot.

"Of course—Hermes comes to Elysium all the time," said Virgo. "He's the Messenger God."

"Not to mention—God of Fashion," announced Hermes, winking into his iGod and taking a picture of himself.

"It's good to see you, Hermes—this is Elliot."

"Mate!" said Hermes, giving Elliot a massive high five. "Nice one."

"I'll introduce you properly later," said Virgo. "But listen, we need your help."

"Babe," interrupted Hermes. "Whatever you want. Gossip. Scandal. Hair that suits your face shape—you name it."

"We need to find Zeus," said Elliot. "It's urgent."

"Babe—I'm your man," said Hermes. "But I'm not being

funny or nuthin', you're not going to get any sense outta me until I've had my nectarchino. Hold tight."

Elliot wasn't confident they were going to get a word of sense out of Hermes at all, but waited patiently while Hermes ordered a skinny-double-frappa-something-or-other and then followed him to a nearby booth.

"Bosh!" shouted Hermes after draining his cup. "Okay—I have a total nightmare keeping track of everyone, I've had to download a new app—it's called Look@Me!"

"What does it do?" asked Elliot.

"It means that friends can show each other where they are every minute of the day. Mate, seriously—dunno what I did without it," said Hermes. "I can spend hours just . . . looking at where people are—it's amazing. Look, I can add you as a friend . . ."

"But I . . ." Elliot protested as Hermes grabbed one of his fingers and pressed it on the screen. A heart icon appeared under his finger.

"Sweet!" Hermes cheered. "That's you. Now if I look on the map . . . here we all are!"

On a map of the Asphodel Fields, Elliot's heart icon flashed in Café Hero next to a star representing Virgo and a pair of wings for Hermes.

"I've got all the family on here," said Hermes, typing "Zeus" into the iGod. "So where's Dad?"

A thunderbolt icon pinged up on the map.

"Apparently, he's in a golf club in the New Forest," said Hermes.

"What's he doing there?" asked Virgo.

"On a Saturday? There's usually only one thing my old man is doing . . ." said Hermes.

He reached into his leather bag and pulled out a rolled-up newspaper, which he handed to Elliot.

"Go to the gossip section—he's nearly always there."

The newspaper was printed on browning parchment, with a large central banner across the top. THE DAILY ARGUS was inscribed in classic Greek type, KEEPING AN EYE ON THE IMMORTAL COMMUNITY. Small boxes around the edges advertised the paper's contents, from the weather forecast by the Meteoracle Office to horoscopes by Cassandra.

Hermes leaned over Elliot's shoulder and read:

DADDY DAY CARE?

By Catullus, Births and Rebirths Correspondent

The Minotaur is proud to announce

Twin baby girls, five pounds and one ounce

His wife isn't happy, it's only been days

He's already lost both the kids in the maze.

"Aw, bless 'im . . ."

"Hermes!" chided Virgo.

"Oh, yeah, sorry, babe, attention span of a goldfish. Blah,

blah, blah—boom! Hold tight, here we are: engagements. Listen to this:

JUST MARRIED . . . AGAIN

By Homer, Society Editor

You've gotta admit it, old Zeus has some faith
He's married more women than Henry the Eighth
His heart has been won by the mortal Petunia
Who's roughly twelve thousand and four years his junior
They're planning a wedding, it's true love of course
Zeus promises this time he got a divorce
Given his record, the bride must be plucky
You know what they say, "Three hundredth time lucky"
The honeymoon's planned for the island of Malta
Provided they make it as far as the altar . . .

"The sly old dog," said Hermes with an admiring shake of his head.

"Why aren't you at your dad's wedding?" asked Elliot.

"Mate—not being funny or anything, but if I went to all my dad's weddings, I'd have spent more on toasters than a sea monster spends on swimming hats."

"I really need to see him," said Virgo. "Can you get us there?"

"Are these cheekbones chiseled?" Hermes announced confidently, positioning a pair of expensive sunglasses on his nose and admiring his reflection in the window.

"Can Charon come with us?" asked Elliot. "After we've seen Zeus, I really need to get home."

"Where's home?" asked Hermes.

Elliot pointed to Little Motbury on Hermes's map.

"Oh, it's on the way," said Hermes. "I'll get you there much quicker than Charon, bless his salty sandals. We'll drop in on Dad, we'll get you home, bosh."

"Well, if you're sure . . ." said Elliot.

"Not even joking, mate," Hermes said, winking. "Let's motor!"

"Ah—Hermes?" chimed Virgo, picking up the messenger's forgotten iGod.

"Babe—you're a lifesaver," sighed Hermes. "I'd forget my head! Then who'd be on the front cover of *Messengers' Health* . . . anyhoo—Kottos! I'll take another nectarchino to go. We've got a wedding to get to! BOOM!"

13

FOR BETTER OR WORSE

Elliot had thought that traveling by constellation was the most terrifying experience he was ever likely to have.

But that was before he had driven with Hermes.

At first, riding in the sidecar of the Messenger God's gleaming motorcycle—all chrome and turquoise sequins—had seemed awesome. Mom had promised she'd teach Elliot to ride a motorcycle when he was old enough, and he couldn't wait to roar along the country lanes.

But Hermes's driving was making Elliot consider a small tricycle instead.

For one thing, Hermes viewed speed limits as a minimum requirement for how fast he should drive. As he whizzed along, warning signs flashed up: SCORPIO SAYS DON'T BE TOO ZIPPY! THE ZODIAC COUNCIL HONORS CAREFUL DRIVERS! But if Hermes noticed them, they had no effect as he revved the bike harder to weave in and out of the immortal traffic, earning him colorful curses from an elderly leprechaun on a mobility scooter and threatening hand gestures from a gnome in a white van.

And for another thing, the road was upside-down.

"I don't understand," Elliot yelled over the roar of the air blasting his ears and the blood rushing to his head. "Why don't we fall down?"

"We're on the low-way—the immortal road system that runs exactly under the mortal one," Hermes shouted back. "You've got, like, a perfectly good network, so we just copied it. Every time you drive down the road, an immortal is probably driving underneath you. You don't fall off the Earth's curve, do you? And you don't fall under it neither. Hold tight!"

In the sidecar, Elliot and Virgo exchanged nervous glances as the bike accelerated again. A voice boomed over a nearby loudspeaker:

"*Vehicle registration: B 0 5 H. Owner: Hermes. Category: Olympian. The Zodiac Council warns you this is your second speeding infringement. One more offense and your vehicle will be disabled and you may face a substantial fine or the forfeiture of a body part. Have a nice day.*"

"Whatevs," yelled Hermes. "Nearly there."

The bike charged along the immortal motorway, finally turning down a country road signposted to the Royal Withering St. Stan's Golf Club. Hermes drove up a ramp, which twisted around until the motorcycle was the right way up, emerging back onto Earth through a set of roadworks.

"Nice of you mortals to keep digging up your roads," said Hermes. "Makes it much easier for us to get in and out. Here we are. Boom!"

He swung into the golf-club parking lot alongside cars

that seemed the size of Elliot's cowshed. At last, the motor-cycle came to a welcome stop. Elliot clambered out, his legs still vibrating from the bike's relentless engine.

"Slumming it again, Dad." Hermes grinned as he took in the grand facade of the clubhouse, a stately home set in acres of lush green golf course. "Shut up! We've got five minutes."

Elliot looked toward an elaborate gold carriage drawn by a beautiful white horse, in which he could see only an enormous white dress. Three salmon-pink bridesmaids were trying to free the bride, but the circumference of the gown had wedged her firmly in the door. As the carriage rocked and jolted, the horse, clothed in an intricately embroidered coat, released an irritated whinny. Elliot could have sworn it actually rolled its eyes.

They joined the gaggles of fancy wedding guests bearing elaborately wrapped gifts. The ladies wore furs, the gentlemen wore tuxedos. Hermes looked woefully at his T-shirt and jeans.

"Nah, mate," he said, producing his iGod and scrolling around the screen. As he rolled the dial in the center, his outfits changed from sportswear to beachwear to a pair of lederhosen.

"Hermes, we don't have time," snapped Virgo. "We need to get to Zeus."

"There's always time to look sharp, babe," said Hermes, finally settling on a designer tuxedo. He offered the iGod hopefully to Elliot and Virgo, taking in Elliot's torn T-shirt and Virgo's backward pants. "Your turn?"

"Hermes!" Virgo hissed.

"Cool, babe," he sighed. "You can lead a unicorn to water . . ."

They snuck in behind two women wearing dead animals around their shoulders.

"So she's finally found Mr. Right," said the one sporting a dead fox.

"About time," said the one draped in dead mink. "She's tried Mr. Wrong, Mr. Stupid, Mr. Boring, and Mr. Married . . ."

They laughed unpleasantly. The dead animals looked mournfully at Elliot. He could see why they were fed up. Not only had they been snatched from the prime of life, but now they were stuck around the necks of these ridiculous women.

"Bride or groom?" asked the usher.

"Neither, you fool," Mrs. Fox announced. "I'm a guest."

"I can't believe it," said Virgo, smoothing her hair. "I'm actually going to meet Zeus! What should I say to impress him?"

"Nothing?" Elliot suggested as they entered the grand room, which was filled with rows of chairs with a narrow aisle between them. It looked as though a wedding had thrown up everywhere. Flowers adorned every surface, pink balloons filled every corner, and there was a huge chocolate fountain with a marshmallow bride and groom dangling their feet in it.

"Now, where's the old boy?" Hermes said, hovering slightly off the ground to see over the crowd. "Ah—Bosh!"

Hermes pointed out someone who, to Elliot, was quite obviously the king of the Gods. Even with his back to them, this tall, broad man had a regal bearing—noble, strong, and brave. As Hermes, Virgo and Elliot fought their way through the chattering guests toward this towering presence, Elliot wondered what he would say to such a great immortal being.

Although as the man turned around, he didn't have to wonder long.

"Champagne, sir?" said the waiter, offering a glass to Hermes.

"Nice one," said Hermes, taking two.

"You'd better fill me up too, old boy," boomed a voice behind him. "Condemned man and all that."

"Zeus!" Virgo gasped as the waiter moved aside to reveal the real king of the Gods.

Mythology was one of the few subjects that Elliot enjoyed at school, and so he was familiar with the classical images of Zeus, all white hair flowing down his broad back and his strapping chest bursting out of a toga as he hurled thunderbolts at his enemies.

So he was rather surprised to find Zeus in a badly fitting light-blue tuxedo with a frilly shirt, holding a ham-and-cheese finger sandwich. The long white hair was there, albeit badly slicked back with hair gel. And it wasn't a strapping chest bursting out so much as a gigantic belly.

"Hermes, my boy!" said Zeus warmly, taking his son into a big bear hug. "So glad you could make it. Such a special day.

This one's a keeper. Whatever her name is. And who do we have here?"

He extended a crumby hand toward Virgo.

"I . . . er . . . w-well . . . I'm . . .," stammered the Constellation, for the first time at a loss for words.

"This is Virgo, from the Zodiac Council," said Hermes.

"Ah—a pencil pusher, eh?" laughed Zeus. "Don't worry, I won't hold it against you. Super to meet you."

"Th . . . argh . . . bler . . ." Virgo burbled.

"And this is my mate Elliot," said Hermes. "Not sure why he's here, but he's rocking the shabby-chic look and that's good enough for me."

"Your Majesty," said Elliot, looking into the smiling eyes set in a lined face. Even with the ridiculous outfit, there was still something about Zeus that exuded almighty power. Elliot recalled the sensation he'd had with Thanatos, the sense that this man could read his mind—but this time it wasn't an unpleasant feeling. It was somehow comforting, familiar, warm. "I'm Elliot Hooper."

"A pleasure, Elliot," boomed Zeus. "Lovely to have you here. I do love a good wedding."

"Shame he doesn't enjoy the marriage part afterward," smirked Hermes.

"Behave, you young whippersnapper," laughed Zeus, hitting Hermes so hard on the back that he fell over. "Good man."

"Your Majesty," said Virgo, dropping into a deep curtsy. "I desperately need your help. I've done something terrible."

"There, there—can't be that bad," said Zeus. "No worse than these finger sandwiches anyway. I've had better food from Tantalus's Takeout. And there's no need for any of that—get up, dear girl."

Just as he helped Virgo to her feet, the organ struck up the opening chords of "Here Comes the Bride."

"Yikes," gulped Zeus, dropping the ham-and-cheese and wiping his hands on his suit. "Here we go. Again."

"But Zeus, I—" started Virgo.

She was drowned out by the chorus of "ahh" announcing that Petunia, the bride, had made it out of the parking lot. Unfortunately, however, she didn't make it much farther, as the almighty dress that had wedged her in the carriage now wedged her halfway down the aisle.

Elliot tried not to laugh as the three miserable bridesmaids unsuccessfully tried to free her.

"Zeus," whispered Virgo. "Zeus, I really need to—"

"Gordon!" the bride sang down the aisle. "Darling, Petunia needs you!"

"Uh-oh—that's me," whispered Zeus, dropping the glass he'd been sipping and running to his bride. "Hold on, my fragrant flower. One. Two. Three!"

Elliot hid his mouth in his hand as Zeus grabbed the bottom hoop and gave the dress an almighty tug. The hoop came unstuck, but such was the width and weight of the gown, the wide skirts merely tipped Petunia backward, leaving her stranded with her legs in the air, flashing her frilly knickers at the congregation.

"Aaaargh! Gordon! Help!"

"Hold on, old girl," said Zeus, grabbing one of her legs. "Hermes—grab the other one for me."

At his father's bidding—and with some difficulty, given the strength, size, and motion of the bride—Hermes grabbed Petunia's other leg.

"You look great, babe," he whispered. "But that dress really needs a bigger heel . . ."

"Right, on my count—one, two, three . . . HEAVE!"

As one, the two Olympians yanked Petunia. And this time it worked—Petunia flew free. Sadly, her dress did not. Now dressed only in her frilly knickers and some underwear that reminded Elliot of an Egyptian mummy, Petunia popped out of her frock like a champagne cork, taking Zeus and Hermes with her as they tumbled down the aisle, and all landed with a splat in the chocolate fountain.

That was when another bride appeared.

Elliot had never been to a wedding before, but he was pretty confident there was only supposed to be the one.

"Frederick!" shouted the second bride. "What is the meaning of this?"

Zeus poked his head out of the fountain and spat out a mouthful of chocolate. "Er . . . oh, hello . . . er . . . Enid." He smiled. "It is Enid, isn't it?"

"Dad—c'mon!" laughed Hermes "You've double-booked your weddings. Again!"

"My angel! You're a vision!" Zeus tried gamely.

"And you're a cheating ratbag!" howled Enid, charging down the aisle, until she was stopped by Petunia's wedding dress. "Wait till I get my hands on you, you old dog!"

With one bride still stuck in the fountain and the other fighting the wedding dress, Zeus let out a shrill whistle, at which the beautiful white horse that Elliot had seen outside drawing the bride's carriage came thundering into the room.

"Pegasus! Over here!" Zeus yelled. "SOS!"

The horse charged down the aisle, elegantly leaping over Enid, the bridesmaids, and the wedding dress like a front-runner in the Kentucky Derby.

"Quickly, up you come," said Zeus, scrabbling onto the horse's back with the help of the embroidered jacket, and lifting Virgo and Elliot in front of him.

The guests were in uproar, with Petunia and Enid's friends fighting over who had the greater claim to the buffet. Zeus winked at Hermes, who nodded and calmly walked into the fray, lightly touching the dead animals that were draped around their owners' large necks. At his touch, the furs sprang to life, filling the room with foxes, minks, and a particularly ferocious badger, snarling at their captors and chasing them around the room, finally taking their revenge. It did the trick. The crowds parted, giving Pegasus a clear run back down the aisle.

"Come on, Peg—step on it," said Zeus, pulling the reins of his magnificent steed. Elliot braced himself as Pegasus lowered his head and charged out of the golf club. With Hermes fluttering discreetly behind, they headed out into the open air, where Pegasus burst out of the embroidered jacket, exposing a magnificent pair of white, feathered wings.

Zeus took a cautious look behind him. "Okay, Peg—up, up, and away!"

"Er, Dad—you might want this, you plum," said Hermes, rummaging around in his bag and producing an engraved bronze helmet that was far too big to have fit inside.

"Good idea," said Zeus, strapping the helmet on. "Belongs to my brother Hades," he explained to Elliot. "Makes the wearer and anything they're touching invisible. Darned useful gadget. Hold on."

As soon as the helmet hit Zeus's head, Elliot felt a tickling sensation as his whole body became transparent. He held up his hand. He could see right through it. It was a very strange feeling, but Elliot didn't have time to dwell on it as Pegasus galloped up the fairway.

The magical horse fully unfurled his gigantic wings and took off into the clear blue afternoon. As the ground dropped away, Elliot saw a chocolate-coated Petunia run out of the golf club in her undies, pelting her empty carriage with ham-and-cheese sandwiches.

14

MYTHS AND LEGENDS

It was the fourth time that day that Elliot had traveled by immortal transport, and flying by horse quickly became his favorite. As Pegasus climbed high into the sky, Elliot was treated to the most beautiful view of the English countryside below.

"There's my farm!" said Elliot after a few minutes, seeing his beloved home like a little model in the fields near Stonehenge.

"I couldn't trouble you for a place to lay my hat, could I, old boy?" Zeus yelled into Elliot's ear. "Need to lie low for a few days."

Elliot was caught off guard. On the one hand, the last thing he needed was another stranger on the farm drawing attention to him and Mom. On the other, Zeus had the Earth Stone—perhaps if he gave him somewhere to stay, he might let Elliot borrow it. Or perhaps Elliot might borrow it anyway. It was worth the risk.

"Of course, Your . . . erm . . . Majesty," he said.

Pegasus touched down in the disused paddock of Home Farm and Elliot immediately jumped off and ran to the farmhouse. It was okay. He could see his mom sitting in the kitchen chatting away to herself. Now he just needed to find somewhere to conceal a handful of immortals.

Zeus removed the invisibility helmet as Virgo dismounted, pinging them back into view. Elliot tried to look away as Zeus struggled to get his considerable girth off his horse. Zeus eventually managed to get both legs pointing in the same direction and plopped inelegantly to the ground. He pulled himself up, ripped off his tux, and revealed bright-orange Bermuda shorts and a red Hawaiian shirt underneath.

"That's better," he said. "Been dying to get rid of that wretched thing."

"The tux or the bride?" asked Hermes, screeching to a halt on his motorcycle.

Virgo dropped into another dutiful low curtsy.

"Oh, enough of that nonsense," boomed Zeus, his bright-blue eyes sparkling like sapphires. "Come here and give your old king a hug."

Virgo ran to Zeus with a relieved smile and was soon enveloped in a vast Hawaiian bear hug.

"That's more like it," laughed Zeus, his twinkling gaze lighting on Elliot. "Wonderful to meet you too, Elliot. Some call me Jupiter, others call me Brontios. To at least five of my ex-wives, I'm a plumber called Bob. But you can call me Zeus."

Elliot accepted a giant handshake, trying not to wince as the God crushed his fingers with his surprising strength.

"And this fine fellow," said Zeus, gesturing toward the winged white stallion, "is my trusty steed, Pegasus."

At the sound of his name, Pegasus trotted over. Elliot had loved the horses they'd had on the farm and this one was truly magnificent. He gently lifted his hand to stroke the horse's elegant head.

"Hey, boy," he whispered softly.

"If you require a dog to fetch you a stick, then please continue," said Pegasus grandly, shocking Elliot into silence. "But if you are referring to me, my name is Pegasus. And I'm gasping for a mineral water."

"You can talk!" exclaimed Elliot.

"I'm a flying horse," said Pegasus pertly. "Talking's the easy part. And I prefer sparkling with a twist of lime."

Elliot looked blankly around him, having never catered for a talking, flying immortal horse.

"Oh, don't mind him," said Zeus dismissively. "Get off your high horse, Peg. There's a water trough over there, that'll do just fine."

Pegasus looked over at the rusty trough filled with murky brown water and released a disdainful whinny.

"I suppose a few ice cubes would be too much to ask," he huffed as he sauntered over, sticking his nose high in the air.

"Zeus—we've got a problem," said Virgo, unable to look him in the eye. "I've done something dreadful."

"I'm sure we can fix it," said Zeus. "I've got a top-notch lawyer if we need one. She could get an Athenian out of a labyrinth and make the Minotaur pay costs. Elliot, is there a good spot to sit and chat, please?"

Instinctively feeling that a chubby God, a flying fashion model, and a talking horse might be too much for Mom, Elliot ushered the immortals toward Bessie's cowshed, where they pulled up some hay bales. Pegasus strode in behind them, earning a flirtatious moo from Bessie as he settled down for a rest on a pile of straw.

"Isn't this delightful!" boomed Zeus, looking around the dilapidated shed as if he were in the Ritz. "So, who is going to fill me in?"

Virgo and Elliot recounted what had happened beneath Stonehenge in as much detail as they could remember, while Hermes and Zeus listened intently.

"And that's when I thought I should find you," said Virgo at the end of their story, hanging her head. "I'm so sorry, Zeus, this is all my fault."

"We'll have no more of that," said Zeus kindly. "If any-one's to blame, it is me."

"Charon said that Thanatos is still alive," said Elliot. "Is that true?"

"Oh, for goodness' sake, Elliot," snapped Virgo. "I'm sorry, Zeus, Charon's been filling his head with—"

"Yes," said Zeus quietly. "Yes, it is."

"What?" gasped Virgo.

"You're 'aving a laugh, Dad!" yelled Hermes. "Since when?"

"Since always," sighed Zeus. "You have to understand,

when I made his father, Erebus, the king of the Daemons, we were like brothers. I'd hoped that the Gods and Daemons could work together to help the mortals. But the Chaos Stones changed Erebus. Made him power-crazed, greedy, blind to anything but his own ambition."

"But you killed him, right?" asked Elliot.

"I did," said Zeus, hanging his head. "It was one of the worst moments of my life. I was younger, angrier, stronger. I saw nothing but my own rage and the next thing I knew . . . Erebus was dead. His wife, Nyx, the Goddess of Night, was so grief-stricken that she was never seen again. But it got worse. As Erebus lay dying, his twin sons Thanatos and Hypnos—barely more than boys themselves—came running to their father's body. I never quite recovered from that sight."

"What happened?" asked Virgo.

"Although Hypnos was the older twin, Erebus handed the Chaos Stones to Thanatos, naming him his heir with his final breaths. Hypnos was furious—the stones were his birthright—but Erebus said Thanatos would make the better king. Hypnos never forgave his brother for that."

"So Thanatos wanted to finish what his father had started?" said Elliot.

"Precisely," said Zeus. "A few centuries later, he wanted to avenge his father—and by now the Chaos Stones had corrupted him too."

"But you killed him in that legendary duel, bosh, job done?" said Hermes. "How can Thanatos still be alive?"

"I went to destroy his kardia and deliver the death blow, but I . . . I couldn't do it," said Zeus. "All I could see was that young boy holding his father's—my friend's—body. I no longer had the stomach for killing. Nor for being king of the Gods. It was why I retired."

"So you hid Thanatos under Stonehenge where no one could find him," said Elliot, everything suddenly making sense. "And the rest of the Daemons?"

"I held the Chaos Stones in my hands and I could feel their dark power flowing through me—I've never experienced anything like it," explained Zeus. "I had planned to take the Daemons' kardia and then wipe them all out with an earthquake or a tsunami—but something stopped me. I realized it wouldn't be a victory. It would be a massacre. I asked my brother Hades to build them a prison in Tartarus. They've been there ever since."

"What happened to the Chaos Stones?" asked Elliot, trying to keep the need out of his voice.

"No worries, mate," said Hermes. "Dad will have them locked up tighter than jeggings in January. Won't you, Dad?"

Zeus's attention was suddenly drawn all around the shed.

"Daaaaaaaad?" asked Hermes suspiciously. "You have got the stones, right?"

"Not . . . exactly," said Zeus sheepishly. "In fact . . . not at all."

Elliot's heart plummeted. He'd been that close to solving his problems.

"So where are they?" he asked.

"There's the rub," said Zeus. "I can admit it now: Thanatos was stronger than me. I just couldn't defeat him while he had the stones. I wasn't able to win them in a fair fight, so I rather . . . well . . . sort of . . ."

"You cheated!" shouted Hermes. "You dirty dog!"

"In a manner of speaking. Well—yes," admitted Zeus. "I remembered the look on Hypnos's face when his father passed him over in favor of Thanatos—it was pure hatred. I knew I could exploit that—and that Hypnos was the only person who could get close enough to Thanatos. They lived together in the Cave of Sleep and Death. So I struck a deal with him. If Hypnos brought me the Chaos Stones, he would escape the fate of his Daemon comrades when I won. He didn't even think about it—the opportunity for revenge was just what he'd been waiting for. He brought me the stones that very hour."

"But . . . but that's not possible," exclaimed Virgo in disbelief. "That's not in our history. You can't have lied?"

"I'm afraid I did," said Zeus, shamefaced. "After all, history is only what the winners wrote down."

Elliot shot a triumphant look at Virgo, which she chose to ignore.

"Once Thanatos and the Daemons were defeated, the power of the stones scared me," said Zeus. "I didn't want them to corrupt me like they had Erebus and Thanatos. I told Hypnos that his brother and the Daemons were dead, then made him swear on the Styx that he wouldn't use the Chaos

Stones himself. I commanded him to hide them where they could never be found—not even by me. I've not seen him nor the stones from that day to this."

"Shut. Up," said Hermes, taking a stunned selfie on his iGod. "You've got to be joking. Seriously. I'm not even joking."

Elliot felt winded. He had less than a week to find twenty thousand pounds and his one ray of hope—the Earth Stone—was fading. He needed that stone—and fast.

"I'm not proud, guys," said Zeus. "But now that Thanatos is free, we must get to those stones before he does. If he gets his hands on them, he can free his Daemon army from Tartarus and then we'll all be in the soup. I'm going to need the girls."

"Which ones?" asked Hermes.

"Athene and Aphrodite," said Zeus firmly. "And Hephaestus, he's always handy in a crisis. It's getting late—we can fetch them tomorrow. Elliot, can we just crash here, if that's okay with you?"

"Sure, why not?" said Elliot, his mind whirring.

"Super! Now," said Zeus, pushing himself to his feet, "give me a tour of this fine home of yours. I could do with stretching my legs after that flight."

They left the shed and Zeus looked out at the overgrown farmlands that had fallen into disuse. Elliot felt embarrassed as he looked at his home through someone else's eyes—the hard soil was thick with weeds, the shed was falling apart, and the farmhouse was a shambles.

"I'm ever so grateful to you, Elliot. I wonder if there is anything I might do to repay your kind hospitality?" Zeus said.

"Are Gods . . . rich?" asked Elliot. "I mean, you've lived for ages. Do you have loads of money?"

"None that's any use to you, my friend," laughed Zeus. "Gods can't keep mortal money. It's against the Sacred Code. We immortals have our own currency—obals, drachma, and mina. Although most of mine goes to my ex-wives anyway . . . Why do you ask?"

"No reason," said Elliot, not comfortable sharing his biggest secret with this complete stranger. Besides, Mom always said it was easier to seek forgiveness than permission. What if the Gods didn't let him use the Earth Stone to save the farm? He'd just "borrow" it the one time, find enough treasure to pay off his debts, then give it straight back. No one needed to know . . .

Elliot again had the sensation that Zeus could see into his thoughts. But it passed in a heartbeat as the God smiled warmly. "My sisters Hestia and Demeter are very good around the house," he said. "With your permission, perhaps they could help you out on the farm?"

"Great. Thanks," Elliot said, and then yawned as the long day caught up with him.

"Good stuff." Zeus smiled again. "You're tired, Elliot—we can manage from here. Why don't you head back inside? Oh, and here," he added, producing a basket that Elliot was sure wasn't there before. "A few leftovers from the wedding. Shame for it all to go to waste. Again."

"Thank you," said Elliot, struggling under the weight of it. "I'll see you in the morning."

"Night," said Zeus as Hermes fluttered down next to him.

The two Gods watched the young boy wander back to the farmhouse with his supper.

"Thank the heavens you found me," said Zeus. "We need to stay close to Elliot—he's in terrible danger."

"What gives?" asked Hermes.

Zeus pulled an ancient piece of parchment from his pocket and handed it to his son.

Hermes's eyes bulged out of his head. "Shut up. It's him, isn't it?"

"It is," said Zeus. "We need to find those stones, and there's not a moment to lose."

"Should we tell him?" asked Hermes.

"No," said Zeus. "Elliot Hooper is the only person who can save the world. And I wouldn't wish that on my worst enemy."

15

A SAFE BET

In the small hours of Sunday morning, Thanatos stood outside the residence of Pythia, Oracle of Delphi and conveyor of prophecies.

"You're sure this is where she lives?" he asked.

"As sure as I've got a spare nose," said Charon. "I go here meself from time to time. I like to play the ponies."

Thanatos looked disdainfully at the neon sign burning in the dawn gloom, announcing that this was BOTTOM DRACHMA BETS in Twitching, Kent.

"I'll go back to the river," said Charon. "Don't be long, mind you—we've got a long way to go if you want to reach Hypnos's place tonight."

Despite the hour, Thanatos could see a faint glow emanating from the apartment above the shop. He pressed the buzzer.

"We're not open" came the crackly reply over the intercom.

"Oh, I think you are," said Thanatos. "Hello, Pythia."

"Is that . . . ?"

Thanatos saw a curtain move upstairs.

"Well, well. You'd better come up," said the voice, buzzing Thanatos in.

Thanatos crunched on discarded takeout cartons up the stairs and into Pythia's cramped room. The oracle sat in an armchair. She appeared to be in a trance.

"What do you seek?" she asked in a monotone.

Thanatos picked up the television remote and switched off the home makeover show she was watching.

"Hey—I was enjoying that," Pythia huffed, heaving herself up and venturing toward the kettle. She eyed Thanatos's black robes. "I see you're still making a big effort to blend in?"

"Some of us still have standards," said Thanatos, peering disapprovingly at Pythia's blotchy complexion, frayed robe, and threadbare pink slippers. "And I shouldn't have to blend in. Besides, my tricks don't work on you."

"True enough," said Pythia. "Cup of tea? The milk's not that lumpy . . ."

"I need to know the prophecy," said Thanatos. "The one you gave Zeus. His last words to me were: 'No immortal can free you. It has been prophesied.' I want the rest."

"Did you bring me an offering?" said Pythia.

"I did, but does it have to be—?"

"No offering, no prophecy," said Pythia flatly, adjusting one of the curlers in her greasy gray hair.

"Don't toy with me," said Thanatos menacingly. "Or I might just—"

"Uh, uh, uh," said Pythia, flashing her glass kardia. "I'm a Neutral. Like you say, your tricks don't work on me."

"Fine," sighed Thanatos. "Here it is." He produced a huge

bucket of fried chicken from his robes in disgust. "Charon insisted I 'go large.'"

"Good man," said Pythia through a mouthful of chicken drumstick. "Oooh—and a toy. Classy. Right—bear with me a second."

She walked over to a battered computer and started searching through her emails.

"Remember, I don't make this stuff up," said Pythia, highlighting the message she sought. "I just give you the odds."

She hit the print button and an aged printer slowly churned out a piece of paper. The oracle handed it to Thanatos and he read his prophecy:

To: oracle@delphi.com

Date: 0016 AD

Subject: Thanatos (Plus how YOU can save on YOUR chariot insurance!)

If Death is contained in a sacred stone portal

He can't be released by a single immortal

The Daemon you place in the shackles of iron

Needs a young mortal child with the heart of a lion

The child can't die from a terrible deed

By the hand of the Daemon he generously freed

But now he could claim the power Death owns

And conquer the world with the help of four stones

Daemon beware! Your life with no end

Might now be cut short by your new mortal friend
So Life will race Death, but who will be faster?
When four stones are one, they will answer one master . . .

"The boy could rule the world?" said Thanatos. "With my Chaos Stones?"

"If it softens the blow, I can give you a great tip on the three-fifteen race at Chepstow," offered Pythia.

"And I can't kill the child?" Thanatos mused. "How inconvenient. Does he defeat me?"

"I'm not psychic," said Pythia, flicking her television program back on. "I can't even tell you if they're going to wallpaper this living room in sixty minutes. But while the mortal child is alive, your odds aren't great."

The conversation was over.

"I see," said Thanatos, retreating back down the staircase. "In which case, Elliot Hooper can't stay alive for very much longer."

16

ALL YOU NEED IS LOVE

Elliot jolted awake with a gasp early Sunday morning. He'd spent a troubled night. When he had made his mom supper the previous evening, he'd found the remains of a cake he hadn't bought. Who had been in the house? He'd tried to find out from Josie what had happened, but the day was already a distant memory and Elliot didn't want to push his mom's tired mind any further.

Even though an owl was still hooting her night music outside his window, Elliot got up to prepare for the day. He felt uneasy leaving Josie again, especially with Patricia Porshley-Plum on the prowl. But he needed to find that Earth Stone to save their home. It was for the best in the long term—once he'd saved Home Farm, he could get back to taking care of Mom.

After he'd sorted the laundry and cleaned the house, he quickly went through what had become his morning routine—making sure that Mom was washed and dressed, cooking her breakfast, and then making a sandwich for her lunch, leaving it on the kitchen table in a clear plastic tub so that it would stay fresh and she could see it.

"Mom—will you fold the laundry while I'm out?" he shouted up.

"Of course, lovely—leave it in the kitchen, I'll see to it after breakfast."

With a grimace, Elliot dumped the neat pile of laundry he'd carefully folded earlier that morning on the kitchen table. He had learned that the best way to keep Josie in the house was to make sure she had something to do. She could spend hours on a single task and Elliot could always sort it out again when he got home.

As soon as Josie was settled in front of her breakfast, Elliot kissed her on the head.

"Remember—that important package is due today, so make sure you stay in," he said.

"Yes, bossypants!" she said as she squeezed him back. Elliot had also discovered that telling his mom there was a reason to stay in the house helped to keep her there, even though she couldn't always remember what the reason was. The fact that it was a Sunday and there was no important package didn't occur to her.

"Good morning, Elliot. Good morning, Josie-Mom," said Virgo cheerfully, untroubled by not being invited in. "Elliot—they're waiting for you in the shed."

"Who's waiting for you, Elly?" said Josie. "And who's this?"

"The handymen, Mom—they've come to fix the shed," said Elliot quickly, wincing at Virgo's spectacular lack of subtlety. "And this is . . ."

"Virgo—we met yesterday," said Virgo, looking confused.

"Did we? I don't . . ."

"Don't worry about it, Mom," said Elliot, pushing Virgo outside. "Stay here. Please. I'll see you later."

"Love you, baby," his mom said, starting on the pile of laundry.

Elliot and Virgo headed toward the cowshed, which was clanking with an orchestra of building noise.

"What is wrong with your mother?" asked Virgo plainly.

"Nothing," said Elliot in reply to the question he had been dreading for so long. "She's just tired."

"She didn't recognize me although I clearly introduced myself yesterday," said Virgo. "I have been researching mortals and this is not normal. *What's What* informs me that mortals are largely friendly creatures who like to discuss the weather and prefer their negative thoughts to be expressed behind someone's back or on social media. Is your mother suboptimal?"

"She's fine," said Elliot defensively. "It's been a tough year."

"Perhaps you should replace her with a mother in full working order?" Virgo suggested.

Elliot laughed sadly. "It doesn't work like that," he said. "You can't replace your mom."

As they walked across the field, Elliot's feet sank into the newly plowed soil, which had been hard as rock just hours ago. But before he had time to unstick his shoe, he was knocked sideways as a fully grown tree, laden with apples the size of bowling balls, burst out of the ground.

"Mind how you go!" laughed a ruddy-faced woman in overalls. "I'm Demeter, Goddess of the Harvest—hope you don't mind if I do a spot of gardening?" She continued to scatter seeds, which immediately sprang up into mouthwatering, oversized fruit and vegetable plants.

"Er, no—thanks." Elliot smiled back as he waded through the field, wondering how he was going to explain giant banana trees in the middle of a damp Wiltshire farm to anyone who came looking.

He pulled open the door to the cowshed, but was immediately knocked down by a swarm of tiny people who came to just above his knees.

"CUSHIONS!" yelled a petite, dark-haired Goddess, dressed in a smart red suit, who was marching around with a clipboard and a pair of golden glasses perched on the end of her nose.

"What the—?" spluttered Elliot, struggling to his feet, only to be bowled over again by another gaggle of pint-sized people whizzing past him in a cloud of smoke.

"Penates," said Virgo as she too was sent flying by the workers, who Elliot could now see were made from clay, wax, silver, or gold. "They work for Hestia, Goddess of the Hearth. What she can't do with plywood and some contact paper isn't worth knowing."

Hestia strode past with a quick smile, muttering about color schemes and creating space.

Zeus was reclining on a makeshift hay sofa reading the

Daily Argus, apparently oblivious to the chaos around him. He gave Elliot a warm grin.

"Morning, good sir!" he roared happily. "Ready for the day?"

"I guess," said Elliot, wondering if today was going to be as mind-blowing as the one before.

"Awesome!" said Zeus, struggling off the sofa before it was swept away by some Penates. "First off, we need to get my daughters Athene and Aphrodite. But I'll need your help—they're a pair of feisty fillies and they might behave better with a dashing new face around. We'll start with Aphrodite. You'll like her. Most boys do."

Elliot had zero interest in girls and Zeus's daughter wasn't going to be any different, but he smiled politely.

"Why have you guys come to England?" asked Elliot. "Why not, like, Barbados or somewhere?"

"We needed a place where a group of eccentric individuals with strange personal habits could fit right in," explained Zeus. "England seemed a natural choice."

"Makes sense," said Elliot with a proud grin.

"Peg!" Zeus hollered at his horse, who was lying down with a pencil in his mouth doing the crossword. "Saddle up!"

"Imbecile!" shouted Pegasus, rising to his hooves.

"Easy there, old chap," scowled Zeus. "I might not be the brightest star in the constellation, but that's a bit . . ."

"Fourteen across—a stupid person, eight letters," explained Pegasus. "Although if the helmet fits . . ."

"Hermes and Virgo, you start tracking down Hypnos—but tread carefully," said Zeus. "The Daemon of Sleep always was as nutty as a squirrel's packed lunch."

"Daemon of Sleep?" said Elliot. "That doesn't sound very scary."

"He was scary all right," said Hermes. "Total psycho. He abused his sleep trumpet to torture mortals and immortals, making them fall asleep, keeping them awake, or giving them impossible dreams and banging nightmares. He's dangerous. I'm not even joking."

"So let's find him," said Virgo, handing Hermes the iGod he was searching for. "We get him, we'll get the Chaos Stones—and put Thanatos back under Stonehenge."

"Nice one. Last one to spot him is last season's sweater dress," said Hermes, grinning.

"That's the ticket," said Zeus amiably. "See you later."

Pegasus knelt to help Zeus and Elliot clamber aboard.

"Come on, Peg—giddyup!" yelled Zeus, strapping on the invisibility helmet before spurring Pegasus on to a gallop. One, two, three giant strides and they were climbing into the morning sky, leaving the industrious immortals far below.

It was another beautiful cruise through the sky. But as they floated over the sunbathed countryside, Elliot voiced a thought that had been playing on his mind overnight.

"What powers do you all have?" he asked. "The Gods, I mean."

"That depends," said Zeus. "Athene is the Goddess of Wisdom, so there's not much she can't figure out—she's also a dab hand at arts and crafts, so she can create anything out of anything. Aphrodite, Goddess of Love—she can make anyone fall in love, often with her. Hephaestus, God of the Forge—he's a bit of a whiz at inventions. Hermes—he's our messenger, but he can also turn himself, or anything else, into whatever he wants. And as for me . . . well, I can do a bit of everything—jack of all trades, master of none . . ."

Elliot sensed that Zeus was being modest, but he had a more pressing question to ask.

"Do any of you have healing powers?" he asked quietly. "Can anyone cure people?"

"I'm afraid not," said Zeus gently, making Elliot wonder again if he could read his mind. "I'm afraid we're often better at creating problems for mortals than solving them."

Elliot's mind flashed back to Stonehenge. "*I can do what the Gods cannot*," Thanatos had said. Was that a lie?

"Thank the heavens Virgo got you out of there yesterday," said Zeus, interrupting Elliot's thoughts.

"Yeah," he groaned. "She's mentioned it once or twice."

"She's quite something," laughed Zeus. "I know legendary heroes who wouldn't have had half her courage. Mind you, I also know twenty-headed monsters who don't talk half as much, but one thing I've learned about women is to take the rough with the smooth. Ah—we're here, right on!"

Elliot clung on to Pegasus as the horse gracefully landed on a quiet patch of sand behind some beach huts.

"Brighton," said Zeus, huffing and puffing off the horse. "How I do like to be by the shore. Back in two ticks, Peg."

"Diet," said Pegasus.

"Beg pardon?" said Zeus.

"Six down—a healthy eating regime, four letters," said Pegasus, pulling the crossword out of his saddlebag with his teeth.

"Hmmm. See you later," said Zeus, taking off his invisibility helmet and wriggling his Hawaiian shirt over his belly as he ushered Elliot across the beach.

They walked up to the promenade and crossed into the winding streets of the town. It had been over three years since Elliot's last trip to the seaside—he and Mom used to camp on the Jurassic Coast, spending every sunny moment on the fossil-filled beaches and every rainy one playing cards as the water hammered down on their cozy tent. The smell of the salty air mingled with salty french fries transported Elliot back to some of his happiest memories.

"Now, Elliot, here's the thing about my girls," Zeus began as they reached a bright-pink door emblazoned with EROS in lipstick-red letters. "They are both beautiful, powerful, intelligent women who are a credit to their old dad. But I can't lie—put them together and they're like two harpies fighting over a half-price handbag. Need to handle this one with kid gloves, if you catch my drift."

"Sure," said Elliot, with precisely no idea what Zeus was talking about.

"Good man, good man," muttered Zeus as he pressed the bright-pink buzzer.

Zeus and Elliot entered the reception area, which looked as though someone had lost a fight with a pink paint can. Everything was pink, from the walls to the ceiling to the lip-shaped chairs dotted around the room.

"Welcome to Eros—where love don't cost a thing. Terms and conditions apply," the receptionist chanted. "I'm Sally."

"Well, aren't you just a pretty little thing?" drawled Zeus. "Can you tell Ms. Venus that her old dad's here? And that I'd like to take her receptionist out for dinner?"

Sally turned a shade of pink that perfectly matched her suit.

"I'll give her a ring," she giggled, picking up the top lip of the pink mouth phone.

"Keep being so beautiful and I'll be giving you the ring, Sarah," said Zeus.

"It's Sally," Sally giggled.

"It's irrelevant." Zeus grinned, picking up her hand and kissing it.

Elliot gazed around the waiting room, which was filled with people who looked . . . single. Photographs of Eros success stories lined the walls, hundreds of married couples grinning at the hopefuls from every surface.

"Daddy!" chimed the most beautiful voice Elliot had ever heard.

"Hello, my little pearl," said Zeus, taking his daughter into a giant hug. "Come and meet my good friend Elliot."

"Hi there, Elliot," said Aphrodite, shimmying toward the boy glued to the floor.

Elliot tried to speak, but all the words evaporated inside his mouth. It was hard to say exactly what made the Goddess of Love the most beautiful woman Elliot had ever seen, but as he gawped at her long golden hair, her twinkling blue eyes, her full lips, and the snug jeans and T-shirt she was dressed in, he didn't honestly care.

Zeus nudged Elliot in the ribs. "Your mouth called, my friend," he whispered. "It wants its tongue back."

But Elliot was deaf to anything but the angel song in his head as Aphrodite glided nearer.

"So you're our little mortal," sang Aphrodite, or so it seemed to Elliot as he drowned in her boundless blue eyes. "Hermes called me last night and told me all about you. Lovely to meet you."

"Hubhurghrumph," garbled Elliot dreamily as he reached for her outstretched hand.

With a twinkle in her look, Aphrodite pulled Elliot toward her and planted a big kiss on his cheek. At the touch of her lips, Elliot felt a blush begin fifty feet below the Earth, surging through the ground before it burst into his shoes and erupted all over his face, making him resemble a thoroughly happy tomato.

"Aphy, could we have a word, please? Bit of business to discuss," said Zeus with a wink.

"Yes, of course—I'm just with a client," she whispered, gesturing to the gentleman in the knitted sweater in her office. "With you in a sec, Colin!"

"Er, right-o, okay, then," replied Colin as he tried to remove his cardigan, banged his knee on the desk, and tripped over the chair, sending his thick black glasses flying. Aphrodite looked lovingly at him.

"Bless his heart. Such a catch," she said, winking.

"Aphrodite Venus?" a voice boomed across the reception. It belonged to quite the tallest and broadest woman Elliot had seen without a shot put, a giantess in a gray suit brandishing a briefcase.

"That's me," said Aphrodite sweetly.

"Millicent Tronglebom," declared the woman, flashing an ID badge. "Health and safety officer. I'm here to inspect your toilets."

"Madam!" Zeus boomed admiringly, much to Sally's annoyance. "You are my kind of gal. You can inspect my toilets anytime!"

Millicent gave Zeus a look that could raise a wart. He shirked against the wall, burbling incoherently.

"Your annual hygiene inspection is overdue," she barked, turning her attention back to Aphrodite.

"Ah. Whoopsie," said Aphrodite mischievously.

"Whoopsie, indeed, Ms. Venus!" roared Millicent, pulling herself up even taller. "It seems you've never been granted license BS666: Operating Toilets Where People Might Need One! And if you can't come up with a reasonable explanation, you can expect a substantial fine!"

"I see," said Aphrodite, looking back at Colin, who was now staggering blindly around the office. "Won't you come through? I'm sure we can sort something out."

With a wicked smile, Aphrodite ushered Millicent into her office, gesturing to Zeus and Elliot to follow. She took a seat at her heart-shaped desk. Colin was crawling around the floor in search of his lost glasses.

"Now, how can I help you?" Aphrodite asked Millicent sweetly, opening a small drawer and removing a pink leather box.

"According to our records, you haven't applied for a toilet license since . . . well, since forever," said Millicent.

"That sounds about right," Aphrodite trilled, opening the box.

"You don't deny it?" said the incredulous Millicent.

"I have nothing to hide," said Aphrodite. "Paperwork is boring. I don't do boring. Besides, I can't pay your fine. My services are free. Money is such silly stuff."

Elliot wanted to argue that it was easy to think that about money when you didn't need it. But everything Aphrodite did was amazing and beautiful and wonderful.

"Don't you have a secretary?" asked Millicent. "Someone to handle vital matters such as toilet licenses?"

"Nope," said Aphrodite absentmindedly, fiddling with whatever was inside the box.

"This is a very serious offense, Ms. Venus," Millicent roared. "You could be facing—"

"Have you met Colin?" said Aphrodite, gesturing to the helpless soul floundering about on the floor.

"No," sneered Millicent, peering down at Colin as if there were a pile of slug vomit at her feet.

"You two should get to know each other," said Aphrodite, suddenly standing up and yanking a pink Taser gun out of the box. "I think you'll get along!"

"What the—?" gasped Millicent, but it was too late. Aphrodite fired the gun and two wires tipped with pink hearts sliced through the air toward their targets—one attaching to Millicent's magnificent bosom, the other to Colin's scrawny butt.

For a moment, both parties tried to overcome the shock of having a Taser fired at them in broad daylight. Elliot noticed that Colin's glasses were lying by his feet, so he handed them to the stunned man, who was plucking the heart from his backside.

Colin rose slowly from the floor, adjusting his glasses to fix his gaze on a dumbstruck Millicent.

"Millicent Tronglebom," she said softly, extending her hand toward a slack-jawed Colin.

"Colin Limpwad," he replied, taking her hand as if it were a holy relic. "You have the most beautiful name I've ever heard. *Millicent Tronglebom.* It's like a choir of heavenly hamsters singing your beauty."

"Why, thank you, Colin," giggled Millicent coyly. "I hope you'll not think me forward, but that's a lovely cardigan."

"Sweet Ms. Tronglebom—my mother knitted it for my forty-third birthday. We live together."

"Oh, Colin—how I've longed to find a man who lives with his mother!"

"Sweet Milly—may I call you Milly?" asked Colin.

"Only if I can call you—Schnookykins!" Millicent blushed.

"You can call me anything you want!" roared Colin, gathering the ample Millicent into his skinny arms. "I have yearned for a woman like you! A woman with grace! A woman with substance! A woman with a bosom I could build our house on! Marry me, Milly!"

"Yes! Yes! A thousand times yes!" screamed Millicent, tearing Aphrodite's file in half. "Let us go to the Little Chapel of Love this very afternoon!"

"If we hurry, we'll catch the next bus!" cried Colin,

picking up his thermos and the cheese sandwich his mom had packed for him. "I'll flag it down!"

"You can flag my bus anytime, my little Colly Flower!" shouted Millicent, shaking her hair free of its bun and scooping Colin up into her arms as they ran out the door and toward wedded bliss.

"And that's why I don't need a secretary." Aphrodite grinned, replacing the Taser in her drawer. "Now. What can I do for you?"

FAMILY MATTERS

Zeus was barely halfway through his explanation of Thanatos's escape when Aphrodite had pulled the keys to her sports car out of her handbag.

"I'm in," she squealed. "Sounds like fun!"

But Athene was going to take more persuading.

Zeus, Elliot, and Aphrodite were in Athene's office at St. Brainiac College at Oxford University, where Athene was an esteemed professor of politics, philosophy, economics, English, French, Spanish, classics, natural sciences, and basket-weaving. It was a delicate negotiation.

"YOU ARE SUCH A BORING-BRAINED, LIBRARY-LAME-O NERD-BUTT!" Aphrodite shouted at her sister across the grand mahogany desk.

"I see you've been studying the *Big Book of Intelligent Insults*," Athene shot back over the top of her tortoiseshell glasses.

Zeus looked at Elliot with raised eyebrows. *See what I mean?* Elliot could hear him say.

"I can't believe you'd rather sit here with your big pointy nose stuck in a book than be out finding the Chaos Stones,"

Aphrodite pouted. "Just because you look like a pensioner doesn't mean that you have to act like one."

Painful as it was to disagree with Aphrodite, Elliot could see that she was being very hard on her sister. Athene would normally be the most beautiful woman in the room: she was slender, with ebony hair piled into an elegant knot, her deep brown eyes radiating intelligence and grace over the rims of her glasses. But Elliot was convinced that all other girls looked like snotty warthogs next to Aphrodite.

"I am a highly regarded academic," said Athene grandly. "Some of us aren't fortunate enough to play boyfriends-and-girlfriends. Some of us improve mortalkind with brilliant thought."

"I've given mortals beauty and joy," replied Aphrodite. "You've given them some boring books for the downstairs bathroom. Besides, you're not so grand when you're cheating on those TV game shows . . ."

"I do not cheat!" said Athene defensively. "I win those competitions fair and square."

"Sure you do," said Aphrodite with a naughty grin. "Although with a few extra millennia to study, any idiot could beat those poor mortals."

"Not *any* idiot," said Athene, looking directly at her sister.

"Come now, girlies, this is no time for squabbling," Zeus chided. "We need to get those Chaos Stones and put Thanatos back in prison where he belongs. We're a team. I need you."

"Yes, Father. Your pact with Hypnos—surely you can't think that was wise?" said Athene, her dark eyes full of disapproval.

"Whatever," yawned Aphrodite. "Prissy-pants, are you in or out?"

"Out," said Athene stubbornly.

Aphrodite opened her mouth to launch another barrage at her sister, but was hushed by her father's hand on her shoulder.

"We could really use your fabulous noggin, sweetie," said Zeus. "But no is no."

With Aphrodite chewing her tongue, Zeus started to usher her out of the door. Elliot didn't have siblings, but he'd seen enough of other people's to know how they worked. Besides, if Athene could help him find the Earth Stone, he needed her on the team.

"I'm sorry you're not coming, Athene," he said.

"I'm sorry too, Elliot, but I wish you well," she said grumpily.

"That's really kind," he said. "Besides, it's probably for the best. This isn't your sort of thing."

"What makes you say that?" bristled Athene.

"Oh, nothing. Just something Aphrodite said. Nice to meet you," he added, starting out of the room under Zeus's admiring gaze.

"Wh-what did she say?" asked Athene, failing to sound as if she didn't care.

"Nothing bad. Just that you preferred reading to fighting—"

"Well, that's not strictly true, I am a Warrior Goddess!"

"And that you probably felt a bit old to fight Daemons—"

"I'm hardly any older than she is!"

"And that she usually comes up with the best plans anyway—"

"SHE SAID WHAT?" shouted Athene, hastily stuffing some books into a large bag. "Aphrodite! Come back here! I'll show you who's the best fighter!"

And in a blaze of fury, the Goddess of Wisdom swept out of the door toward Aphrodite's sports car.

"Good stuff, my boy!" Zeus winked as they headed out of the university behind her.

With the squabbling Athene and Aphrodite dispatched to fetch Hephaestus, God of the Forge, from his job fixing supermarket self-service machines, Elliot and Zeus flew back to Home Farm. Elliot looked in on his mom, who was happily chatting with Hestia about wallpaper textures in the living room. All was well—or at least no sign of the Horse's-Bum—so Elliot hurried back to the cowshed to find out how he was going to get the Earth Stone and save his home.

"Boom, you're back!" shouted Hermes. "We've been busier

than Photoshop in Fashion Week. We've found Hypnos in a list of the Earth's richest mortals."

"How can you be sure?" said Athene sharply, striding into the barn with Aphrodite and a short, stocky man whose right shoulder was slightly higher than his left. He reminded Elliot of a troll action figure he'd enjoyed playing with when he was younger, although when he saw the huge bronze ax hanging inside the man's brown trench coat, he quickly decided he wouldn't tell him that.

"Ah—you're here!" boomed Zeus happily.

The troll inclined his head in greeting.

"Marnin'," he said.

"Hephy, my man, this is Elliot, a marvelous new friend. Elliot, this handsome dude is Hephaestus, inventor and builder extraordinaire."

"How do," said Hephaestus coolly, but not unkindly.

"Hi, Hef . . . Hefist . . . Hefor . . ." bumbled Elliot, unable to get his mouth around the name.

"Heff. Ice. Tus," Zeus whispered in his ear. "Darn awkward name."

"Nothing wrong with me hearing, though," said Hephaestus, producing a massive hammer from his coat before wandering over to the other side of the shed to look at Bessie's broken water feeder.

"Hypnos will have dissembled into a mortal form," Athene continued. "He won't look like the Daemon we knew."

"Hold tight," said Hermes, putting his palm up to Athene. "Now where is my iGod? You're gonna love this."

"Snordlesnot!" yelped Hephaestus, hitting his thumb with the hammer as he fixed the feeder.

Hermes scrabbled around in his small bag, his whole arm delving in up to the shoulder. He threw out unwanted items, including a stuffed panda, a green macaroon, and the 1994 edition of the London street map, the last of which hit Hephaestus on the head, bringing the golden hammer down on his thumb for a second time.

"Snordlesnot!" cried the immortal blacksmith again as he whipped the throbbing thumb to his mouth, immediately dropping the offending hammer on his foot.

"SNORDLESNOT!" he bellowed for the third time, not knowing which injury to treat first, leaving him awkwardly sucking his thumb and hopping on his good foot for the five seconds it took him to fall over and bang his head.

"What does 'Snordlesnot' mean?" Elliot grinned.

"Ah, well. It's not a word one usually hears in polite company," said Virgo disapprovingly. "It's an ancient Titan curse. It's tricky to translate, but roughly it means, 'May the Gods forever poke you in the rear end with a pointy potato and throw monkey poop at your sister.'"

"Don't all rush at once, I'm fine," grumbled Hephaestus, struggling to his feet.

"Seriously, where did I leave it . . . here it is!" said Hermes triumphantly, spotting the tortoiseshell iGod on the floor.

"So this is just wicked. I downloaded a new app from the Golden Apple Store just the other day. It's called Veritum— when you tap on a photograph, it shows you the true essence of the person in the picture. Bosh!"

Hermes tapped the picture of the first billionaire on the iGod, a bald, bespectacled man who had made his fortune in computers. At his touch, the photograph changed from a middle-aged man to a scrawny-looking chicken. Hermes nearly fell off his bale laughing. "Boom! You should see what happens when you Veritum some Hollywood actors—it's disgusting. Now then . . ."

Hermes went down the list, tapping the pictures. The images variously changed from snakes to toads to rats, while one famous model turned out to be nothing more than a pair of plastic jugs.

"What about this one?" said Aphrodite. "Richard M. Trumpington, founder of 1Born, online gambling site."

"Quite righty, Aphrodite," chimed Hermes, prodding Trumpington's unremarkable mortal features. The picture instantly changed into a gaunt, wild-eyed young man, whose face was locked in a crazy and quite terrifying grimace. At first glance, his chaotic white hair encircled his head like a warped halo. But on closer inspection, it was in fact a mass of tiny feathers in the shape of a pair of wings on either side of his head. In his hands, he clutched a curved ivory trumpet.

"That's him," said Zeus quietly. "That's Hypnos."

"Wow, he hasn't exactly had a rough time of it," said

Hermes, dropping his iGod on the hay bale. "Estimated wealth of five hundred billion pounds. He lives in a seventy-five-bedroom mansion in the Scottish Highlands. What a show-off."

"I thought immortals can't keep mortal money?" said Elliot.

"*We* can't," sighed Zeus. "We all had to swear on the Styx to adhere to the Sacred Code. But the Zodiac Council didn't know Hypnos was alive—he wasn't made to take the oath. Our rules don't apply to him. Lucky dude . . ."

"If we can find him this easily, so can Thanatos," said Athene, as a copy of the *Daily Argus* flew into the cowshed out of nowhere, hitting Hephaestus, who dropped the hammer on his thumb in a symphony of "Snordlesnots." "We need to get to Hypnos first while we've got the element of surprise."

"You can forget about that," said Pegasus, eyeing the front page of the *Daily Argus*.

Elliot surveyed the newspaper. The lead story was illustrated with a black-and-brown picture in the style Elliot had seen on the side of Greek vases. At first he couldn't make out what it depicted, but when he looked more closely, he saw that the picture was of Thanatos dangling Virgo by the hair while Elliot cowered in front of him.

MORTAL PERIL!

By Ovid, Current Affairs Correspondent

The *Argus* has just come across

The great escape of Thanatos
Virgo met the ancient crook
And let the Daemon sling his hook
The Virgo girl was only due
To visit Prisoner Forty-Two
She took the drink for him to sup
And then she royally screwed it up
'Cause when she crossed the sacred portal
Stupid Virgo brought a mortal
The human child broke the spell
Now Thanatos will give us 'ell
The Daemon villain's on the loose
Those silly kids have cooked our goose.

"We've got a mole!" shouted an outraged Athene.

"Are you accusing one of us of leaking the story?" huffed Aphrodite.

"No," said Athene, picking up a shovel and whacking a small mound of earth next to her. "We've got a mole."

A slightly dazed mole holding a notepad and pencil stuck his head out of the soil before scuttling back underground.

"I'd better call the Zodiac Council and let them know," said Virgo. "May I borrow your iGod, Hermes?"

"Bosh," said Hermes, dialing the number before replacing the device on a bale. "Not being funny, the signal is THE worst. It might cut out."

After a few rings, a flickering hologram of Pisces's fishy face was projected onto the wall of Bessie's pen.

"Ah, Pisces—Virgo here, I thought I'd better update you on a development in the ongoing situation vis-à-vis the Daemons . . ."

"UPDATE US!" hollered the projection of Pisces. "The phones are ringing off the hook! We're inundated with panicked immortals! There hasn't been a stink like this since the Titans' last pork and beans night!"

Intrigued by the noise, Bessie strolled out of her pen and went to sniff at Pisces's face.

"Young lady!" Pisces went on, his face now projected on Bessie's backside. "Have you any idea of the mess you have created?"

Virgo tried not to be distracted by Hermes and Aphrodite's giggles.

"No," she said innocently.

"We're still trying to get to the bottom of it!" shouted Pisces, the angry bubbles from his lips looking as though they were coming out of Bessie's butt. "You've really landed us in the poop!"

"I'm sorry," said Virgo, trying to make herself heard over Hermes and Aphrodite's guffaws. "I have taken steps to ensure that Thanatos is recaptured immediately. I have sought the assistance of the Olympians."

"Ha!" scoffed Pisces. "Those old has-beens! They couldn't catch a cold!"

Aphrodite and Hermes stopped laughing.

"I'm warning you, Virgo," said Pisces, flickering violently and starting to fade. "You are wet behind the ears! My pants are older than you! I will not have a whiff of scandal!"

"Sorry?" said Virgo. "You cut out. I didn't catch that . . ."

"I said," huffed the fish over the crackling signal, "I . . . wet . . . my . . . pants . . . I . . . whiff . . ."

Pisces's face disappeared as the signal dropped out altogether.

"Yikes!" cried Zeus. "Hermes, get yourself to Hypnos's mansion, quick smart. Find out where he hid those stones. We have to get to them before Thanatos does."

"Bosh! I love a good spy," said Hermes, as his motorcycle whizzed into the shed by itself. "I'll take the low road— Scotland, hold tight!"

And he raced his motorcycle out of the barn in a flash, leaving a blizzard of hay in his wake.

"Well, that's that," said Zeus. "Now what about some security measures? Hephaestus—we need something around the farm, something that will keep Elliot safe inside and everyone else out, something big and tall, something strong, something . . . something like . . ."

"A fence?" suggested Hephaestus dryly as he wrapped his bright red thumb in a dirty rag.

"That's the ticket!" boomed Zeus, as if Hephaestus had just invented the wheel. "Get to it, my friend, good work."

"I get all the good jobs, me," grumbled the blacksmith,

heading out of the shed with a golden tape measure, just as Bessie's water feeder started to work beautifully.

Zeus glanced over at Elliot, who suddenly couldn't keep his exhausted eyes open.

"You go and rest," he said. "You're going to need your wits about you. Virgo, you stay with Elliot at all times—until we know what Thanatos has in mind, we have to be on constant alert."

"Wait!" said Elliot. "I have to go to school tomorrow. I have a stupid history test."

"What an admirable attitude," said Athene, who was weaving sumptuous silk sheets out of straw.

"Don't bother," said Aphrodite, pulling a face behind Athene's back. "All the best stuff you learn outside school."

"If I don't go to school, they'll come looking for me here," said Elliot. "And none of us need that."

"He's right," said Zeus. "And the less disruption to Elliot's life, the better. Virgo, you will go to school and protect him."

"Excellent," said Virgo. "I look forward to spending time in an illuminating mortal educational establishment."

"Shame you're coming to my school, then," muttered Elliot.

"You have to promise us you'll stay safe, my boy," said Zeus. "Now go and sleep well, it's been a long day."

"I'll walk the kids back to the house—make sure they get there safely," gabbled Aphrodite, hustling Elliot and Virgo out of the shed before anyone could object.

Virgo and Aphrodite chatted away while a tongue-tied Elliot walked a few paces behind them. But when they reached the farmhouse, Aphrodite held Elliot back, waiting until Virgo was out of earshot before speaking.

"Now listen, Elly," she said, opening a locket around her neck and producing a heart-shaped pearl from inside it. "Ignore the Fun Police back there; here's some real help for your test."

She handed Elliot the pearl, which he turned slowly in his palm.

"This wishing pearl will grant you anything you want—but only once a day and only for seven minutes. Seven's my lucky number," she said, her eyes twinkling. "Keep it near you and make a wish at the start of the test—you'll ace it."

"Wow—thanks," said Elliot, stringing together his longest sentence to the Goddess.

"You're welcome, sweetie," Aphrodite said, winking.

And with a musical giggle, she sashayed back to the cowshed, leaving a happy pink boy so dazed that he didn't notice an especially nosy neighbor lurking in the shadows, a neighbor who had been spying on the strange new guests and who was determined to find out what was really going on at Home Farm.

18

AN OLD FIEND

Until very recently, life had been a blast for Hypnos, the Daemon of Sleep. In fact, several lives had been a blast, as he was now enjoying his twenty-ninth incarnation.

Blessed, as all Daemons were, with the ability to dissemble into any shape at will, for the past two thousand years the Daemon of Sleep had enjoyed making history—and money—as some of the world's most notorious characters. Emperor Nero, Genghis Khan, Napoleon, Rasputin, Al Capone—Hypnos had been them all, "dying" when he'd had enough and reincarnating in a new guise. With the Zodiac Council unaware that he was still alive, Hypnos was free from the Sacred Code and able to do as he pleased. Life was a game. And Hypnos was the winner.

Nothing mattered to Hypnos more than winning. The moment his father, Erebus, had robbed him of his destiny as king of the Daemons, Hypnos had become obsessed with beating Thanatos. The deal with Zeus had made his yellow, bloodshot eyes dance with vengeful glee. Indeed, his victory over his brother had excited Hypnos so much that he hadn't been able to sleep—for two thousand years. It didn't matter—his insomnia gave him a buzz, a manic energy, a hyper edge that hadn't wiped the smile from his face in two millennia.

But winning had proven dangerously addictive. Once Thanatos was defeated, Hypnos discovered that he needed to find more and bigger victories. He tried dissembling into sportsmen, but his Daemon strength gave him such an advantage, it was pointless. Winning was only fun when it was unexpected.

And that's how Hypnos discovered gambling.

Now the thrill of the unpredictable win could be his every day—or could it? That was the buzz. There was nothing Hypnos wouldn't bet on—horse races, roulette wheels, which raindrop would reach the window ledge first . . . The losses made the wins that much sweeter, and he could afford both. In his current guise as Richard M. Trumpington, his online gambling business 1Born provided yet another way for Hypnos to cheat mortals out of their money, torturing them with dreams of big wins and making their worst nightmares come true when they lost everything. Nothing gave him greater pleasure. Hypnos had everything just the way he wanted it. The Daemon of Sleep was having the time of his lives.

Or at least he was until yesterday. He never normally paid much attention to the *Daily Argus*, having no interest in the immortal losers featured within. But yesterday's front page had filled him with a fear he hadn't known in twenty-nine lifetimes. Zeus had lied. Thanatos was alive. And Hypnos knew that his twin would be coming straight for him. Most things were a joke to the psychotic Daemon. The thought of being killed by his brother was not.

Hypnos immediately hired the best security guards money could buy and gave every single one strict instructions not to let anyone in. It didn't matter if someone claimed to be his long-lost son or his dying mother—only Richard M. Trumpington was allowed in his Scottish mansion.

So the guards thought nothing of allowing Richard M. Trumpington through the massive gates early the next morning. His butler happily opened the door to allow Richard M. Trumpington into the house while Trent, his personal bodyguard, gladly unlocked the door to the office when Mr. Trumpington said he had forgotten his key. Had they all checked with one another, they would have realized that Richard M. Trumpington had never left his office in the first place. But by the time Thanatos had tricked them all and was standing in Hypnos's office, it was far too late.

"Hello, brother," said Thanatos eventually, after an eternal silence while each twin tried to read the other.

Beneath his laughing stare, Hypnos was frantically calculating how to stay alive.

"Hi, yourself," he said at last. "You're looking well."

"How kind," said Thanatos coldly. "Two thousand years imprisoned beneath the Earth doesn't do a lot for one's social life, but it certainly restricts poor lifestyle choices. But we have more important matters to discuss. May I?"

Thanatos pulled a tacky golden chair back from the desk and sat on the edge of the seat. He surveyed the opulent room with a sneer.

"They say that money can't buy you taste," he said. "How kind of you to prove them right."

"They say that you're dead." Hypnos grinned. "How inconvenient of you to prove them wrong."

The two brothers stared intensely at each other.

"So how are you?" Hypnos inquired.

"Can't complain," said Thanatos. "Although perhaps I can? It's not every day you are betrayed by your own twin brother . . ."

"Yeah—about that." Hypnos smiled cheekily. "If I hadn't accepted Zeus's deal, one of the other Daemons probably would have. Seemed a shame to let the Chaos Stones leave the family . . ."

"WHERE ARE THEY?" roared Thanatos, jumping out of the gold chair, sending it clattering across the room. "Tell me, or I'll kill you this second."

"If I tell you, you'll kill me that second," said Hypnos, his wild stare challenging his brother. Maybe Hypnos could blink. Maybe he couldn't. No one had ever kept their eyes open long enough to find out.

"I'm going to count to one," said Thanatos.

"You haven't thought this through . . ." chirped the Daemon of Sleep, his eyes as wide as his laughing mouth.

"One," said Thanatos reaching over the desk toward Hypnos's slender neck.

"I always was faster," cackled Hypnos, deftly dodging the hand by taking flight with his winged head. "Catch me if you can!"

Thanatos lunged repeatedly over the desk, trying to grab his brother, who taunted him by flying away with split-second timing.

"Too slow!" laughed Hypnos. "You've lost your—"

The remaining words were knocked out of Hypnos's smug face as Thanatos landed a colossal punch on his cheek.

"I always was stronger," said Thanatos, and he grabbed his twin by the neck with one hand and twisted his kardia with the other. "Where are my Chaos Stones?"

"If I die, you'll never know," rasped Hypnos.

"Then you'd better start talking," said Thanatos, lifting his brother clean off the floor and pulling the kardia away from his neck.

"*I . . . know . . . something . . . you . . . don't . . . know,*" sang Hypnos, his eyes still laughing despite his face turning a fearful shade of puce.

"TELL ME!" said Thanatos, shaking his breathless twin.

Hypnos shook his grinning head, no longer able to speak.

"Oh, for . . ."

Thanatos released the kardia and threw his brother down in disgust. Despite his desperate gasps for air, Hypnos was delighted that Thanatos realized he'd sooner die than lose. He threw back his sore neck and screamed with dark laughter.

"In a funny way, I've missed you," Hypnos said, wiping the tears from his eyes as he returned to his seat.

"If you're never going to tell me, I may as well kill you now," said Thanatos, calmly retrieving the chair and sitting down.

"And then you'll never know," said Hypnos. "Fun, isn't it?"

"Where are they?" Thanatos asked again slowly.

"Tell you what I'm going to do," said Hypnos, his fingers dancing across the table. "I'll tell you where they are one at a time. That way, you get your stones, I get to stay alive."

"Until I get them all," said Thanatos. "Then I'm going to kill you."

"I hoped we might have a side bet on that." Hypnos grinned. "You need someone to kill the mortal child. You can't."

"How do you know that?"

"A chicken gyro, some fries, and a tub of OMG! Marshmallow Ice Cream," said Hypnos.

"You've spoken to Pythia?" said Thanatos.

"I'm her best customer." Hypnos replied. "I bet you I can kill the child. You must swear on the Styx you won't kill me if I win."

Hypnos loved watching Thanatos trying to quell his murderous rage. He knew his brother had no choice.

"Done," said Thanatos darkly. "Start talking."

"Oh, I had such fun hiding them!" whispered Hypnos. "But it's going to be even better getting them back! Let's start with the Earth Stone—that one was tricky. Every time I buried it underground, some greedy mortal would dig it up again and I'd have to . . . persuade them to give it back. But then I found a great spot for it . . ."

Hypnos watched gleefully as Thanatos hung on his words.

"It's in . . . the Tower of London!" he whispered with a giggle. "It's an impenetrable mortal fortress and I hid the Earth Stone there—smack in the middle of the Crown Jewels!"

"Marvelous," said Thanatos.

"I first had the idea when I was a character called Colonel Thomas Blood in the seventeenth century," said Hypnos, stretching out and putting his feet up on the desk. "I made friends with the guard, then knocked him out and shot him while I stole the jewels. Only I wasn't stealing them—I put the Earth Stone in there! Various jewelers have moved it around—at the moment, it's slapped on the front of the Imperial State Crown."

"If this tower is impenetrable, how are you going to get my stone back?" hissed Thanatos.

"Your timing is impeccable, brother," squealed Hypnos. "I have a golden opportunity this very week. Once a year the crown is worn by the Queen—she's an important mortal the other mortals like to print on things—and she will have it in her palace in a few days! Taking it from her will be a breeze. It'll be like stealing a hot water bottle from a granny!"

"Then go and fetch it," said Thanatos.

"First I'll kill the child," said Hypnos, flying over to a safe concealed behind the *Mona Lisa* on his wall. "Shouldn't be too hard. Then I'll get your stone."

"I'll be at our old home in the Underworld, the Cave of Sleep and Death," said Thanatos. "Until my stones are returned, I'll be keeping a low profile. Meet me there with my Earth Stone. Don't fail me."

"What fun!" squealed Hypnos, pulling his ivory trumpet out of the safe and kissing it. "Come on, baby, we've got work to do. I'll take my private jet. The boy will be resting in peace in no time."

"He'd better be," said Thanatos.

"Have a nice day, sir," said Trent the bodyguard as Thanatos swept past him, disguised once again as Richard M. Trumpington.

"Have a nice day, sir," said Trent again as a second Richard M. Trumpington raced out of the office, looking exactly like the first.

Trent removed his shades and wiped his eyes. He'd been guarding the office all night. Clearly he needed a coffee. He closed the door on the empty room.

Or at least, it appeared to be empty.

In his paranoia about who might enter his office, Hypnos hadn't given any thought to what might already be inside it.

Had he paid closer attention, Hypnos might have noticed that among the expensive bric-a-brac, a new and especially good-looking jewel-encrusted Grecian urn had appeared the night before. And had he looked more closely still, he would have observed that the large handles on the side of the urn looked remarkably like a big pair of ears, flapping around to hear what might be said. The urn now started to wobble and shake, finally falling to the ground, where it immediately transformed back into the gasping form of Hermes.

"Shut uuuup!" he whispered. "The Earth Stone! Elliot! Everything! I'm not even joking. Where's my iGod, I gotta call home!"

Hermes delved into his bag and groped around its bottomless depths. He pulled out a sock, a chandelier, a riding saddle, and a ferret, but with each desperate grasp, he couldn't find his phone.

"No, mate! Anti-bosh!" he hissed.

The Messenger God recalled his hasty departure from the cowshed—he'd left his iGod on the hay bale. He had no way of contacting the Gods, but he needed to warn Elliot—right now.

Hermes ran to the door to escape the tacky horror of Hypnos's office before transforming into the guise of Richard M. Trumpington.

"Have a nice day, sir," said Trent to the third identical man to walk out of the room.

He rubbed his eyes again. He didn't need a coffee. He needed a doctor.

Back on the low-way, Hermes revved his motorcycle as hard as it would go. He dodged in and out of traffic, jumping over the occasional cyclist as he careered back toward Home Farm at the opposite end of the country.

"Come on, babe," he urged the bike. "Let's go . . ."

He revved the bike again, but was shocked when it started to decelerate instead.

"What . . . seriously?" he said as he came to a shuddering halt on the side of the road.

"Vehicle registration: B 0 5 H. Owner: Hermes. Category: Olympian," boomed the nearest loudspeaker. *"Libra calculates that this is your third speeding infringement. Your vehicle has been disabled. It's only fair!"*

"You're joking!" shouted Hermes, and he kicked his bike in frustration. "I'm hundreds of miles away. It'll take me . . . Urgh . . ."

He delved into his bag and pulled out a pair of winged sneakers, which he swapped with the winged biker boots he'd been wearing.

"Looks like I'm going old-school," he said as he fluttered into the air. "I hope I've still got it."

And with a whoosh, Hermes took off, flying back to Home Farm and Elliot's endangered life.

19

BE CAREFUL WHAT YOU WISH FOR

By Monday morning, Elliot was starting to appreciate living with a cowshed full of immortals.

In a single day, Hestia, the Goddess of the Hearth, had transformed Elliot's shabby farm into a home that looked like it had jumped out of the pages of a magazine. Some changes were simply the result of a good eye for interior design—the peeling walls were covered in fresh coats of bright paint, sumptuous fabrics covered the plush new sofas and armchairs, and the bedrooms now had enormous fluffy beds that sank a foot when you lay on them.

Other alterations, however, suggested that this was no average DIY job. The bathroom had a shower that flowed like a warm, scented waterfall, with a bathtub that was big enough to swim in, permanently filled with hot, bubbly water. Even the toilets played a Mozart piano concerto when you sat on them. But Elliot's favorite changes were in the kitchen, which boasted a self-emptying dishwasher, a washing machine that dried, ironed, and folded clothes before spiriting them back into their drawers, and—Elliot's personal favorites—a fridge and a kitchen cupboard that always contained exactly what you wanted to eat.

Josie had accepted Elliot's explanation that some friends were staying to help with the farm, even when Virgo had staggered into the kitchen under a tomato the size of a satellite dish, or when Hestia transformed their black-and-white set into a flat-screen HD TV with that expensive game console Elliot had fancied. If anything, Elliot thought Mom seemed better for having the Gods around, chatting to her about life on the farm, none of them batting an eyelid when she asked the same question several times or forgot something they'd just told her. It was a huge relief that someone could watch her while he was at school, and for the first time in ages, Elliot was feeling the benefits of having some help.

But no matter how great the house looked, he was still going to lose it unless he could find twenty thousand pounds by Friday. There had been no word from Hermes, and without the Earth Stone, Elliot had no idea how he was going to conjure up the money. He wondered if he should confide in the Gods—he was running out of time. Could he trust them . . . ?

Elliot didn't know for sure. Until he did, it was safer to stay quiet.

While the cowshed was alive with Hestia's building works—much to Bessie's bemusement—and Hephaestus was working on the new fence, the other Olympians came up to the farmhouse for breakfast, which would have fed a small army for a week. As Virgo was coming to school with Elliot, Athene had woven two perfect Brysmore uniforms, consigning Elliot's threadbare old one to the garbage.

"I intend to make the most of this opportunity to broaden my mind," said Virgo, admiring herself in her new uniform.

"Try a microscope," said Elliot, tucking into his third bacon sandwich.

With Josie sleeping in, Aphrodite doing his paper route in her car, some extra sleep, and the fullest stomach Elliot could remember, he felt in pretty decent shape for a Monday morning.

Until there was an irritating knock at the door.

"Coo-eee," trilled the unmistakable whinny of Patricia Porshley-Plum.

"Hello, Mrs. Porshley-Plum," groaned Elliot. "Can't chat now, I was just—"

"Goodness, it's busy around here!" Patricia smiled with her dead eyes. "It's like Clapham Junction. That is still a train station, isn't it? I always take taxis; public transport is so . . . public."

"Yes—we're having some . . . home improvements," said Elliot, quickly turning Patricia around so she couldn't see the dishwasher Frisbeeing plates back into the cupboard. "But I have to get to school . . ."

"Of course, my little pookums," said Patricia. "I just wanted a quick word with Momsypops?"

"Er . . . she's—" started Elliot.

"Lucky to have such a foxy friend," drawled Zeus, wiggling his eyebrows..

"And who is this?" she asked with another empty smile.

"I'm Elliot's uncle," said Zeus smoothly. "I'm a plumber called Bob."

"Well . . . Bob," said Patricia, "I was hoping to catch . . ."

Elliot shook his head behind her back to warn Zeus she was dangerous. Zeus winked discreetly and ushered Patricia out of the house.

"Drat and double balderdash." He smiled, shutting the door firmly behind them. "Josie's away for the day."

"Away?" said Patricia, a fraction too high. "Wherever has she gone?"

"Shopping," lied Zeus effortlessly. "Heaven help her credit card . . . Hephaestus? How are you coming along with that fence?"

"I'll be done by lunchtime," grumbled the blacksmith, heaving a fence post into place.

"Marvelous," said Zeus to Patricia, tucking her reluctant arm into the crook of his elbow. "You can't be too careful these days—never know who might want to get in."

"Quite," said Patricia, as she was half dragged up the path and out of the gate. "If you could let Josie know I came by?"

"Of course," said Zeus, his eyes narrowing. "Mind how you go."

"You too," said Patricia, her eyes narrower still, as Elliot and Virgo brushed past her to set off over the fields to school.

Zeus had secured Virgo's place at Brysmore with a phone call to Call Me Graham early that morning, pretending to be the headmaster of a prestigious girls' boarding school. He spun a story that Virgo was Elliot's cousin, a brilliant student who had just moved to the area and needed to continue her schooling. Clutching the certificates that Aphrodite had expertly forged, Elliot and Virgo walked up Brysmore's grand driveway.

"You need to keep a low profile today," said Elliot. "I can't have any trouble."

"I thought you'd be more concerned about this test," said Virgo. "I've been studying all night and I still don't think I can possibly pass it. Mortal history is weird."

"Thing is, Virgo," said Elliot smugly, thinking of the wishing pearl in his backpack, "you've either got it or you haven't."

"Got what?" said Virgo suspiciously, as Elliot swaggered toward the school.

"Morning, Mr. Boil," he said to the teacher squeezing out of a compact car that smelled like old fish.

"Be quiet, Hooper," sneered Boil as he finally freed his backside from the door frame. "Who's this?"

"This is my cousin . . . er . . ."

"Anna Hooper," said Virgo moodily, unhappy with the mortal name Zeus had chosen for her.

"Urgh—another Hooper, just what we need," said Boil unpleasantly. "Well, Miss Hooper, clearly there are a few things you need to learn about the Brysmore rules . . ."

"Excellent. I always follow the rules," Virgo said, nodding.

"Unless you change your hair color by tomorrow, you'll earn yourself a detention."

"Whatever's wrong with my hair?" asked Virgo, running her hands through her long silver locks.

"Silver hair is against the Brysmore rules," pronounced Boil.

"Then the Brysmore rules are ridiculous," said Virgo plainly, making Mr. Boil gasp at her blasphemy. "I have no more control over my hair color than you do over your hair loss."

"How—how dare you!" exploded Boil.

"Don't mind my cousin, sir," said Elliot, steering Virgo away. "She's from . . . a long way away. Where she comes from, baldness is a sign of greatness."

"No, it—" Virgo started.

"Nice to see you, sir," called Elliot.

"I'll be watching you today, Hooper," Boil shouted. "Both of you."

"Great way to keep a low profile," sighed Elliot, as they made their way into school.

"What a funny little man," said Virgo. "Is he always that much of a Minotaur dropping or was today a special occasion?"

"Nah," said Elliot. "He's always like that. Hates my guts."

"Why?" asked Virgo. "What have your guts done to him?"

"He doesn't like anyone who thinks for themselves," said Elliot. "And it's possible that last year I sewed sardines in his car seats. But he's determined to get me kicked out—and I can't start a new school. They'd ask too many questions about . . ."

"Josie-Mom," said Virgo quietly. "Athene explained it to me. Mortal children aren't allowed to remain with suboptimal parents."

"You have a gift with words," said Elliot. "But Boil needn't worry. These exams will get rid of me. He knows I'll never get eighty-five percent."

"All the more reason to prove him wrong," Virgo said.

"Absolutely." He grinned, tapping his backpack.

Elliot and Virgo walked to the exam hall, where a straggle of fellow pupils were trembling outside, clearly exhausted after a sleepless night of frantic study.

"Suckers," Elliot muttered as Brainy Briony burst into tears and her boyfriend Dummy Dominic threw up in a wastepaper basket.

The waft of old vegetable soup announced that Boil had arrived. The sad gaggle of students trudged into the hall, holding their breath to walk beneath Boil's smelly armpit as he held the door to count them all in.

When they'd taken their seats, Boil slammed an exam paper down on each individual's desk, delighting in making his petrified students jump as the thuds ricocheted around the hall.

"You have one hour," he announced with a ghoulish grin. "You may begin."

Elliot watched scornfully as his classmates whipped over their papers in horror and started furiously scribbling away. Elliot casually turned over his test. He didn't have a clue how to answer a single question. But then he didn't have to. He waited until the patrolling Mr. Boil had walked past his desk.

"I wish," he whispered as quietly as he could, "to pass this test."

There was a tiny tinkling from his backpack.

Elliot sat completely motionless, his eyes closed, waiting for his mind to fill with inspired historical knowledge.

But nothing happened.

He cautiously opened one eye to see if the test paper had simply written itself. It was completely blank. He didn't understand. Surely Aphrodite wouldn't give him something that didn't work?

Suddenly, Elliot's hands snapped to his desk and grabbed hold of his paper. He darted his head around to check that Boil hadn't noticed, but the history teacher was too busy looming over tearful Briony, narrowly missing Dominic's second puddle of vomit. Elliot didn't get it—how was this going to pass the test? He tried to let go of the paper, but he no longer appeared to have any command over his hands.

"What are you doing?" cut Virgo, seeing Elliot shake next to her.

"I don't know," whispered Elliot. "I can't help it."

"SILENCE!" roared Boil from the back of the hall, making everyone jump in their seats.

Elliot tried desperately to release the paper, but now his hands seemed determined to raise it off the desk.

"No, no, no," whispered Elliot as his arms lifted off the table and veered sharply to the right, bringing Elliot to his feet and pulling him over to Virgo's desk.

"What the blazes are you doing, Hooper? Sit down!" shouted Boil as he charged toward Elliot.

But Elliot was utterly powerless. His hands plonked his test paper heavily in front of Virgo.

"Ow!" she yelped. "What's the matter with you?"

"Silence!" said Boil, arriving at her desk in a fury. "Hooper! You have precisely two seconds to return to your seat before I give you an automatic fail."

"Sorry, sir," said Elliot, relieved to be free of the paper and turning back to his own desk. But his hands suddenly sprang to life again, grabbing Virgo's test and jerking toward the table in front of her. This time they forced him to deposit Virgo's paper on Briony's desk, who duly burst into tears again. The other students watched in bemusement as Elliot worked his way around the hall, picking up test papers and passing them on to the next person with increasing speed.

"Everyone get back to work!" puffed a flaming red Boil as he chased Elliot. "Hooper, I'll have your hide for this!"

But Elliot was completely out of control, frantically running from one desk to the next, passing exam papers around the room as Aphrodite's pearl granted his wish to the letter.

"Help me," he panted at Virgo as he completed his third circuit. "Make it stop."

Virgo ran over to restrain him, but she was powerless against the Olympian's wishing pearl. Elliot darted from her grip and carried on passing the test from person to person, with a panting Boil shouting threats a few feet behind him.

"THIS EXAM IS OVER!" Boil eventually roared amid the chaos.

At his words, Elliot's hands immediately dropped the paper he was holding and returned limply to his side, allowing the exhausted boy to crumple to the floor.

"You've all failed!" Boil spat to a chorus of groans as every last one of Elliot's classmates shot him filthy looks. "Hoopers! You're both coming with me!"

"But I haven't—" started Virgo.

"Silence!" screamed Boil, dragging Elliot up by the back of his blazer and frog-marching him and Virgo straight to the headmaster's office.

20

THE PERFECT PARENTS

Call Me Graham was renowned for being a soft touch, and Elliot had always managed to talk himself out of serious punishment. But this time, Mr. Boil stayed too and no amount of sob stories was going to help.

"Elliot, I'm very sorry to hear that your great-aunt has died. Again," said Call Me Graham, nervously flicking his bangs. "But Mr. Boil is right, this time you have gone too far. You will have to be disciplined."

"Expelled!" cried Boil triumphantly.

"Oh, r-really?" stammered Graham, turning to look at Mr. Boil. "I was thinking more along the lines of a stern letter home. Maybe. If that's okay?"

"The boy is a menace," said Boil, not taking his piggy eyes from Elliot's angry face. "And the girl has 'Trouble' written on her like white on rice."

"I can assure you that my physical composition has nothing to do with cereal grains," said Virgo disdainfully. "I am a carbon-based entity who—"

"You see!" screamed Boil. "I will not see the Brysmore name dragged into the dirt. You're both expelled!"

"But that's ridiculous!" cried Virgo, nudging a belligerent Elliot into defending himself. "It wasn't even a real exam."

"Not another word!" yelled Boil. "The headmaster's decision is final!"

"Er—I haven't actually made a decision," Call Me Graham piped up.

"Yes, you have. And an excellent one it is too," said Boil, slamming his hand on Call Me Graham's shoulder in approval.

"Right. Oh. Well, then. I'll need to see your parents," said the headmaster, and Boil gave an enthusiastic wobble.

Elliot's blood froze. This was exactly what he'd been trying to avoid. There was no way Mom could come to the school. If Call Me Graham found out about Elliot's home life, the headmaster would have to tell the authorities, and then all the months he'd spent trying to keep Mom safe would have been in vain. He looked desperately at Virgo.

"Why. Don't. You. Call. My. Parents?" said Virgo loudly, with spectacularly bad acting skills.

Of course. The Gods. Elliot asked permission to telephone Home Farm from the school office.

"Helloooo," Aphrodite breathed down the line after a few rings.

"It's me," he whispered furiously. "We're in trouble."

"Thanatos?" gasped Aphrodite.

"No. School," said Elliot, "We need some parents, quick."

"Hang in there, sweetie," said Aphrodite, instantly catching his drift. "Two prize parentals coming up."

"Thanks, Aphrodite," he said, hurrying back to Call Me Graham's office before Virgo's mouth could get them into any more trouble.

Ten minutes later, the screech of Aphrodite's car tires broke the tense silence in the headmaster's office. There was a thundering knock on the door and Mr. Boil sprang to answer it, clearly delighted to have a ringside seat at Elliot's expulsion.

"Hi," boomed a vast man enthusiastically, grabbing Boil's hand in a handshake so violent it made him wobble like Jell-O. If the huge, muscular body and cropped hair were unfamiliar to Elliot, the orange Bermuda shorts and red shirt were not. He tried not to laugh at Zeus's disguise. "I'm Brad. And this little cutie is my wife, er . . ."

"Bridget," purred Aphrodite, extending her lovely hand toward Boil's sweaty paw, just giving him time to adjust the glasses that Zeus-Brad's shaking had dislodged. "You must be Mr. Boil. I'd know that handsome face anywhere from Elliot's description."

Aphrodite shot the youngsters a shifty wink as she walked toward them.

"Now what have you two scamps been up to?" she said, waggling a finger at Elliot and Virgo as she perched on the edge of the headmaster's desk. "You know how seriously I take your education."

"Welcome to Brysmore School," said Graham. "I'm Mr. Sopweed. But please, call me Graham . . ."

Call Me Graham came out from behind the desk to shake hands, allowing Boil to breeze past him and sit in his chair, leaving the headmaster looking rather lost in the middle of his own office.

"So," murmured Call Me Graham as he took a seat on a footstool to one side, "I'm afraid the children have disrupted a school examination."

"And been insolent to a teacher! And it would take me all day to list your nephew's crimes!" roared Boil.

"I'd happily spend all day with you, Mr. Boil. All night too, if necessary," said Aphrodite breathily, leaning so far over the desk that Boil spat out the mouthful of the tea he'd just slurped.

"Now, kids," said Zeus-Brad, maneuvering his huge frame behind Mr. Boil at the desk. "Sounds like you owe Mr. Wart here an apology."

"It's Boil," shouted Boil, tempering his volume when he considered the size of the man behind him. "And an apology won't come close. What little I've seen of your daughter doesn't impress me, but Elliot Hooper is a disgrace to the Brysmore name and must be expelled!"

"Oh, come on now, Graham," boomed Zeus-Brad sternly, moving to the headmaster and bringing a hand the weight of a bowling bowl crashing down on his skinny shoulder. "I'm sure we can work this out. They're just a couple of excited kids."

"I love the way your chins wobble," said Aphrodite to Boil, perching on the desk so that her lovely legs were right in front of Boil's third chin. "And the way the spit glistens on your lips is just heavenly. But expelled—that's so, so final. Is there any way I could persuade you to give our little Elly one more chance?"

"Absolutely not," gasped Boil, not taking his eyes from Aphrodite's long legs. "He's had too many chances."

"Aw, you seem like a reasonable guy," said Zeus-Brad, squeezing his huge hand on Call Me Graham's shoulder, releasing a pained whimper from the headmaster. "Let's not be hasty."

"Please," implored Aphrodite, puffing her lips into an irresistible pout.

"Well—I—the Brysmore rules state—" spluttered Call Me Graham, earning him another painful squeeze from the hulk of a man behind him.

"Pretty please," said Aphrodite, batting her luscious eyelashes.

"I s-s-suppose Mr. Boil here might have been a little harsh," he stammered, wiping the sweat from his brow with a frilly handkerchief.

"Wh-WHAT?!" shouted Boil. "No, headmaster, expulsion is the only possible consequence—"

"I think you'll find that Graham here has spoken," said Zeus-Brad, striding over to Mr. Boil and towering over him. "Unless there's anything you wanna add?"

"No—no," whimpered a gibbering Boil. "But they are both suspended. I don't want to see either of these children until the end-of-term exams next month. And if they get half a mark beneath eighty-five percent, they'll be out of this school."

"Oh, thank you," cried Aphrodite, leaping off the desk and planting a big kiss on Call me Graham's clammy cheek, turning him a shade of pink that put Elliot's blushes to shame. "You won't regret it. Now come along, you naughty children, let's get you home."

"Yes, Mommy," droned Virgo, showing little improvement in her acting ability.

"Yes, Aunty Bridget," squeaked Elliot, running from the room before exploding with laughter in the corridor.

"Good to meet you, Wart," boomed Zeus-Brad, his blue eyes as cold as steel. Mr. Boil winced in his handshake. "I'll be keeping my eye on everything, don't you worry."

"IT'S BOIL!" shouted the incensed history teacher as Zeus slammed the door in his livid red face, blocking the hysterical laughter coming from outside.

"Well, I think I handled that very nicely," said Call Me Graham quietly from his footstool. "Time for lunch."

As the head tripped over some fresh air on the way to the cafeteria, Mr. Boil looked out of the window to where the quartet was piling into Aphrodite's car in giggling fits.

"You wait, Hooper," he muttered under his pungent breath. "The last laugh will be mine."

Zeus, Aphrodite, Elliot, and Virgo couldn't stop giggling all the way home. But when they reached the farm, Athene didn't see the joke.

"Suspension is a very serious business," she said sternly to the four, who hung their heads before her. "Think of all the school they'll miss. Why did you give Elliot that pearl?"

"Oh, be quiet." Aphrodite pouted guiltily. "I was only trying to help Elly rub that pig-faced buffoon's nose in it. Besides, this suspension is just what we need—it's too dangerous letting them out of the house until we know where Thanatos and Hypnos are. They're safer here and you know it."

"Let's talk in the shed," said Athene, looking over at Josie, who was happily knitting a colorful scarf in the kitchen.

From outside, there was nothing apart from the fixed roof to show that Demeter, Hestia, and their teams of Penates had touched the shed at all. But as Athene swung the door open, it took Elliot a moment to comprehend what he saw. His run-down old cowshed had turned into a marble-floored palace, complete with fountain, statues, and rows of olive trees growing inside the barn. On an upper level were the Olympians' opulent sleeping quarters, with a library for Athene.

Although the outside appeared no larger, the inside of the shed now seemed vast, not least because of the two lush meadows growing on either side. To the left was Pegasus's residence, a hay-lined golden stable with a mineral-water fountain, where the splendid horse reclined on a velvet bed reading *Black Beauty*. To the right was Bessie's new home, with a luxurious hay-bed and giant water feeder set in the softest grass. Elliot's pet cow was clearly delighted with her new pad—although perhaps less pleased with the pink frilly knickers Aphrodite had put over her udders—and was happily leaping around thanks to a new golden splint on her lame leg. Elliot could hear the chink of hammer on iron in Hephaestus's new forge underneath the shed, and despite the cold, gray weather, inside the barn it felt warm and sunny.

"Hope you don't mind the alterations," said Zeus, struggling to maneuver his portly frame onto a comfy chair. "Hestia tends to go a bit overboard. If there's anything you don't like, pipe up."

"It's awesome," gasped Elliot. "Thanks."

"Hephy, how's the fence coming along?" shouted Zeus.

"All done," said Hephaestus, lumbering into the shed. "Not bad, if I say so meself. Which I'll have to. It's a smart fence, so it knows who you are. The gate'll only open automatically for Elliot's family and ours. Everyone else needs our permission. Or they're in for a surprise . . ."

"Nice job, old boy!" Zeus grinned, giving Hephaestus a back slap that could have dislodged a lung.

"But you 'ave to tell it to shut behind you," warned Hephaestus. "Zodiac Council won't give me planning permission anymore for self-closing gates in case anyone gets squashed. 'Elth and safety gone mad, if you ask me. It was only the one time . . ."

"Perfect!" boomed Zeus. "Now has anyone heard from Herm—"

An explosion of feathers cut Zeus short as Hermes blasted into the shed and landed in the marble fountain, knocking it sideways.

"Maaaaaaaate! Hypnos is coming! Not even joking!" the bedraggled messenger yelled, spitting out a mouthful of water. He lifted his panting, soaking head and saw Elliot, alive and well.

"Boom!" he cheered as he propelled himself toward him. Elliot tried to retreat from the approaching hug, but within seconds, he and Hermes were one big, wet heap.

"Nice one!" Hermes laughed. "You're alive! You're— mate—absolutely soaking. Anyone got a towel?"

As soon as Hermes was refreshed by a nectarchino to-go from Café Hero, the six immortals and Elliot crowded around Hermes's iGod.

"So Hypnos said he's going to steal the crown from the Queen's home this week, but why and when?" said Hermes, tapping away on his device. "Blah, blah, blah—ah, here we go—'The Imperial State Crown is worn by Her Majesty the Queen at the State Opening of Parliament. This ceremonial occasion usually takes place in the summer months, but this year will be on the eighteenth of November, due to the early general election.' Boom."

"That's this Thursday!" said Athene.

"What is this 'general election'?" asked Virgo.

"It's how we decide who runs the country," explained Elliot. "Every five years there's a big vote."

"Every five years!" snorted Virgo. "What a ridiculous system! What if you don't like the people you chose? What if they prove terrible at the job?"

"Then you're stuck with them," said Elliot. "Unless you have another election. Or a revolution or something."

"That's just silly," scoffed Virgo. "On the Zodiac Council, we change leaders every month, so everyone gets a turn. If you don't like what the last person did, you just change it."

"How do you get anything done?" asked Elliot.

"Quickly," said Virgo.

"'On the morning of the State Opening, the crown is escorted to Buckingham Palace to allow the Queen to become accustomed to its weight,'" read Hermes.

"So if Hypnos is planning to steal the crown from Buckingham Palace, we need to get to it first," said Athene. "Which means we need to intercept it at . . ."

"The Tower of London!" laughed Elliot. "You're going to steal the Crown Jewels! Epic . . ."

"Stealing it is going to be harder than my abs," said Hermes. "Security at the Tower of London is super tight."

"I should hope so too," huffed Athene. "Besides, we can't steal it. Breaking a mortal law is against the Sacred Code."

"Fat lot of use the code's going to be when Thanatos is pelting the mortals with mountains, genius," said Aphrodite sarcastically. "Sorry, Elly, no offense," she added with a dazzling smile.

"None taken," mumbled Elliot, immediately bursting into his Aphrodite blush.

"It's a good point," Zeus conceded, and Athene smiled smugly at her sister. "Hypnos can steal the crown, we can't. But we must get our hands on the Earth Stone first."

Everyone waited for inspiration. Elliot's mind was whirring. He was good at finding ways around rules. There must be a loophole. He watched as Hephaestus skillfully fixed the broken fountain.

"What if we just swapped the crown?" he said. "That wouldn't break the Sacred Code. Hephaestus, would you be able to make a replica?"

"I can make a bloody better one," snorted Hephaestus, mildly miffed.

"You're welcome to use my jewelry collection," offered Aphrodite. "Admirers are always giving me tokens of gratitude . . ."

"For leaving them alone?" murmured Athene. "But Elliot's right. All we have to do is swap the original for our replica and we've got the Earth Stone. Tomorrow's Tuesday. We only have two days."

"How will we do it?" asked Elliot.

"*We're* not doing anything," said Athene. "There's absolutely no way you are coming on such a perilous mission."

"Yes, I am!" said Elliot, looking to Zeus and Aphrodite for support. But for once, all the Gods were in agreement.

"It's too dangerous, Elly," said Aphrodite, coming over and giving him a squeeze. "We have to keep you safe."

"The girls are right," said Zeus. "The best thing you can do is take care of yourself; leave the silly stuff to us. Nothing and no one can get past Hephaestus's new fence. You'll be safer here."

"A mortal simply isn't equipped for something as risky as this," added Virgo condescendingly. "Your place is here."

"So's yours," said Aphrodite.

"What?" cried Virgo. "But for the mission to be optimal, surely I'm coming with you?"

"No, you're not, old girl," said Zeus softly, but firmly. "You need to stay here with Elliot. You two are sitting this one out."

"Well, that's not . . . I should . . . you all . . . fine. That's just fine," snapped Virgo as she strode out of the barn.

"Are you all right, dear boy?" Zeus asked Elliot with one of his soul-piercing looks. "Aphy's little gizmo must have been quite an ordeal."

"I'm fine," said Elliot. "And thanks for helping out at school. I just don't want them to—"

"You don't have to explain anything," said Zeus knowingly. "We're here to help."

"Thanks," said Elliot quietly, his fears about the farm on the tip of his tongue again.

"Er . . . Zeus?" he began.

"Yes?" said Zeus gently.

But the words were still unable to find their way to Elliot's lips.

"Nothing," he said, and he wandered up the path to the farmhouse with the weight of the worlds on his shoulders.

That night, when Elliot was tucking his mom into bed, his brain felt like a beehive. Mom, the farm, the Earth Stone, Patricia Porshley-Plum, school . . . all his worries buzzed around his head, deafening his clarity with their drone.

He felt a soft hand on his cheek.

"Penny for your thoughts?" Mom smiled.

"I'm fine," Elliot sighed.

"You sure?" she sang, pulling back the quilt and patting the space next to her invitingly.

Elliot hesitated. Every now and again, Mom had these moments—moments where she seemed just like her old self. The first time it happened, he had let himself hope that she was cured, that her illness had simply gone away, that he had his mom back. Elliot had experienced many new emotions over the past year—grief, fear, rage. But when Mom wandered off that very same night, he'd learned that hope could be the cruelest of them all.

"What are the rules of the bed?" she cajoled with a cheeky smirk.

Elliot grinned in surrender as he clambered in next to her.

"No shoes, no lies, no farts," they recited together.

Mom pulled the quilt over them both and Elliot snuggled into her arms.

"If I don't know, I can't help," she whispered.

"Do you ever get scared?" Elliot asked eventually.

"Moms are always scared," she laughed. "Comes with the job."

"How do you stop it?"

"You don't. You embrace fear like an old friend."

"Why?"

"Because if you are afraid, you are alive," she said, squeezing him tight. "You make your fears. They don't make you."

"What are you afraid of?" Elliot asked.

"A single day without you," said Mom softly, kissing his hair.

They lay in silence for a while. Elliot bathed in the calming peace of his mom's hug as his mind finally quieted. It had been so long since he'd been able to confide in her. Perhaps he was wrong to keep so much from her? Mom was still his mom. She'd know what to do. She always did.

"Mom," he began quietly. "There's something I need to tell you."

"Anything, my darling."

"It's about that loan . . ." said Elliot, his heart thumping.

"Loan?" laughed Josie. "I wouldn't take out a loan. Remember what Grandad says—neither a borrower nor a lender be . . ."

"You did," said Elliot gently, as he felt Josie's arms tense around him, "to pay for Grandad's funeral."

"What do you mean?" she said anxiously, her voice trembling as she pulled away from Elliot and ran her hands through her hair. "Funeral? What are you talking about? Grandad's outside, feeding the chickens, why are you . . . ?"

Elliot climbed silently out of the bed. It was cold outside the covers.

"Shhhh. Don't worry, Mom—my mistake," he whispered, smoothing the quilt until it looked as though he'd never been there. "Time to sleep."

She instantly calmed down and settled back into bed. He kissed her on the forehead and stroked her hair.

"Are you all right, Elly?" She smiled sleepily. "You look worried. Penny for your thoughts?"

"I'm fine, Mom," whispered Elliot. Turning away, he switched out the light and wiped his cheek. "Night night."

21

ON THE LOOKOUT

Elliot's eyes sprang open very early on Thursday morning. It was the day of the State Opening of Parliament.

"What have you and your friends got planned today, Elly?" asked Josie as Elliot loaded the dishwasher with their breakfast things.

"Not much." Elliot smiled, cheekily throwing a dishcloth at his mom, who threw it back with a giggle. He was only planning to talk his way on to a mission to steal the Crown Jewels and save their home. Not much at all.

Last night, a grimy, sweaty Hephaestus, having locked himself in his forge beneath the cowshed since Monday, had finally emerged, proudly bearing a beautiful crown that was the spitting image of the Imperial State Crown. The blacksmith gave a demonstration of the "improvements" he had made to the original, before reluctantly handing it to Aphrodite, who was eventually persuaded to take it off her own head and place it in Hermes's bottomless bag.

The Olympians had rehearsed their plan down to the very last second. They had been practicing endlessly, enacting every moment in meticulous detail, thanks to the security vans and guards that Hermes was able to create from wheelbar rows and mice. By Thursday morning, the Gods were confident nothing could stop them.

But no amount of begging could persuade them to take Elliot and Virgo along. As the Olympians prepared to leave for London, they were watched by two very grumpy onlookers.

"We'll be back by lunchtime," said Zeus.

"You will get the Earth Stone, won't you?" asked Elliot. The Really Scary Letter's deadline was tomorrow. This was his only chance to find twenty thousand pounds, or he was going to lose his home.

"Of course!" Zeus grinned. "We've got hours. I can get married, divorced, and wed the bride's sister in half the time."

"What a ridiculous outfit," said Pegasus, who was decked out in full ceremonial regalia.

"Nonsense, you look splendid," said Zeus as he mounted his steed dressed as a red Beefeater guard.

"I wasn't talking about mine," snorted Pegasus.

"Behave yourselves, you little monkeys," giggled Aphrodite to the children, as she and Athene squabbled over who was driving, with Hermes and Hephaestus squashed in the back. "Hold tight everyone, here we goooooooo!"

Elliot and Virgo watched with faces like thunder as Aphrodite's car raced down the track toward the nearest road for the low-way.

"Off we go!" cried Zeus as Pegasus soared into the sky, remembering at the last minute to wear the invisibility helmet, vanishing himself and Pegasus into thin air.

"So," grumbled Virgo, as she and Elliot walked back through the gate and commanded it to close, "do you want to go over that homework Athene left us?"

"No," sulked Elliot, kicking a stone in frustration. "It's not fair, we should be going too. I . . . we need that stone. Today."

"I know," said Virgo. "We were managing perfectly well ourselves. In a kind of releasing-a-Death-Daemon sort of way."

They gave each other a sullen glance. But one look at each other's miserable faces was enough to make them burst out laughing.

"Come on," said Elliot as they reached the shed. "Perhaps if we get this algebra done, Sergeant Athene will give us the night off."

Out of nowhere, a rolled-up copy of the *Daily Argus* landed at their feet.

"I wish my paper route was that easy," said Elliot, picking up the newspaper and unfurling its pages.

"The one that Aphrodite has been doing for you every day?" scoffed Virgo.

But Elliot didn't answer. He was reading the front page.

"Uh-oh," he whispered at last. "Virgo, listen to this . . ."

CROWNING GLORY

By Cicero, News Editor

The *Argus* can't see any reason nor rhyme
Why Zeus and his gang are resorting to crime
Word reaches our paper that those crazy fools
Are planning to pinch one of England's Crown Jewels
This morning they travel to fair London town
To sightsee, then nab the Imperial Crown
Hephaestus has made one from silver and gold
And Hermes will swap this new crown for the old
Her Majesty's gonna be mad as a snake
To find that her crown is a lousy old fake
This terrible heist truly beggars belief
The king of the Gods is a dirty old thief . . .

"This is not good," said Elliot.

"No, it is not," agreed Virgo, whacking another mole with a notepad as it hastily retreated from the shed. "The standard of journalism at the *Daily Argus* is utterly reprehensible—it has moles everywhere, but this level of press intrusion—"

"Who cares?" snapped Elliot. "If we're reading this, then so is every other immortal in the world, including Hypnos and Thanatos! They'll know the plan to swap the Imperial State Crown at the Tower! We have to warn the Gods!"

"All right, they won't have gotten far—we'll call Hermes," said Virgo.

"No, we won't," said Elliot, pointing at the forgotten iGod on the sofa next to a copy of *Salve!* magazine.

"Not again! And they've taken all the transport with them. Unless we take Hermes's bike? The AAA finally towed it back."

"The AAA?" asked Elliot.

"Amazing Amazonian Autorepairs," said Virgo. "Those ladies are ferocious with a wrench. Can you drive?"

"I'm twelve, you prune," said Elliot. "Charon?"

"He's on strike until this evening," said Virgo, pointing at the paper. "The Argonauts are launching a cheaper service. Come on! You know how things work here, how else can we get to London?"

"The train!" cried Elliot. "If we run, we might just catch the 6:42 from Little Motbury!"

"Hurry up, then," shouted Virgo, as the gate opened for her to race down the track. "Let's go!"

"Wait for me!" said Elliot, grabbing his backpack in such a rush that he neither remembered to shut the new fence nor noticed the winged figure lurking in the shadows, which quickly dissembled into a rat and sniggered behind them all the way to the train station.

Patricia Porshley-Plum had a problem. She was not accustomed to problems—problems were something she paid other people to deal with, thank you very much. But if she wanted Home Farm—and she really did—she was going to have to overcome this one. And the problem was that dirty great fence.

Five days after their luncheon (lunch was for common people, and anyone who called the midday meal "dinner" deserved to be shot), Patricia Porshley-Plum needed to see Josie Hooper again to conclude last Saturday's arrangements. Patricia could feel that land—and the hundreds of thousands of pounds it could yield her—within her avaricious grasp. She just needed to get to Josie one more time to put everything in place.

Patricia was a firm believer in the basic right to privacy. So she always made sure her telescope was positioned where no one else could look at it—she loathed nosy parkers. Through the telescope, she had been watching the developments on her neighbors' land over the past few days with considerable concern. No one had come to the farm for months; she knew that the Hoopers didn't have two brass farthings to rub together, and yet suddenly they could afford teams of workers to undertake landscaping and refurbishment. Had they come into some money? Had they already paid off their debt? And who were these strange new relatives? She hadn't seen them at the funerals of . . . whatever the grandparents were called, so why show up now? Something strange was going on.

That pesky—if rather dashing—chap had held her off on Monday, so Patricia had been determined to go back that night and get hold of Josie herself. But when she arrived at

Home Farm, a huge wooden fence had sprung up around the property. She knocked, called, shouted, and kicked the wretched thing, but the gate wouldn't open—Patricia even thought she heard the faint sound of a raspberry being blown.

Patricia wasn't one to let anything stand in her way. After all, she'd not become chair of the parish committee by backing down when she lost the election. Grit, determination, and the strategic use of a shotgun had won the day that time—and Patricia would win the day again.

So she did what any respectful neighbor would do. She hitched her tweed skirt in her knickers and tried to climb over the fence, but immediately erupted in bright blue boils.

On Tuesday, she tried to take a pair of bolt cutters to the gate. The moment they made contact with the lock, Patricia discovered she could only speak Swahili for the rest of the day.

On Wednesday she had tried to chainsaw the fence, but was rewarded with twenty-four hours of earsplitting farts, which nearly burned a hole in her sofa.

But finally on Thursday, with only a day before Home Farm was lost, her moment arrived. As Elliot raced out of the farm, he was so intent on catching the train, he didn't notice that he'd left the fence open. But Patricia Porshley-Plum never missed a trick.

Before Elliot reached the station, Patricia had Josie dressed and in her car. And as Elliot and Virgo's train started the journey to London, Patricia had Josie Hooper right where she wanted her.

22

ON THE WRONG TRACK

Nearly a week into her first visit to Earth, Virgo felt she was making outstanding progress with her mortal research. They were a curious category, but she found their endless diversity fascinating. Being aboard the "train" was another opportunity to observe mortals in action, and she felt an unfamiliar sensation, a tingling in her stomach, at the prospect of something new.

"I'm hungry," moaned Elliot less than an hour into the journey, confirming Virgo's observation that young mortal boys ate more than a hundred-headed Hydra. "I'm going to the buffet car. Stay here and don't be weird."

Content for a short while to sit and watch the English countryside go whizzing past the window, it wasn't long before Virgo's curiosity demanded a look around the train. There was nothing "weird" about her perfectly natural desire to explore her new habitat, and Virgo was perfectly satisfied with her decision to ignore Elliot's rule.

The train was an intriguing mixed bag of mortals. There was the large lady in car C who had locked herself in the "toilet"—Virgo was still unsure of the purpose of these small rooms, but the smell from the "toilet" in car F deterred her from investigating further. In car J, a small child put on a spectacular performance, making pink milk erupt from his mouth. Strangely, the mortal in the suit opposite him didn't seem to enjoy the show, nor appreciate Virgo's enthusiastic applause.

Many mortals seemed displeased that the train was running fifteen minutes late. Time was a big concern in the mortal mind, which was odd because they didn't appear to have anything particularly important to do. As Virgo arrived back at her seat, she wondered what it must be like to live in this strange, imperfect world. A man carrying a box around his neck stomped up to her seat.

"Tickets, please," he barked.

"Sorry?" asked Virgo, startled.

"Your ticket," snapped the mortal rudely. "I want it."

"Oh, I see," said Virgo, her brow furrowed in confusion. "But it's mine."

This annoyed the mortal. Mortals often became annoyed extremely quickly over nothing. Virgo suspected it was because their clothing was too tight—this mortal could barely fit his rear end into his pants.

"Miss, if you cannot produce a valid ticket for your journey, I will be forced to charge you a penalty fare. Do you have a ticket or not?" he huffed.

"Yes, I have it here," said Virgo, pulling her train ticket from her pants pocket. "So you want this?"

"Yes," sighed the man.

"You want me to give you my ticket?"

"YES!" he shouted more loudly and quite unnecessarily.

"All right," said Virgo, holding the ticket out.

"Thank you," sighed the man, reaching for it.

Virgo whipped the ticket away again.

"That'll be nine pounds and fifty pence," she said.

The mortal gave her a look that could unblock a drain. "What?"

"My ticket," said Virgo. "If you really want it, it'll cost you nine pounds and fifty pence, the same as it cost Elliot. Be grateful I'm not adding a surcharge for your appalling manner and the front-row view of your backside."

"I am not going to pay for your ticket!" shouted the man. "Just give it to me!"

Now Virgo was a guest in this realm, but she was not about to have her property stolen, particularly by someone incapable of purchasing the optimal pants. This simply would not do.

"I will not," said the indignant Constellation, putting her ticket back in her pocket. "We've all paid good money just to sit on your train—which is covered in some revolting pink mess, by the way—and yet here you come, refusing to pay a penny and stealing everyone's tickets. It's a disgrace."

"That's it!" cried the man, throwing his hat on the floor. "Get off my train! Get off, you rude, obnoxious—"

"Come to think of it," said Virgo, "I don't see why we should have to pay for this journey at all. The train was going to London anyway. Why should we have to pay for a service that you are using for free? No, not only will I not give you my ticket, I insist upon a full refund . . ."

As he wound his way back down the speeding train, Elliot could hear some choice language coming from the car ahead of him.

"Please not," he whispered, praying that it had nothing to do with Virgo.

But as he opened the door, he was greeted by the sight of the Constellation standing on a table, trying to encourage fellow passengers to rise against the tyranny of South Coast Trains while the conductor jumped on his hat in a temper.

Before Elliot could calm the situation, the train jolted so violently it threw Virgo from the table where she had been holding forth.

"Ow! What was that?" cried Virgo from the floor, rubbing her silver head.

"I don't know," said Elliot, bracing himself between the seats as the train made another sudden jolt. "But I'm guessing it isn't train traffic ahead."

"What the 'ell's going on?" shouted the conductor down the emergency intercom to the driver.

"Er—Brian. There's someone in my cab," yawned the driver. "He's blowing a trumpet at me and I'm . . . I . . . er . . . I'm feeling a bit . . . zzzzzz . . ."

"Kevin? Kevin? You need to—" The train lurched violently again, dislodging a suitcase from the luggage rack onto Brian's head and knocking him out cold.

"Hypnos!" cried Elliot and Virgo, stepping over the unconscious Brian to race to the front of the train.

Thrown from one side of the train to the other, they forced their way through the screaming passengers, the suitcases littering the floor, and the scalding-hot coffee that flew at them with every shudder. Eventually they burst into the driver's cab. The wind from the open window nearly blew them straight out again, but they forced their way in. The driver was comatose in his chair and outside the window was Hypnos, waving his trumpet.

"Have fun, kids!" he laughed. "I'm off to see your buddies at the Tower. Choo-choo!"

He dissembled into a wasp and buzzed away.

"He's crazy!" Elliot shouted above the noise of the wind. "He's going to kill us all!"

"How do you stop this thing?" yelled Virgo.

She frantically pulled all the levers and jabbed the buttons on the train's dashboard, but nothing would slow the train down. It shot through a station with a gust that threw the waiting passengers all over the platform. Elliot and Virgo were smashed against the dashboard, and Elliot felt his father's watch crack in his pocket.

"How many people can you carry in your star-ball?" he yelled.

"For the last time—I can't use my powers!" shouted Virgo as the train shot through another signal.

"But just say you could—in an emergency—how many?"

"Barely one," Virgo yelled. "But there must be another way to get you off this train . . ."

"It's not just me—what about all these people?" said Elliot. "We have to stop the train!"

Elliot and Virgo frantically searched for anything that might show them what to do as they charged on through red signals, sending alarms ringing inside the train and out. Elliot racked his brain, desperately trying to think of something, anything that might save them. Virgo grabbed hold of his arm.

"What?" he cried.

Virgo pointed ahead. Elliot could see nothing but a small black blob on the horizon.

"Wha—?" he started again, as the sound of a distant whistle gave him the terrible answer. The black blob was taking shape . . .

It was another train. And they were heading straight for it.

"Elliot, we have to get you off this train!" screamed Virgo.

"We can't leave all these people!" Elliot shouted back.

"You have to save yourself!" Virgo screamed again. "Oh . . . I wish Zeus were here."

There was a tiny jingle from Elliot's backpack—and with a loud pop, the bemused king of the Gods appeared next to the train, flying on Pegasus.

"What—where—Winifred . . ." he burbled, scratching his bottom.

"Zeus?" said Virgo. "How did you—?"

"The wishing pearl! It's in my bag—it must have heard you!" cried Elliot. He looked at his smashed watch. "We've only got seven minutes before he disappears again."

"Then hurry up and get on Pegasus," said Virgo, watching the black blob growing on the horizon. "You can fly to safety."

"That's it!" cried Elliot, leaning out of the window to shout instructions.

"Great idea!" Zeus yelled back, spurring Pegasus on to the front of the train.

"What are you doing?" demanded Virgo.

"Get off!" said Elliot as she tried to stick her head out next to his.

"I need to know the plan," she insisted.

"Stop it—you're going to—"

The train rocked violently again as it shot past another signal, and the sudden movement pushed Virgo's hand down on the handle, opening the door and sending Elliot flying out of the train, just clinging to the window.

"Elliot!" Virgo screamed. "Zeus! Zeus!"

But plainly Zeus could hear nothing over the roar of the engine as he tried to secure Pegasus's reins to the front of the train.

"HELLLLP!" Elliot howled as the track whizzed perilously under his feet. His fingers were burning from the strain of holding on as he was slammed against the side of the train. He clung on with all his might—but his grip was starting to slip . . .

Virgo searched her jeans pockets for anything that would help. The other train was approaching fast. She found her *What's What*.

"Help!" she screamed at the blank parchment.

Help, the parchment started to scribble. *The need for assistance, often urgently, from someone or something in a moment of particular need.*

"Aaaaargh!" said Virgo. "You are SO suboptimal! You're lucky I don't throw you out of the window! Wait . . ."

She looked at Zeus up ahead, before leaning out of the other door and taking aim at the Olympian. She hurled the roll of parchment with all her might and landed it perfectly on the back of Zeus's skull.

"What the blazes—?" shouted Zeus, turning to see Virgo gesturing wildly at Elliot.

"I . . . can't . . . hold . . . on!" said Elliot as his white fingers lost their final grip on the window. He shut his eyes and prepared to drop to his doom.

"Gotcha!" boomed a huge voice as a strong arm grabbed his backpack and hauled Elliot onto the back of Pegasus.

He looked at the sundial on his wrist. "We've only got five minutes—let's get a move on! Virgo—tie these to the door!"

He threw Pegasus's reins to the Constellation, who did as she was asked in a flash.

"I've done it! But I don't—"

"Up, up, and away!" yelled Zeus, and he spurred Pegasus up into the sky. The flying horse gave an almighty groan as he took the strain of the train, lifting the front wheels off the track.

"Good boy!" said Zeus, patting his immortal steed's neck. "Heave, Peg! Heave!"

"It's too late!" cried Virgo as they continued on their collision course with the approaching train. But Pegasus responded to Zeus's cries with a great surge up into the heavens.

Car by car, the train gracefully came away from the track and climbed into the air, flowing behind Pegasus like the ribbon on a kite. Zeus replaced his invisibility helmet, and the battered commuters, who had been screaming their prayers and curses, suddenly fell silent as the 6:42 to London Waterloo flew invisibly up into the sky, just missing the train that would have smashed them all to smithereens.

Four minutes later, the invisible train made a graceful landing just outside platform ten at Waterloo station, fifteen minutes ahead of schedule. Zeus wandered through the train spraying a bottle of Aphrodite's perfume, which immediately calmed all the passengers and made them forget the past six minutes of their lives.

Elliot and Virgo were tending to Brian, the conductor, who had regained consciousness somewhere over Vauxhall. As the paramedics arrived to take him away, concerned that his concussion had left him feeling like the train had been flying, the two youngsters jumped off the train.

"Next time, we'll take the bus," said Elliot, pulling his father's watch sadly out of his pocket. It was completely smashed. "Thanks."

"My pleasure, old chap," said Zeus. "But you two ne'er-do-wells were supposed to stay at the farm . . ."

"We had to find you," said Virgo. "Hypnos knows about the plan—"

"Arghhh!" growled Zeus, bundling them both on board Pegasus. "We need to saddle up. By my reckoning, the wishing pearl runs out in three . . . two . . . one . . ."

And with a great big pop, the pearl pinged them away into thin air.

23

CROWNING GLORY

The Tower of London rose majestically from the early-morning fog on the banks of the river Thames. Elliot, Virgo, Zeus, and Pegasus popped back to the exact spot in the sky from which the wishing pearl had snatched Zeus, and flew down to where the other Olympians were hiding by the Beauchamp Tower, one of the smaller towers that lined the main courtyard.

"Where did you go?" said an annoyed Aphrodite. "We had to climb over the wall! I nearly gave myself a hernia getting Brainiac over . . ."

"I'm all muscle," whispered Athene. "Why are the children here?"

"We had a train to catch," said Zeus, winking at Elliot. "But look lively—Hypnos is onto us. What's the score?"

"The crown's about to leave the Jewel House!" whispered Hermes. "This is our last chance before it goes to Buckingham Palace! Not even joking."

"This is magnificent," said Virgo, looking around the historic grounds of the fortress. "What was it for?"

"Chopping people's heads off," said Elliot.

"Urgh—mortals are barbaric," said Virgo. "Our punishments are civilized. Fines . . . imprisonment . . . your organs feasted upon by an immortal eagle . . ."

"Shhhhhh!" chided Athene.

They all peered out from their hiding place again. Three armored trucks stood outside the Jewel House, surrounded by heavily armed soldiers.

"How big is this crown?" asked Virgo, looking at the three huge vehicles.

"Only one will carry the crown," said Athene. "The other two are decoys. We need to swap the crown before it's loaded into the truck."

Nearby, four Beefeater guards were leaning on their pikes, enjoying a quiet cup of coffee: one very tall man, one very short man, one rather distinguished man, and one rather scruffy lady.

"Right—children—you go and find Hephaestus outside and wait for us there," ordered Athene, to an outcry from the youngsters. "No arguments! Places, everyone! Aphrodite, you create a distraction. Daddy, you and I will tackle the soldiers. Hermes, disguise yourself as a guard and swap the crowns."

Elliot and Virgo reluctantly climbed aboard Pegasus and strapped the invisibility helmet on Elliot's head, shimmering them out of sight. They were about to take off over the wall when a raven swooped down and landed on Athene's shoulder.

"But what about me?" it whined. "I wanna play."

They all whipped around as Hypnos dissembled back to himself.

"It's horribly early, isn't it?" said the Daemon of Sleep, raising his ivory trumpet to his lips and blowing a thick fog of black smoke toward the Gods. "Perhaps you'd like a little sleep?"

The Olympians scattered away from Hypnos's blast, tumbling across the grass on Tower Green, hidden from the soldiers' view by the White Tower.

"Oh, please," whispered Aphrodite, getting back to her feet. "There's only one of you. There are four of us. How hard do you like your butt kicked?"

"Good point, cutie," laughed Hypnos. "Only fair that we even up the teams."

The Daemon aimed his trumpet toward the four Beef-eaters and blew another almighty cloud of black smoke their way. It wafted around their big navy-blue hats, splitting into four small cyclones that circled over their heads for a second before simultaneously sucking into their left ears. The strange sensation made them all instinctively put their hands to their heads, but then, as one, they snapped to attention, drew their pikes, and started marching slowly toward the Gods with their weapons aimed at their enemies.

"Ex-e-cute," they droned together. "Ex-e-cute."

"Look—the crown!" whispered Elliot to Virgo. "It's coming out of the Jewel House!"

They both strained their necks to see the Imperial State Crown as a security guard carried it out on a red cushion.

The purple velvet cap at the center was encased by a frame of gold, platinum, and silver. Every kind of gemstone covered the crown—rubies, emeralds, pearls, and sapphires. And in the center shone the most brilliant diamond.

"There's the Earth Stone!" gasped Elliot.

Even in the morning mist, the diamond outsparkled its companion gems with a penetrating, otherworldly light.

"Ex-e-cute," moaned the Beefeaters as they marched on the Gods. "Ex-e-cute."

"What's he done to them?" asked Hermes.

"They're sleepwalking," said Athene.

With the Gods rooted to the spot, Hypnos raised his trumpet to his lips to blast them again. Elliot dug his heels into Pegasus's side and cantered toward Hypnos.

"I'll have that, thanks," he said, and snatched the trumpet from Hypnos's hands.

"Wha—? Who's there?" hissed the Daemon of Sleep as his trumpet vanished into thin air. "Don't play with me . . ."

"Where's the crown?" said Elliot, making Hypnos spin around to find the direction of the unseen voice.

"I can't see," said Virgo. "We need to get closer."

"Is that you, child?" Hypnos grinned. "So you wanna game of hide-and-seek? You're it."

Elliot put his fingers to his lips to silence Virgo as Hypnos put his hands in front of him to feel for the invisible thieves.

The Beefeaters were now just feet away from the Gods.

"Looks like it's time for some good old-fashioned fisti-cuffs," said Zeus, rolling up his sleeves. "Back in the day we enjoyed a good scrap."

"We have to be gentle with them," said Athene. "They don't know what they're doing."

Elliot smiled as Hypnos walked straight past him. The Gods were going to nail this.

"Forget fisticuffs," said Hermes, drawing his lean body into a low crouch with his hands raised. "I can handle this . . . Beefeaters! Hold tight! I am the Karate King! I am a trained master in kicking butt and taking names! Though I already know what to call you, so let's get right to the kicking of butts! Bosh!"

Hermes performed an elaborate series of martial-arts moves, kicking and lunging with a chorus of high-pitched cries.

"H-iiii-ya!" he yelled each time, kicking his right leg higher with each shout. "H-iiii-ya! H-iiii-ya!"

The Beefeaters stopped and stared.

"Scared now, aren't you?" shouted Hermes, drawing his leg back for even bigger kicks. "Well, then check this action out— H-iiii-ya! H-iiii-ya! H . . . AMSTRING! HAMSTRING! OW! OW! OW!"

Hermes yelped painfully across the grass, clutching his injured thigh.

Elliot gently urged Pegasus on to get a better view of the crown. But the moment the horse's hooves hit the cobblestones, Hypnos flew over. They froze as he felt around, barely a few feet from Pegasus's head.

"Here I come, ready or not . . ." sang the Daemon.

Elliot looked to the Gods for help, but the Beefeaters had their full attention.

"Theney—we've got this," said Aphrodite, signaling to her sister as two of the Beefeaters reached them. "Remember the old routine?"

"As if it were yesterday," said Athene confidently, retreating across the grass to give herself a long run-up. "You throw me up, I'll take two of them down with a flying somersault before you cartwheel over and flip the other two over your head. Ready?"

"Ready," said Aphrodite, kneeling down and cupping her hands.

Athene sprinted toward her sister, ready to be boosted into the air. But halfway there, confusion clouded her face.

"We use my right foot? No, my left, right?" she called as she hurtled toward her sister.

"Right!" shouted Aphrodite.

"Right as in the foot, or right as in 'Yes, it's your left'?"

"Right!" yelled Aphrodite as Athene charged on.

"Which right?" screamed Athene. "You need to give clearer instructions!"

"Your right!"

"I'm right about what?" screeched Athene. "Too late!"

She put her left foot in Aphrodite's hands.

"Seriously!" Aphrodite groaned as she attempted to fling her sister into the air. "What have you been eating?"

"I'm the perfect weight for my—aaargh!"

With a heave, Athene tried to leap gracefully into the air. But on the wrong foot and with all momentum lost, Athene splatted backward onto her bottom, kicking her sister in the head with her right foot. The two Goddesses sprawled across the green.

"Come out, come out, wherever you are . . ." cooed Hypnos.

As the Daemon groped toward Pegasus, Elliot tapped the horse's neck and pointed to the sky. Pegasus winked and, lightly as a feather, leapt into the air, just as Hypnos grabbed at the empty space in front of him.

"You . . . boron!" yelled Aphrodite, holding her hand to her swollen nose, forgetting all about the Beefeaters.

"They seem a little . . . suboptimal," whispered Virgo, looking down on the Gods.

"They suck," groaned Elliot, as the Imperial State Crown started its solemn procession toward the trucks. "And they need to hurry up."

The female Beefeater marched toward Zeus.

"Ex-e-cute . . . Ex-e-cute . . ."

"I will not fight a lady," said Zeus, snatching her pike and throwing it down. "It would be unfair, unchivalrous, and un—"

The lady Beefeater grabbed Zeus by the chest, lifted him over her head like a paper dumbbell, and threw him to the floor with a thud.

"And quite uncomfortable," he groaned as he crashed to the ground. "Ooooof—my back . . ."

"Listen up," said Athene, holding Aphrodite's head at arm's length. "We're out of shape. We'll have to do this another way. We need to get into their minds, break the sleepwalking spell . . ."

Elliot stifled a frustrated groan. He checked that Hypnos was still creeping around below. Maybe he could snatch the crown himself? He looked at the team of soldiers and their machine guns. Maybe not. But as long as he kept his eye on where the crown was, the Gods would still be able to swap it.

"Ex-e-cute," droned the older Beefeater, lifting his pike and aiming it at Athene.

Athene put her hands to her brilliant head, searching her brain for a solution.

"When was the Tower built?" she suddenly shouted.

The Beefeater immediately snapped to attention and instinctively launched into his guided tour.

"The Tower is believed to have been begun in 1078 at the behest of William the Conqueror," he recited, still keeping Athene at the end of his pike. "The first building was the White Tower, which is an impressive thirty yards high. Now if you'd like to follow me, the toilets are this way . . ."

With Hermes still rolling around clutching his hamstring, the tall and short Beefeaters marched on Aphrodite.

"Ex-e-cute . . . Ex-e-cute . . ."

Inspiration struck the Goddess of Love. She blew two kisses. The kisses floated through the air as pink wafts before settling gently on the Beefeaters' lips. They stopped and inhaled the sweet scent of pure love.

"Jim—in all the years we've been working together, I've never told you what a great friend you are," said the taller one. "I don't appreciate you nearly often enough."

"Oh, stop, Steve," blushed Jim. "You're my best mate. I don't know what I would have done without you when Fulham were relegated out of the league last season."

"There's something I need to say to you," said Steve, welling up.

"There's something I need to say too," choked Jim.

"I really love you, man!" blurted Steve.

"I really love you too!" sobbed Jim. "We don't spend enough time together. Let's call the wives and arrange a holiday for the four of us!"

"Great idea!" howled Steve. "Is the house next door to yours still up for sale?"

"It is," sniffed Jim. "Wonderful loft conversion . . ."

"I'm gonna move in!" cried Steve.

"LET'S BUY A CARAVAN TOGETHER!" cried Jim, pulling Steve and Aphrodite into a huge, bromantic hug.

With Aphrodite trapped between the two sobbing Beefeaters, Elliot looked down to see the crown being loaded into a big black box. Hypnos was directly beneath him, pouncing intermittently at thin air. Zeus was still on the ground, with the lady Beefeater ready to spear her prey with her pike.

"Ex-e-cute!"

"Stop!" cried Zeus, holding his hand to the end of her weapon. "In the name of love!"

She halted as Zeus stared longingly into her eyes.

"Speak to me, my darling," drawled Zeus. "Tell me what name the angels gave you when they crafted you from starlight?"

The Beefeater's pike quivered.

"Janet," she whimpered.

"Janet!" sang Zeus, searching desperately for lyrical inspiration. "Janet . . . Janet . . . you . . . have . . . a . . . bum like a planet . . ."

"What?" snapped Janet, returning her pike to Zeus's throat.

"Janet! If you don't love me—skewer me now!" Zeus exclaimed, pushing the pike away gently with his palm. "I have already been struck by Cupid's arrow—another wound can't hurt me . . ."

As Zeus's words fought Hypnos's spell, Janet lowered her pike.

"Do you like cats?" she asked shakily.

"Like them!" roared Zeus. "Only one thing pains me more than the thought of a kitty without a warm lap. Do you know what I fear, Janet? Do you know what agony tears my soul apart? Do you know the one torture I cannot bear?"

"Musical theater?" Janet ventured.

"My life without you!" boomed Zeus, sitting bolt upright and clutching his lower spine. "Tell me you feel it! Tell me you sense this connection between us! Tell me how many cats you have!"

"SIXTEEN!" shrieked Janet, flinging off her Beefeater hat to reveal an astonishing case of hat hair. "Come here, handsome!"

Zeus gasped as Janet lunged and bent him backward for a spectacular make-out session.

"Euuuuurgh! Gross!" heaved Elliot.

"That large a saliva exchange cannot be hygienic," whispered Virgo with her head cocked.

Elliot turned away to see the crown being loaded into the middle of the three trucks.

"Gotcha!" he said out loud.

"And I've got you!" screeched Hypnos, suddenly appearing in front of them in midair and grabbing at them. The shock made Elliot drop the trumpet, which became visible again the moment it left his hands.

Hypnos swooped and caught his trumpet, bringing it straight to his mouth and sending a great black blast toward Pegasus. The flying horse elegantly swerved in the air, missing the smoke. Hypnos tried again, but he was still unable to see his invisible enemy. Pegasus dodged the blast again.

"Well played!" said Hypnos as the rumble of engines

started up below. "But I'll get you in the next round. I'm due at another game . . ."

Hypnos dissembled back into the raven and flew over the high Tower walls.

"No!" cried Elliot. "The crown's leaving!"

Elliot and Virgo watched in horror as the three trucks rumbled slowly across the cobblestones and out of the Tower in a row.

"Which truck is it in?" said Virgo.

"It was the middle one," said Elliot.

"Which one's the middle one?" said Virgo.

"I don't know," shouted Elliot as the three identical trucks rolled down the hill.

"Quick," said Virgo. "Let's get the others."

They looked around the green to where Hermes was yelping like a wounded kitten, Athene was being marched into the gift shop with a pike at her back, Aphrodite was jammed between Steve, Jim, and a caravan catalog, and Zeus was in a headlock looking at cat selfies.

"No time!" said Elliot, grabbing Hermes's bag and jumping back on Pegasus. "We have to get to Buckingham Palace before Hypnos. Pegasus—take us to the Queen!"

24

BY ROYAL COMMAND

Under the cover of the invisibility helmet, Pegasus flew above the security trucks all the way to Buckingham Palace. Riding on the horse's back, Elliot and Virgo looked out for Hypnos in case he tried to attack again, but there was no sign of the Daemon anywhere. Thirty minutes later, they were peering through the windows of the Queen's London home. It was quite a view—they could see a maid pocketing some of the silver cutlery she was supposed to be polishing in the kitchen, and a footman trying on the Queen's dresses in the robing room.

They found Queen Elizabeth II in her private parlor around the back of the palace. Dressed in an elegant white gown with a purple sash draped from her right shoulder to her left hip, the Queen was reading the newspaper and slicing a crumpet with the Sword of State. The Imperial Crown sparkled brilliantly on top of her regal head. Elliot looked at the beautiful Earth Stone shimmering in the center. The answer to all his problems. It was so close. Which meant Hypnos must be too.

"What do we do now?" asked Virgo. "Shall we smash through the window?"

"I think we'd better knock," said Elliot, unsure of the correct protocol for approaching the Queen of Great Britain on a flying horse. With Pegasus hovering steadily outside the window, Elliot leaned over and tapped as politely as he could manage on the glass.

The Queen looked straight at Elliot and Virgo, but returned to her paper.

"We've just been blanked by the Queen," said Elliot indignantly. "And to think my nan had a mug with her picture on it."

"That invisibility helmet suits you," said Virgo with a sigh. "It matches your invisible brain."

Elliot snatched off the helmet, making sure that Virgo received a good nudge in the ribs, took a deep breath, and knocked once more.

The Queen looked up again. If she was startled to see two children on a flying horse outside her window, she had the good manners not to show it. Elliot smiled politely and Virgo gave her an enthusiastic wave, which the Queen courteously returned with an elegant swivel of her wrist. Not taking her eyes from the window, she slowly removed her glasses and put her newspaper down on the golden tea table in front of her. She walked over to the window and opened it.

"Good morning," she said calmly to her visitors. "May I help you?"

"Er—good morning, Your Majesty," said Elliot, attempting

a clumsy bow on Pegasus's back. "Can we come in, please? We have something really important to ask you."

"I see," said the Queen. "To whom does one have the pleasure of speaking?"

"One is . . . whom are . . . am a . . . I'm Elliot," he said, quickly abandoning any attempt at talking poshly. "Elliot Hooper. And this is Virgo. She's an immortal."

"Hello, the Queen," chirped Virgo with a big grin.

"How do you do?" said the Queen. "You'd better come in."

As Her Majesty helped Elliot and Virgo to dismount from Pegasus and clamber through the window, Elliot became aware of an insistent snorting behind him.

"And this is Pegasus," said Elliot as he landed on the soft carpet of the Queen's parlor. "He's a flying horse," he added, quickly realizing that the Queen had probably worked that out for herself.

"Your Majesty," said Pegasus grandly, dropping into an elegant bow.

"Welcome, Mr. Pegasus," said the Queen, acknowledging his bow with a gracious nod of her head. "I can honestly say that you are the most magnificent horse I have ever seen."

"I can honestly say that you are correct," said Pegasus, sweeping into another bow as Elliot leaned out of the window and put the invisibility helmet over his white head to conceal him from view.

Elliot and Virgo fidgeted awkwardly in the middle of

the parlor as the Queen closed the window and turned to greet her visitors.

"May I offer you some tea and crumpets?" she asked.

"No, thank you, we don't have much time—" started Virgo.

"Oh, yeah," belted Elliot, whose stomach had been rumbling since the Tower. "With some peanut butter. If . . . you . . . have . . . some . . . please . . . Your Majesty," he trailed off, as a subzero look from Virgo reminded him that this wasn't really the time.

"I'll see what I can do, Mr. Hooper." The Queen smiled, her eyes sparkling as she rang a small silver bell on the table. She sat back down in her chair, neatly repositioned her flowing white gown, and straightened the purple sash across her right shoulder.

"Now," she said, folding her hands in her lap. "What can I do for you?"

"Right," Elliot began slowly. "There's no easy way to say this, so I'm going to get straight to the point. That crown you're wearing contains a diamond that's really a Chaos Stone and has the power to control the Earth. It's that one, there."

Elliot reached out and pointed at the stone, his fingers tantalizingly close to his home's salvation.

"We need to take it so that a Death Daemon called Thanatos can't get his hands on it—nor the other three Chaos Stones, which we're also trying to find—and release his

Daemon army and attack mortals and Immortals with earth quakes and floods and fires and plagues and other really bad stuff." He sighed at the lunacy of his own tale. "You think I'm insane and you're going to lock me up in the Tower of London, aren't you?"

The Queen calmly took a sip of her tea and stared intently at the young boy before her.

"Your tale is incredible indeed, Mr. Hooper," she said evenly. "But you'd be surprised what one might believe from two children who have arrived on a flying horse. And for the record, I prefer to lock people up in Windsor Castle these days," she added with a twinkle. "The heating's rather better."

She picked up the small silver bell and rang it again.

"I can't think what's taking Jeffers so long. He's normally so prompt," she said, looking at the white double doors. Elliot wondered if Jeffers was the man they had seen in the robing room, who was probably struggling to undo the zipper on the pink frock he'd been wearing a few minutes ago.

"But to return to your request, Mr. Hooper, do I understand correctly that you would like me to give you the Imperial State Crown, so that you may guard this Earth Stone from Thanatos?" said the Queen.

"Yes," said Elliot, slightly surprised that his garbled explanation had been that clear.

"We'd replace it," said Virgo, pointing at Hermes's bag.

"Oh—yes," said Elliot, plunging his hand into the bag,

which seemed to go on forever before something met his grasp. "We'd like to exchange it—for this."

He pulled his hand out with a proud flourish, expecting the new crown to be met with gasps of delight from the Queen. But upon seeing her politely confused expression and hearing Virgo's groan, he looked more closely at what he had produced from the bag. In return for the priceless Imperial State Crown atop Her Majesty's head, Elliot Hooper was now standing in her private parlor offering the Queen a large rubber chicken.

"Oh, sorry," he said, thrusting the chicken back in the bag. Virgo rolled her eyes. Elliot had another rummage around before pulling his hand out again, this time producing the replica crown. "I meant *this.*"

Now the Queen gasped on cue at Hephaestus's astonishing work. The crowns were identical.

"May I?" asked the Queen.

"Sure," said Elliot, bringing the new crown to her, deciding a small curtsy would be appropriate as he handed it over.

The Queen turned the replica Imperial State Crown in her hands, looking highly impressed.

"It's certainly much lighter than this old lump," she said, raising her eyes. "I must admit I've never cared much for it; it's far too heavy. This is exquisite."

"Oh, and another thing," said Elliot, remembering the blacksmith's demonstration the night before. "Hephaestus, that's the man—well, God, really—who made it, thought you might like this."

Elliot placed the crown on the table in front of the Queen and pressed a large ruby on the side. The crown quietly started to rumble, a small wisp of steam twirling from the top for a few moments until there was a gentle ping. Elliot lifted the crown to reveal a small golden cup and saucer, which was filled to the brim with steaming tea.

"The sapphire on the back makes coffee and every turn of the cross on the top will give you a lump of sugar," he said nervously as the Queen stared at the crown in amazement. "Do you like it?"

"I think it's quite wonderful, Mr. Hooper. But speaking of tea, what on Earth has become of yours? This really is most unlike Jeffers," she said, insistently ringing her bell again.

"So. Can we swap it for yours?" asked Virgo impatiently. "We'll return the rest of the crown."

"Well," said the Queen, "it's a little difficult . . ."

She was interrupted as a footman, whom Elliot presumed must be the delayed Jeffers, flung the white doors open with a flourish.

"Heeeeeeere's Jeffers!" he sang, throwing his arms wide open.

"Er . . . Jeffers," said the Queen cautiously. "Would you be so kind as to fetch my guests—"

"Get it yourself, Granny," Jeffers laughed, looking from one crown to the other.

"I beg your pardon?" said the Queen.

"Which one's got the Earth Stone?" Jeffers grinned, holding out his hand. "Give it."

"I can't say I care for your tone, Jeffers," said the Queen warily, rising to her feet. "Whatever's got into you?"

"That would be me!" screeched the footman, his face growing wings and wildness as he dissembled back into Hypnos. "Now hand over the goods, you wrinkly royal."

If the Queen had any thoughts about her footman melting into a wing-headed Daemon, she kept them to herself. Elliot looked around the room to see what he could use to defend his elderly monarch. He had placed Her Majesty in great danger. It was down to him to protect her.

"Give me the crown and I'll let you get back to your nap, Nana," Hypnos said, winking.

"You'll have to get through us first, Hypnos," shouted Virgo, charging at Hypnos, hoping to knock him off his feet. But her small frame was useless against the Daemon of Sleep, who picked her up and threw her against the wall like a used tissue.

"Have it your way!" Hypnos snapped at the Queen, pushing her aside to get to Elliot, leaving the monarch in a pile of lace petticoats on the floor. "I'll deal with you in a minute, Queen. First things first."

Hypnos seized Elliot by the neck. Grabbing the nearest thing at hand, Elliot hit the Daemon with a gold cake stand, but he may as well have attacked him with a banana. Without even flinching, Hypnos lifted Elliot off the ground and started to choke him.

"Thanatos says hi." He smiled, raising his trumpet to his lips. "Sleep well."

"No, you don't!" screamed Virgo, running at the Daemon again, jumping on his back, and smashing the Queen's teapot on his head.

Hypnos dropped Elliot and the trumpet to the floor with a shriek, holding his burning head in his hands. Virgo kicked his trumpet away.

"Playtime's over!" he shouted, wiping scalding tea from his eyes. He walked menacingly toward the window that Elliot and Virgo were struggling to open, while Pegasus kicked at the glass. Hypnos reached them before they could make their escape and towered over them, holding his fists aloft.

"Sorry, kids," he said, winking, as he drew himself up to put his full weight behind the blow, "this is gonna hurt."

But at that moment, a heavy object flew across the room and smacked him hard on the back of the head.

"Oi!" he shouted, spinning around to see what had clobbered him.

"One doesn't think so, Hypnos!" declared the furious Queen, her neat hair disheveled where she had pulled the Imperial State Crown from her head and hurled it at the Daemon. "Prepare yourself for a right royal kicking!"

And with a great wrench, the Queen whipped off her full white dress to reveal a black ninja outfit beneath.

Unencumbered by her gown, she leapt up into the air and backflipped across the room, hitting Hypnos square in the chest with a flying double-footed kick. Elliot and Virgo just had time to jump out of the way before Hypnos crashed against the wall, winded by the Queen's attack.

Hypnos reached for his trumpet, but the Queen sprang off her back to her feet with a neat flick, spinning her purple sash around to expose four throwing stars on the back. She aimed them expertly at the Daemon, who defended himself with a priceless vase. When all four had been thrown, Hypnos retaliated by hurling the chipped vase at the Queen, who smashed it with a yell and a spinning kick on the heel of her court shoe. Hypnos ran at the tea table and threw it blindly at the Queen. But Her Majesty simply cartwheeled across the room and caught it, snapping it over her knee and twirling the golden legs threateningly at the Daemon.

Elliot and Virgo watched with mouths the size of dinner plates as the Daemon of Sleep and the Queen of the United Kingdom of Great Britain and Northern Ireland, Her other Realms and Territories, Head of the Commonwealth and Defender of the Faith, circled around the room, neither taking their eyes from the other as they waited to see who would make the first move.

Hypnos was the first to strike, with a clumsy lunge that the Queen easily sidestepped, thwacking the Daemon on the back with both table legs as he passed. But Hypnos recovered more quickly than she expected and immediately lunged again, this time catching the Queen off guard and snatching one of her table legs. A furious duel began, Hypnos and the Queen fighting each other with table legs like swords, chips of wood flying everywhere as they thrust and parried around the room.

"Elliot, duck!" cried Virgo as another vase got caught up in the battle and hurtled toward Elliot's head, smashing against the wall behind him a split second after he dived out of the way. The frantic battle continued, Hypnos's brute strength an even match for the Queen's skilled swordsmanship. With an almighty swing, Hypnos blasted the table leg from the Queen's hand, forcing her to dive across the carpet to avoid being smashed by Hypnos's weapon.

"Mr. Hooper?" called the Queen politely, as she ran up the wall and crouched on the top of a cabinet. "Would you be so kind as to pass one the Sword of State, please?"

Elliot saw the ornate red-and-gold scabbard at his feet. He picked it up and threw it to the Queen.

"Thank you so much," she said with a smile, catching the sword midair as she performed a flying front somersault from the top of cabinet, mere seconds before Hypnos smashed into it.

The two warriors paused for a moment on opposite sides of the room. The Queen unsheathed the Sword of State to reveal the brilliant silver blade. She raised the sword above her head and prepared to charge.

"HYPNOS!" she bellowed, her eyes ablaze with fury. "KISS ONE'S ROYAL BOTTOM! AAARRGHGH!"

Her Majesty ran at the terrified Daemon, who raised a splinter of a chair leg to defend himself from the murderous monarch before thinking better of it and running away. The Queen chased Hypnos three times around the parlor, holding her sword above her head and roaring her terrifying battle cry. Hypnos tried to grab his trumpet, but the Queen was too fast. He made for the window and launched himself headlong at it. Wood and glass shattered everywhere as the Daemon of Sleep threw himself outside, dissembled into a pigeon, and flew out of sight.

Elliot and Virgo turned back to the demolished room, where the Queen was zipping up her white gown and smoothing the worst of her disheveled hair. She picked up the two halves of her broken teapot.

"I never really liked this set anyway," she said as the real Jeffers burst into the room, still in the pink dress, but with a lump the size of an apple on his head.

"Your Majesty!" he cried, taking in the destruction of the sitting room. "Are you all right, ma'am?"

"We are fine, thank you, Jeffers," said the Queen calmly. "But Mr. Hooper would like some crumpets and peanut butter. And we might need a new table."

"Yes, ma'am," said a confused Jeffers, who backed out of the room, rubbing his wounded head and trying not to trip on the hem of his dress.

Elliot picked up Hypnos's trumpet and put it into Hermes's satchel.

The Queen walked over to the original Imperial State Crown and handed it to Elliot.

"I think you had better take this, Mr. Hooper. Clearly it could do great harm in the wrong hands."

Elliot took the crown reverently in his hands. He had it. He could save Home Farm.

"Thank you, ma'am," he said quietly. "Sorry about the mess."

"Don't worry about that," said the Queen. "And good luck finding the other stones. If I can be of any further assistance, you know where to find me."

"Yes, ma'am," said Elliot, as Jeffers reappeared with a plate of buttered crumpets and a silver pot of peanut butter. "Thanks."

"Now if you'll excuse me," said the Queen, "I must prepare for the ceremony. I can't possibly open Parliament with my hair like this."

She extended a hand to Elliot and Virgo. "Good-bye, Miss Virgo; good-bye, Mr. Hooper. I've a feeling we're going to be seeing a lot more of you."

And with a regal smile, Queen Elizabeth II turned to leave the room, crunching over broken glass and china with every elegant step.

"Your Majesty?" Elliot said admiringly to her retreating figure. "You rock."

"One knows," said the Queen with a wink.

The rest of the Queen's day passed as planned, the State Opening of Parliament proceeding without a hitch. Most observers wouldn't have noticed anything extraordinary as the Queen watched serenely over the proceedings, playing her regal role to absolute perfection.

But toward the end of the ceremony, the keenest of eyes might not only have noticed the tiny curl of white steam escaping from the top of the Imperial State Crown, but also Her Majesty's contented smile at the thought of the lovely cup of Earl Grey she was going to enjoy in the carriage on her way home.

25

ALL THAT GLISTERS . . .

As Pegasus touched down at Home Farm, Virgo leapt triumphantly off his back.

"I can't wait for the others to get back!" she cried. "We have to celebrate!"

Elliot held the bag containing the crown tightly to his beating chest. Celebrating would have to wait. There was something he had to do first.

"I need to check on Mom," he said quickly. "You wait in the shed and tell them the good news. I'll come up when I'm done."

"Oooooh—the Jacuzzi!" said Virgo, running toward the shed. "I can't get near it when Hermes is here . . ."

"I'd better go and fetch the old boy," said Pegasus, launching into the sky. "No rest for the wonderful . . ."

Checking that no one was watching, Elliot slunk away to the relative privacy of the fields behind the farmhouse. With a deep breath, he reverently pulled the crown out of the bag.

Elliot stared at the magnificent diamond at its heart. The Earth Stone was the size of a small apple and had been cut with countless flat edges, which refracted the afternoon sun into a hundred rainbows on the ground. How could something this beautiful corrupt anyone? It could surely only be a force for good?

Elliot slowly reached out and touched the huge diamond. As his fingers made contact with the Earth Stone, it immediately started to glow with the strength of a thousand sunbeams. He snatched his hand away as if he'd been bitten. The glow disappeared.

"Whoa," whispered Elliot. It was true. He really had the mystical Earth Stone at his command. For the first time in his life, Elliot had an inkling of what real power felt like.

He reached out again, this time placing his whole palm on the Earth Stone. As he connected with the diamond, it felt like it had been made for his hand alone. The incandescent glow illuminated the field, and for a moment, there was nothing in the world but Elliot and the Earth Stone. It was a good feeling.

He tightened his grasp around the Earth Stone, and as he pulled his hand back, the huge diamond came away from the crown like a head from a pillow. Elliot tossed the useless crown on the ground and cupped his hands around the Earth Stone. He closed his eyes.

"Find me treasure," he whispered, experiencing a sensation the likes of which he'd never known. A million tingling atoms flowed through his veins at the command, empowering every inch of his body. He felt bigger. He felt stronger. He felt . . . invincible.

As the Earth Stone's rays hit the ground, it began to tremble and shudder beneath Elliot's feet. A distant rumble became slowly louder as the diamond glowed brighter in his hand, blinding him with its supernatural glow. Elliot had to resist the urge to roar with the power that surged through his body.

A thin black line snaked along the ground in front of him. The rumble became stronger; the line widened and the quaking Earth started to open up. Elliot just had time to step aside before there was a jolt, as if the soil were about to be violently ill, then it suddenly exploded in a shower of rubble, propelling him across the grass. Elliot instinctively covered his face with his hands, dropping the Earth Stone, which immediately extinguished.

The explosion passed. Elliot waved his hand to clear the air and spat a mouthful of grit from his lips. What had just happened?

As the dust floated back to the Earth, Elliot struggled to comprehend the scene before him. Scattered all around, as if they had fallen from the sky, were unimaginable precious treasures. Some were buried artifacts, others raw gemstones from the ground. There was gold, silver—he couldn't even name some of the shining lumps that littered the farmyard. But Elliot didn't care. Whatever they were, they were worth a fortune. He'd become a frequent customer at Mr. Macgregor's pawn shop in the village, where he'd sold all of Nan's jewelry and anything else of value over the past months to raise some cash. He thought of Mr. Macgregor's eyes bursting out of his head when he saw this haul.

"Epic," whispered Elliot as he gathered armfuls of the precious loot and put the Earth Stone carefully into his pocket. Imagine what else he could do with its power? He could find gold and jewels anywhere. He and Mom could be rich beyond their wildest dreams. And never have to eat beans again. Perhaps the Earth Stone could be borrowed on a more permanent basis . . .

But these were matters for another time. Right now he had to let those stupid loan people know that he had their money. He exhaled weeks of pent-up worry into the dusty air. At last. Home Farm was safe.

Elliot sprinted toward his front door, stopping only to collect the bits of booty that fell from his arms. He burst into the farmhouse, laden with his treasure.

"Mom! Mom! We're celebrating!" he cried. "I've got . . ."

"Hello, honeypot," chirped Patricia Porshley-Plum, blocking his path to the kitchen, her eyes as warm as winter. "Ooh—are you playing pirates?"

"How did you get in here?" Elliot asked suspiciously.

"You should be more careful, munchkin," trilled Patricia. "Leaving that gate wide open like that? Anyone could have gotten in . . ."

"Are you okay, Mom?" said Elliot, pushing past Patricia to where his mom was sitting happily in the kitchen.

"Oh, we've had the lovellest time, haven't we, Josie?" said Patricia, looming behind her and squeezing her shoulders.

"Lovely, Elly. We had scones."

"Of course we did, dear. We're not animals," said Patricia.

"You look tired, Mom," Elliot said, glancing at Patricia. "Why don't you go upstairs and lie down?"

"What a lovely idea, Josie. That way Elly and I can have a little chat about our busy-bee day."

Pausing only to give her son a loving squeeze on her way past, Josie headed quietly upstairs to her bedroom.

"Ellykins. I know what's been going on," said Patricia gravely, as soon as Josie was out of earshot. "You poor, poor little pickle! What a lot you've had to deal with! You should have asked me for help."

"We're fine, thank you," said Elliot, sensing greater danger from this awful woman.

"Of course you are, sugarplumplum. Or at least you will be now."

Elliot's blood cooled by several degrees.

"What do you mean?"

"Well . . . Momsy and I were talking over lunch the other day—you know, girl talk—and she told me about your . . . money worries." She whispered them like the dirty words that they were. "I know about the house."

"Mom doesn't know about the house," said Elliot. "So how could she tell you?"

"Mommies know everything, pumpkin," said Patricia, her eyes betraying that she'd slipped up. "But you don't need to worry about that silly loan anymore."

"Why?" asked Elliot suspiciously.

"To think they sent that horrid ickle-bickle letter threatening your home—some people have no shame," she said with her monkey-bottom pout.

"I don't understand."

"The loan. The twenty thousand pounds. It's history, all gone, pffff!" trilled Patricia, with a voice like a frantic merry-go-round. "I've paid off your debt in full."

Elliot couldn't believe it. How could he get someone so wrong? All this time he'd thought Patricia was a rotten, interfering harridan. And yet she'd given them this wonderful gift. His gut instincts were never normally this off. But he'd never been happier to be wrong in all his life.

"Mrs. Porshley-Plum—I don't know how to thank you," he said.

"Oh, no need to worry about that, my little porkie pie," said Patricia. "Anything to see you and Momsy happy."

"That's—that's amazing." Elliot smiled. He couldn't believe it. After all that, salvation was living next door. Life was full of surprises.

"Virtue is its own reward," said Patricia, standing to leave. "And besides, Mommy has already thanked me in a super-special way . . ."

"Sorry?" said Elliot.

"I'm sure it's for the best—this place must be so much work for you . . ."

"What do you mean?" asked Elliot, his blood temperature starting to dip once more.

"All that cleaning and all those bills to worry about. Not to mention finding some more suitable . . . care for Mommypoos."

"What's for the best?" asked Elliot, now practically a Popsicle inside. "What have you done?"

"It's good news, dumpling," said Patricia, pulling a sheaf of papers from her handbag and tossing them on the kitchen table. "We've finalized all the paperwork today."

"What—what are these?" said Elliot, his panic blurring the legal gobbledygook before his eyes.

"It's so exciting, pookie!" shrieked Patricia. "Mommy's sold me your farm!"

Elliot choked back the sickness that spewed up his throat.

"No—no—you don't understand!" he cried. "She—she's not well! She doesn't know what she's doing! She'd never sell the farm! She's . . ."

He held all the treasure in his arms out to Patricia.

"Here—take this, let me buy it back," he said, tears filling his eyes. "You can have it all—I can get you more. I can get you anything you want. Just . . . please . . ."

"Oh, there, there, there," said Patricia, chucking Elliot a paper towel to dry his eyes. "There's no need to do that. Besides, you're going to need that money."

"Why?" choked Elliot.

Patricia's face lit up like a jack-o'-lantern.

"To find somewhere else to live," she sneered. "I have legally purchased Home Farm"—Patricia chuckled as she played her final ace—"for twenty pounds."

There was a scream in Elliot's head as a roar of blood rushed to his brain.

"Get out!" he yelled as his fingers tightened around the Earth Stone in his pocket.

"Elly?" said Josie sleepily, wandering back into the kitchen. "What's all the noise?"

"That's no way to talk to your elders and betters," said Patricia, ignoring Josie as she parked her handbag on her arm. "My lawyer says the house sale should take about four weeks. I suggest you start packing . . ."

"Packing for what?" said Josie anxiously. "What house sale? Where are we going, Elly? What's happening?"

"Get. Out," said Elliot menacingly, wishing the ground would open up and swallow Patricia whole. The diamond began to glow in his palm.

"Urgh," snorted Patricia, taking a disdainful look around the kitchen. "This really is a mercy killing. The rats must be complaining to the public health board about this place . . ."

"Elly, I don't understand," said Josie. "Why is she saying—?"

"I said . . . GET OUT!" yelled Elliot, his body igniting with the power of the stone. As his voice exploded into the air, the kitchen filled with the diamond's light. The ground beneath Patricia's feet burst open, nearly sending her tumbling into the small ravine it created in the middle of the kitchen.

"Elliot?" cried Josie in disbelief.

"What the . . . ! This place is a death trap!" shrieked Patricia as she teetered over the chasm.

Elliot stood panting in the middle of the kitchen, his blue eyes darkened with the tint of pure hatred.

"I think you should leave, Patricia," said Josie, rushing to her son and pulling him into her arms. Elliot dropped the Earth Stone to the floor and collapsed into his mother's embrace.

"Fine with me." Patricia scowled. "But mark my words. So long as there is breath in this body, in four weeks the pair of you will be where you belong—out on the street!"

Patricia stormed out of the farm, leaving Elliot crying in his mother's arms. He stayed in her embrace for an eternity, shaking with agonized sobs.

"I can't do it, Mom!" he gasped eventually. "I can't do it anymore!"

"Shhhh," soothed Josie, stroking his head. "I'm sure we can make it better. Now tell me what's happened. Something at school?"

Elliot looked tearfully into his mother's calm face. She'd already forgotten.

But he couldn't. In four weeks, Elliot and Josie would lose Home Farm.

Patricia Porshley-Plum had won.

26

THE CAVE OF SLEEP AND DEATH

"So let me get this straight," said Thanatos, arching his long, thin fingers beneath his chin as he stretched out on his throne of bones. "You have failed to kill the child. You have failed to fight a woman in her nineties. And you've failed to bring me my Earth Stone."

"And I've lost my beautiful trumpet," sulked Hypnos as he reclined on his sumptuous fur-lined bed in the Cave of Sleep and Death. His shrill voice echoed around the dark, barren chambers of the cave. Outside, the river Lethe murmured and the poppies at the cave's mouth rustled. "But looking around this place, you failed to understand the basics of interior decor. Would a little wallpaper be too much to ask . . . ?"

"MY PATIENCE WEARS THIN!" roared Thanatos, leaping from his throne and flinging aside the black, wispy drapes surrounding his brother's bed. "If I thought for one minute you were double-crossing me . . ."

"Where's the fun in that?" Hypnos smiled, his brother's fury immediately cheering him up. "It's all under control—trust me. You're far too suspicious . . ."

"I wonder why," said Thanatos, pinning his twin against the wall and grabbing his kardia. "I'm warning you, brother. Betray me again and I—"

"Can't kill me!" Hypnos grinned. "You swore an oath . . ."

"Which I will uphold as I tear you apart, piece by piece, leaving only your loud mouth to tell me where my Chaos Stones are. Perhaps I should start now to remind you where your loyalties lie . . . ?"

"Thanatos?" said a new voice outside the cave, cutting through the air like a moonbeam.

Thanatos spun around.

"Who's there?" he shouted.

"Too slow!" taunted Hypnos, taking advantage of his brother's distraction to free himself from his grip.

"Get back here," snarled Thanatos. "I'm not done with you."

"Well, maybe I'm done with you," trilled Hypnos. "You're not the boss of me. And you're no fun anymore. See ya."

And the Daemon of Sleep unfurled his wings and whizzed out of the cave with a whoop, shaking the sea of poppies that wafted at the cave's entrance.

"Who is it?" Thanatos demanded again. "Reveal yourself."

The intruder stepped into the cave.

"Well, well, well. How did you find me?" Thanatos smiled admiringly.

"Charon," said Elliot, walking into the darkness. "It's amazing what he'll do for three bottle tops and a pen cap."

"You'll have to excuse me—I rarely entertain mortals," said Thanatos, pulling up a chair for Elliot. "Not live ones, anyway. The Underworld doesn't seem to . . . agree with them. To what do I owe the pleasure?"

Elliot wiped his puffy eyes. This was his only hope, the only way to keep Mom safe. He'd told himself that all the way here. He placed the Earth Stone on the table between them. Thanatos's eyes flickered with desire.

"I thought you'd be interested in this," said Elliot, trying to keep the fear from his voice. He couldn't quite believe what he was about to do. It was so risky. But he had no choice. He had to do it for Mom. She couldn't carry on like this. And neither could he.

"You have gone to great lengths to get the Earth Stone before me and now you are simply going to hand it over?" said Thanatos with a raised eyebrow.

"I need something in return," said Elliot. "Something only you can do."

"Your mother." Thanatos smiled knowingly. "You want me to cure your mother."

"You said at Stonehenge that you can do things the Gods cannot," said Elliot. "Was that true?"

"Like you wouldn't believe," said Thanatos. "Why do you think Zeus is so afraid of me? Because he knows I'm more powerful than him. And you could be too . . ."

"What do you mean?" asked Elliot.

"He hasn't told you?" said Thanatos.

"Told me what?" said Elliot.

"How interesting." Thanatos leaned back in his bone throne. "But tell me—since you have stolen the Earth Stone, why not keep it for yourself? You could be a very rich young man, never work a day. You could afford the best doctors mortal money can buy."

"She doesn't need a doctor," said Elliot. "She needs herself. Can you give her that back?"

Thanatos stared deep into Elliot's eyes. "If you give me *that*," he said at last, gesturing to the Earth Stone. "And its three companions."

Elliot turned the diamond over in his hand. It was a high price. What would this mean for the world? But Mom was his world. He needed her back.

"Swear it," said Elliot.

"I swear on the Styx," said Thanatos solemnly. "Bring me my Chaos Stones and I will give you your mother back."

"Then it's a deal," said Elliot quietly, his stomach in knots.

Thanatos poured two glasses of water from a black stone jug on the table.

"Let us drink a toast," he said. "Here's to a fresh start. Time to forget the past."

Elliot hesitated as he looked down at his water. It was so clear it was as if there were nothing there at all. But life was teaching him to be suspicious.

"It's not poisoned," laughed Thanatos, draining his glass in a single gulp. "I swear on the Styx. Take it or leave it."

Elliot looked thirstily at the water. The oppressive air of the cave was making him sleepy. A cool drink was just what he needed. And if it wasn't deadly . . . He drank.

"I need to go," he said, putting the Earth Stone back in his pocket and standing up shakily. He held the table for balance. Everything was swimming. "Everyone will be wondering where I am."

He walked unsteadily to the cave's entrance.

"Er—Elliot," said Thanatos, settling back onto his throne. "Aren't we forgetting something? My Earth Stone?"

"You'll get it with the rest," said Elliot, suddenly afraid at the thought of losing the diamond. "I need it. I need to buy a new house. You'll get it soon enough . . ."

Elliot teetered toward the exit. At a click of Thanatos's fingers, the poppies at the cave's mouth suddenly grew taller and thicker, tangling over the entrance to form a thick wall, blocking Elliot's only way out.

"Oh, I think I'll have it now," said Thanatos, rising from the throne and walking slowly toward him.

Elliot felt the dark fear rising through him. He stamped it down. He was in control here.

"No," he said as firmly as he was able.

"Then I'll just have to take it," said Thanatos.

Elliot flinched as Thanatos lunged toward him. But as soon as he got close to Elliot's body, the Daemon was knocked away by the same invisible force as beneath Stonehenge.

"You can't touch me," Elliot realized aloud.

"So it seems," drawled Thanatos. "It would appear we are at a stalemate."

Elliot waited for the cave entrance to open. It didn't. His head started to feel strangely fuzzy, and another yawn escaped his lips.

"I fear that you and I got off on the wrong foot, young Elliot," said Thanatos, returning to his throne. "I'm sure that your . . . friends have told you all manner of lies. But I assure you, my motives are entirely honorable."

His words swarmed in Elliot's head. It was difficult to concentrate through this tiredness. His eyes wandered around the cave, up to the roof covered in enormous stalactites. They were the ones that hung from the ceiling. Mom had taught him that.

"Honorable?" said Elliot. "You want to kill mortals."

"Not all of them," said Thanatos. "I intend to keep some. The place will need looking after. Besides, no point in ruling the world if no one is there. Look at your realm, Elliot. The Earth is overrun. Millions of mortals without homes, not enough food, no clean water, sanitation, education. All I want to do is balance the books."

"By murdering?" asked Elliot, unable to stifle a yawn.

"Murder is premeditated and deliberate," said Thanatos. "I would use the Chaos Stones for more of a . . . cull. A necessary evil to control the species. It isn't personal. After all, what is more impartial than death? An earthquake can't see the color of your skin. A tsunami doesn't know your religion. A hurricane doesn't care about your money. Which makes me about the fairest individual you'll ever meet. It's for your own good."

"What about the Gods?" said Elliot, his eyelids sagging.

"Ah," said Thanatos. "Now, that is personal. Zeus killed my father and locked me away for two thousand years like a dirty little secret. I'm not proud to admit it; I want revenge."

The oppressively warm air of the cave was making Elliot feel unbearably heavy. He stumbled forward as his body started to droop.

"Gracious, Elliot, you are weary," said Thanatos. "Are you quite all right?"

"What?" said Elliot. "Yes, yes, I'm fine. Just a bit . . . tired."

"Of course," said Thanatos. "And look—here is a lovely warm bed. Wouldn't that be so comfortable?"

Elliot looked at the corner of the cave where Hypnos's opulent bed was calling him. Perhaps if he could just lay his head down for a moment . . . No. He had to leave.

"Let me go . . . er . . ."

"Thanatos," said the Daemon of Death. "You seem to be struggling with your memory."

"Nothing wrong with my memory," said Elliot through half-closed eyes.

"Remind me of your name again?"

"It's . . . well, it's . . . it's . . . of course I know my . . . what did you say?"

"Oh, silly me," gasped Thanatos, picking up the glass that Elliot had dropped on the floor. "What a terrible host. It appears I've served you water from the river Lethe outside. Like I said, it can't kill you. Packed with natural minerals, in fact. It just has the one unfortunate side effect. You're going to forget everything. Everything you know, who you are—you'll even forget how to stay awake. In one hour, that water will be absorbed into your blood forever. You will spend the rest of your life in unconscious oblivion."

"Don't be ridiculous," yawned Elliot. "If I just have a quick nap, I'll be . . ."

"What a marvelous idea," said Thanatos. "Why don't you lie down and have a lovely sleep? And while you're lying there, sleeping until you die, I can take that Earth Stone from you. Gods can't travel to the Underworld. There's no one to rescue you."

The Earth Stone? Elliot knew that was really important. He just wasn't entirely sure why. He stumbled over to the bed and lay down. That felt so good . . .

"Perhaps next time, you'll think twice before presuming to negotiate with me," sneered Thanatos from his throne. "Except there won't be a next time. Go to sleep."

Sleep. Yes. That's what Elliot needed. A nice long sleep . . .

"As if I need a mortal child to find my Chaos Stones," scoffed Thanatos. "They will be mine. I will have my revenge. And with you eternally asleep, I'm also free of my oath to your mother."

Mother. The word pierced Elliot's last drop of consciousness like a spear.

"Mother," Elliot repeated.

"Shhhhh," said Thanatos. "Go to sleep, Elliot. Go to
sleep. Forever."

Mother. Mom. The words tumbled around Elliot's mind,
fighting back the encroaching oblivion.

"Mom," he said more loudly, his mind searching for the
answer to the question on his lips. He had a mom. His mom.
He couldn't stay here. He needed to get back to her. He
needed to get home. He tried to stand.

"No, no, no," said Thanatos with a smirk. "Don't fight it."

Elliot raised his leaden eyes over Thanatos's pale head, to
the field of stalactites that clung to the roof above him.

"Drop," he said in the quietest whisper, a faint image of
Josie's smile forcing its way into his mind. He looked at the
ceiling, but the stalactites stayed firmly in place. "Drop."

"Oh, do shut up," sighed Thanatos. "Epic poems have
ended faster . . ."

"Drop," said Elliot more firmly, feeling the warmth of his
mother's arms around him and her laughter singing in his ears.

"What's that?" said Thanatos, leaning from his throne.
"What are you doing?"

Elliot felt his love for his mom shoot up inside him like
volcanic lava. The sensation radiated from his heart into every
corner of his body, giving him a surge of power for one last
effort.

"I said, DROP!" he roared with every last bit of strength he had, holding up the Earth Stone. The light from the diamond exploded into the cave.

"What the—?"

As Thanatos leapt up from his throne, an enormous stalactite came loose with a deafening crack and dropped to the floor, sinking deep into the ground directly in front of the Death Daemon, barring his path.

"Too little, too late," he snarled. "You're still going to—"

Another massive rock cracked from the ceiling, holding Thanatos back once again. He moved to avoid a third falling on him, but every way he turned, an enormous stalactite fell to block his way.

"This won't save you!" he screamed at Elliot. "You'll rot here anyway!"

But his curses were futile—the stalactites kept falling all around his throne, creating a solid stone circle around the livid Daemon, who raged at the mortal who had cheated him of his Earth Stone.

"This won't hold me!" yelled Thanatos. "I will find you! I will find the stones! You cannot defeat me!"

"Oh, do shut up," murmured Elliot, holding the Earth Stone high above his head to send a final shower of stalactites down onto Thanatos, silencing the Daemon beneath the rockfall.

Elliot flopped off the bed and dragged his heavy body across the floor of the cave to where the poppies were wilting as Thanatos's spell weakened. He held one of Charon's cards between his fingers, desperate to summon the ferryman at the riverbank. He was nearly there. But he was just so, so tired.

Elliot reached his trembling fingers toward the river and stretched his arms as far as he could, dropping the card with a whispered prayer. It landed on the blade of grass nearest to the water. He had missed. Elliot's head slumped to the ground. He could go no farther. He'd failed. He'd failed the Gods. He'd failed himself. He'd failed Mom.

He let out an anguished sigh. So this was it. He took one last look at the lonely grave around him before closing his leaden eyes for the final time.

27

SNORDLESNOT

"I don't understand—he was here before . . ." said Virgo.

"He's not in the house," said Aphrodite, running back to the circle of worried immortals. "And I can't find Josie either. The back door was open."

"Athene and Hephaestus—search the farm for Josie," ordered Zeus. "The gate was shut, she can't have gone far."

The two Gods nodded and ran off in opposite directions across the fields.

"It's been hours," said Virgo, looking gravely at Zeus. "It's all my fault, I should have stayed with him. The jacuzzi isn't even that comfortable. I can't tell you where the bubbles went . . ."

"I'm sure it'll all be fine," said Zeus unconvincingly. "Where could he be?"

"Look at me!" Virgo shouted suddenly.

"It's not about you right now, babe . . ." said Hermes.

"No—your app," said Virgo, returning the forgotten iGod to Hermes. "You put Elliot on it, remember? You can find him!"

"MEGA BOSH!" cheered Hermes, his fingers punching at the iGod with lightning speed. "Where are you, mate . . . ?"

"Josie!" Zeus exclaimed.

The immortals ran over to where Athene was escorting a shaking Josie in her arms. Aphrodite rubbed Josie's frozen hands in hers while Zeus put his jacket around her shoulders.

"I found her roaming around the fields," said Athene. "Along with this . . ."

Athene handed her father the discarded Imperial Crown—minus the Earth Stone. They exchanged a worried glance.

"I don't . . . I don't . . . What have I done?" cried Josie, pulling at her hair as the tears ran down her face. In her other hand was the contract of sale for Home Farm. "It says I've . . . Where's Elly? I can't find him . . ."

"It's okay, Josie, we're here now," soothed Athene as Zeus gently took the papers from Josie's trembling hands. "We'll find him. I promise."

"Oh, no," said Zeus, riffling through the contract. "Poor Elliot! Why didn't he tell us?"

"Let me see," said Athene, reading the document aghast. "No! That awful woman! How could she—?"

"Not being funny," said Hermes, hitting his iGod with his palm. "Look@Me isn't working."

"No signal?" said Aphrodite.

"It's not that, babe: it says it's found Elliot," said Hermes. "But it says he's in the Underworld. That can't be right , ,"

"Let me see!" said Virgo, grabbing the iGod.

"It's insisting," said Hermes, as Virgo threw the device back to him. "Why would he go down there?"

"Thanatos," said Zeus grimly. "Elliot's desperate. I should have seen the signs . . . We have to get him out of there."

"Seriously," said Hermes. "But how? We can't go to the Underworld."

"The wishing pearl!" cried Aphrodite. "We can wish him home!"

"It's already been used once today," said Athene. "You said Thanatos can't kill him."

"But there are plenty of other things he *can* do," said Zeus. "Virgo, you're the only one of us who can travel to the Underworld. You're going to have to—"

"I think she already has," said Athene, looking at the open gate and the silver dot on the horizon that was sprinting toward the river.

"Can't you go any faster?" Virgo yelled at Charon.

"Listen, it ain't my fault there were river works all along the Acheron," said Charon as he rowed along the gloomy river Lethe. "And that two-knot average speed check is doing my head in; you need to have a word with the council . . .

Anyway, you don't need me, you could just whiz down here in your star-ball."

"It's a CONSTELLATION!" screamed Virgo. "And I can't unless I want to lose my kardia and spend the rest of my shortened days as a mortal! What were you *thinking*, taking Elliot to Thanatos?"

"I just take the jobs, mate—none of my business who's doing what to whom," said Charon. "All I ask is that you pay your fare, specify your preferred route, and don't be sick in me boat. It's a nightmare when someone vomits on me floorboards . . ."

"Fine—just . . . hurry up!" hissed Virgo, looking along the banks of the Lethe for any sign of her lost mortal friend.

"Next stop—Cave of Sleep and Death," announced Charon.

"Elliot! Elliot! Where are you?" shouted Virgo along the murky riverbank. "Oh, this is no good, I can't see a thing. If only I could use my glow . . ."

Virgo's mind wrestled with itself. Would that count as breaking the rules? Her face screwed up with indecision.

"I know that feeling," said Charon softly.

"You do?" said Virgo. "What should I do?"

"Get yourself some concentrated prune juice," said Charon brightly. "Clears out constipation like Daedalus's dynamite . . ."

"You're no help," huffed Virgo. "Look. It's only a tiny power and there are no mortals to see . . ."

She cautiously pulled her palms apart to illuminate her body and cast a ray of starlight over the riverbank.

"Where are you?" she moaned.

Suddenly, her glow caught a glimmer on the riverbank, sending tiny rainbows bursting through the darkness. It was the Earth Stone. And just beyond it lay Elliot's comatose body . . .

"There he is!" shouted Virgo. "Over there!"

Charon steered the boat to the shore and Virgo bounded to Elliot's side.

"Elliot!" she screamed, shaking his body. "Elliot, wake up!"

She looked around for any sign of Thanatos or his twin, but the unconscious boy was the only life there. Although it didn't look as though he had much life in him. Virgo turned Elliot over and slapped his pale cheeks, but he lay motionless in her arms. She put her face to his chest, an unpleasant sensation fluttering around her own. Her nose caught a scent and she sniffed Elliot's face.

"Lethe water!" she cried. "I can smell it on his breath. We have to get it out of him before it's too late—how fast can you get back to Earth?"

"You saw the state of the traffic, darlin'—could take an hour or more," said Charon.

"He doesn't have an hour!" cried Virgo. "If the water gets into his blood . . . I don't know what to do! Elliot! Come on, Elliot, you have to wake up!"

But Elliot didn't flicker. He needed the Gods. If Virgo was going to save him, she had only one option. It must be the right thing to do. Surely the council would understand . . . ?

"Oh, SNORDLESNOT!" yelled Virgo.

Throwing her arms wide, she transformed into her constellation, scooped Elliot up in her starry glow, whizzed past Charon in his boat, and raced through the realms at top speed.

"Elliot!" shouted Zeus, seeing the unconscious boy floating down to Home Farm in Virgo's constellation.

In a mad scramble of arms and hands, the immortals lifted Elliot down and laid him on the ground.

"He's drunk water from the Lethe," cried Virgo bleakly. "I tried to get him here as fast as I could, but . . ."

"We have to get that water out of him. Father—put your hands like this," commanded Athene, placing her hands on Elliot's ribs. "When I nod, gently press down on his rib cage."

As Hermes shot into the air to check that Josie was still safely in the farmhouse, Athene started blowing rhythmic breaths into Elliot's mouth, signaling to Zeus to pump his chest.

"Come on, Elliot," panted Zeus. "Spit it out. Come back to us."

The other immortals stood frozen around Elliot's body, barely drawing breath as Athene and Zeus tried to force the water of oblivion from Elliot's body. They looked on in desperate hope, watching for a flicker of consciousness, a movement, a sound, any sign that Elliot was going to wake up. But the pale boy lay comatose on the floor and gave not so much as a finger twitch in response to the Gods' desperate efforts to revive him. After several endless minutes, Athene stopped her breaths.

"It's too late," she said quietly. Zeus put a heavy hand on her shoulder.

Virgo hung her head. She was experiencing another unpleasant new sensation in her chest, a kind of hollow, twisting feeling that spread darkness around her body and forced drops of liquid out of her eyes. As the leakage ran down her face, she had never felt so suboptimal.

A tearstained Aphrodite forced her way to Elliot's side.

"CALL THAT A KISS OF LIFE?!" she screamed wildly, pushing her father and sister out of the way. "Come on, Elly, time to come home!"

And with a tearful sob, Aphrodite lifted Elliot's head from the ground and planted an enormous and very long kiss square on his pale lips.

Everything was silent, the still air broken only by Virgo's sobs. Zeus pulled her to him.

"He's at peace," he said gently.

"He's been through so much," said Athene, biting back the tears that shone from her brown eyes.

"He's a hero," said Hephaestus, shaking his head.

"He's . . . he's blushing," said Hermes. "Not being funny or anything . . ."

Everyone craned their necks to stare at Elliot's face. Hermes was right—the face that had been a sickly shade of gray just moments before was becoming steadily more scarlet, as if it were being filled from the chin with fruit punch.

"Elly!" cried Aphrodite, breaking from the kiss. "Elly, are you there?"

With an almighty belch, Elliot sat bolt upright and spewed the Lethe water volcanically out of his body.

"Elliot!" screamed Virgo, freeing herself from Zeus's embrace and hurtling toward her friend, knocking him flying with a diving hug and impulsively kissing him on the cheek with relief.

"I preferred it when she did it," croaked Elliot, still gasping for air and now rubbing a sore head from Virgo's enthusiastic welcome.

"Elly!" screamed Aphrodite, diving in as well to hug him senseless.

"EPIC BOSH!" yelled Hermes, joining the fray.

"Give the boy some air, for goodness' sake," said a relieved Athene, wiping a tear from her eye. "Oh, what the heck!" and she too threw herself at the pile of people on the ground and gave Elliot a delighted squeeze.

"Well done," said Zeus softly to Virgo, who beamed with pride.

When Elliot was finally allowed to his feet, he slunk over to Zeus and handed him the Earth Stone with his eyes glued to the ground. Zeus lifted Elliot's chin and answered his guilty glance with a reassuring smile. Now was not the time for words. Not those ones.

Hermes's iGod rang in the background.

"Virgo, babe—call for you," he said. "It's the Zodiac Council."

"Ah," said Virgo with a satisfied smile as Hermes projected the hologram of the council table into the evening air. "Calling to congratulate me, no doubt. Hello, everyone."

"Virgo!" roared Pisces, with a look that didn't seem very congratulatory at all. "I thought we made ourselves perfectly clear! You were forbidden from using your Constellation powers!"

"I was, however—" said Virgo.

"It seems that you have developed a callous disregard for authority," huffed Aries. "The rules are there to be obeyed!"

"Yes, b-but—" stammered Virgo.

"There will be no more buts from you, young lady!" shouted Taurus. "But I have a big but!"

"You're not wrong," muttered Leo as the other Zodiac Councillors sniggered behind their papers.

"She saved my life," said Elliot, looking gratefully at his friend.

"Silence!" shouted Pisces. "Virgo, this is very serious indeed. You have proven, once again, that you cannot be trusted to follow a simple set of rules."

"Of course I can, it's just that—"

"Just what?" demanded Sagittarius.

"It's just that . . . maybe sometimes, on certain extremely rare occasions, when no other viable alternative presents itself, then and only then, perhaps . . . OUR RULES SUCK!" Virgo blurted out, immediately clasping her hand to her mouth.

The council gasped in horror as Aphrodite and Hermes high-fived in the background.

"I can see you have been spending too much time around mortals and their strange, lawless ways," said Scorpio.

"Indeed," said Aquarius. "Well, let's see how you manage among them on a more permanent basis . . ."

"Now hang on a minute," said Zeus, "she was only trying to—"

"I'm sorry, Your Majesty," said Pisces. "But Virgo has left us no alternative. Nor staples—we can't find a single one. Virgo, Constellation of the Zodiac Council and *former* Guardian of the Stationery Cupboard, I hereby strip you of your kardia. You will be suspended from immortality pending a formal trial upon completion of forms X4suf Recategorizing of an Immortal, VF4gl Breaking of an Arbitrary Rule and Gh74p Because We Feel Like It."

"No . . . please!" cried Virgo as a thin stream of stars appeared around her neck and unfastened her kardia.

"We will fight this!" shouted Athene as the kardia came away from Virgo's neck and floated up into the sky.

"Mate!" said Hermes, trying unsuccessfully to grab it midair.

"Give it back to her, you bureaucratic butthead!" yelled Aphrodite.

"You can make your case at the trial," said Pisces. "But until then, Virgo will live her life as a mortal, with all the dangers and discomforts that brings."

"But . . . but that's not fair," said Virgo weakly.

"Life isn't fair," said Pisces as his hologram faded away. "As you're about to find out. Good-bye, Virgo."

28

TESTING TIMES

The Brysmore exams came around quickly in early December, but after four weeks of Athene's tuition—and without the wishing pearl that the Goddess of Wisdom had confiscated—Elliot went into them better prepared than he could ever have imagined.

His English exam was easy as pie as he recalled the Gods' memorable performance of *Romeo and Juliet*, with Hermes playing the tragic heroine. Latin was a cinch: He had to translate a passage about Perseus, who had dropped by during his world tour to sing a ballad about Medusa called "Heart of Stone." Even history was a gift: Elliot had to write an essay about the Roman wars against Carthage, which Athene had reenacted a few days previously, transforming an ant colony into a full-scale Roman battlefield, with a wood louse taking the role of Hannibal.

The results were to be posted on the school bulletin board on Thursday morning, the last day of term. Elliot barely slept a wink on Wednesday night. At first he'd felt the exams had gone well, but now he'd had some time to reflect on them, had the French comprehension really been about some talking pigs? And had he actually gotten Nigeria muddled up with Norfolk in geography?

But Elliot also had bigger things to worry about. Since the Gods discovered the sale of Home Farm, they had worked night and day to find a way to get it back. They had explored every legal—and at least one illegal—possibility that Elliot could take, but they couldn't find a way to stop the sale. Patricia had legitimately exchanged contracts on the farm, and if they didn't do something, the sale would complete the next day.

"We'll think of something, old boy," Zeus kept saying, reading Elliot's sad face every time he thought of losing his beloved home.

"I don't know what's wrong with me," said Virgo, breaking Elliot's thoughts as she banged around the kitchen in a flap, dropping eggs, spreading jam on her cereal, and putting three big spoonfuls of salt in her tea. "Since becoming a mortal, I have this curious sensation demanding that I fill my stomach with food every hour of the day. But today, all the food just wants to leave my body by the nearest exit."

Virgo was still struggling to come to terms with her newfound mortality. Elliot found the things she was struggling with highly amusing, smiling to himself as she ran to the toilet for the umpteenth time that morning.

"Whoever thought of this system should be locked up in Tartarus," she yelled from the downstairs bathroom. "I wish I'd never found out what this room was for . . ."

The Gods came into the kitchen, looking every bit as nervous as the two students before them.

"How are you feeling?" said Zeus, attempting to sound cheery as he paced around the kitchen.

"Okay," said Elliot unconvincingly.

"WE'RE FINE!" shouted Virgo angrily from the bathroom. "Snordlesnot! Just remembered I got that photosynthesis question wrong. That's it, I've failed. I am totally suboptimal."

"I'm sure you've both done your best," said Athene, who looked like she hadn't slept, despite the fact that she hardly ever did.

"You'll be amazing, Elly," said Josie, giving Elliot a hug. "You are always are."

"Well said, Jo-Jo. Will you all just calm down," said Aphrodite, perching on the kitchen table and taking a bite of Elliot's toast, the only Olympian to appear entirely relaxed. "So you get kicked out of school, big deal. Don't stress, Elly, we'll look after you."

"That's all he needs," muttered Athene, who had now taken to pacing around the kitchen behind Zeus.

"Oh, come on, let's get you to school and put you out of your misery," said Aphrodite, magically summoning her car keys. "I'll let you drive."

Elliot had been enjoying this secret part of his daily trip to school down the quiet country lanes, but even he knew that today it would be particularly unwise for a sleepless, anxious twelve-year-old to get behind the wheel. He threw his backpack into Aphrodite's car, which had been transformed into a luxurious pink 4x4 as a more suitable vehicle for the English winter, and sat in silence as Aphrodite drove them both to the school gates.

"Good luck, Virgo; good luck, Elly," she said cheerily as Virgo threw up her breakfast on the side of road. "I'll see you later. We're proud of you whatever happens."

The two friends trudged toward the school as if they were walking down death row, their nerves keeping them silent as they entered Brysmore through the grand wooden doors.

A crowd of pale students hung around the bulletin board, awaiting their fate with dread. Briony and Dominic comforted each other in a corner, each holding a tissue in case one cried and the other threw up.

The staff room door opened with a long, slow creak, every head spinning toward the shaking figure that emerged. Call Me Graham tottered nervously to the board, apparently surprised to find a large group of children in his school. He quickly stapled the results sheets up, then hurried away, looking like he might cry.

There was a moment's stillness as everyone froze, not wanting to make the first move toward their doom. But the slightest twitch of someone's foot was enough to send the entire crowd racing over to the board.

Elliot and Virgo held back, watching pupils peel away from the crowd with cheers or tears. They waited until the last person had left, before walking side by side to the board. They looked over every sheet of paper, taking in the information on each one, before turning to each other once more.

"Snordlesnot," they chimed in unison.

Back at the farm, the Gods paced around the kitchen in anxious silence, staring at Hermes's iGod—Virgo had promised to contact them with the phone Aphrodite had smuggled to her.

"Not being funny," moaned Hermes, fluttering from one end of the room to the other. "But I haven't been this nervous since I last ate carbs."

"He's a smart cookie," said Aphrodite, painting Josie's nails. "Prissy-pants has been stuffing his head with this nonsense for weeks; he'll ace it."

"I don't know," said Athene. "He was a long way behind; if only I'd had more time."

"You've done everything you can," said Zeus. "The rest is up to Elliot."

"My boy will be brilliant." Josie smiled. "He always is."

Hermes's iGod beeped a text message, making all the Gods jump. They stood and stared at the phone, no one daring to read the news.

"Well, go on, for the heavens' sake!" shrieked Aphrodite, all illusion of calm now gone. "Read it!"

"No way, babe!" said Hermes. "What if it's bad news?"

"We'll never know unless you read it," snapped Athene.

"You read it, then," said Hermes, throwing her the phone.

"Well, I, it's not my— Father, you should read it," said Athene, passing the iGod to her father.

"Not on your life," said Zeus, pushing the device toward Aphrodite. "My nerves are shot. Aphy—go on, open the darn message."

"Oh, give it 'ere," said Hephaestus, who had been fixing the damage to the kitchen floor caused by the Earth Stone. "I'll read the bloomin' thing."

He stormed over to the iGod and snatched it up.

"Mate, seriously, any chance you could wash your hands before you . . . Nope, never mind." Hermes winced at the blacksmith's filthy fingers smearing his screen.

Hephaestus scanned the text.

"Well, I'll be—" he grunted.

"WHAT?" screamed the Gods in unison.

"The boy done good." Hephaestus smiled. "Average of ninety-two percent across the board, with ninety-six percent in history."

The Gods exploded into a chorus of whoops and yells.

"Told you so," laughed Josie as Hermes hugged her in midair.

"Well, this calls for a celebration!" cheered Zeus. "Let's go and pick up Elliot in style."

Later that day, Zeus, Athene, Aphrodite, and Josie stood by the enormous pink limo created from Aphrodite's car. Zeus was dressed in his light-blue tuxedo with the frilly white shirt, his white hair slicked back. Aphrodite sported a bright-pink strapless evening dress, while her sister wore a more modest dark-blue satin off-the-shoulder gown. They had dressed Josie in her favorite red dress and had delighted in doing her hair and makeup. The car was filled with balloons decorated with Elliot and Virgo's faces and was laid out inside with a banquet of all their favorite food.

"Hurry up, Hermy, we're going to be late," Aphrodite called inside the shed, as they waited for Hermes and Hephaestus.

Hermes floated elegantly out of the shed in his designer tuxedo, abandoning his usual winged hat for some expensive sunglasses with little gold wings on the side.

"Hold tight," he announced. "May I present your driver for this evening, the grump with a hump, Mr. Heph-aes-tus! Boom!"

"I am not going out like this," huffed a moody voice from inside the shed.

"Oh, mate, you look great," grinned Hermes. "Not even joking. C'mon . . . out."

Heaving a sigh, Hephaestus trudged to the car. The other Olympians bit their lips at the sight of his shiny gold chauffeur's outfit, complete with a gold hat that had CONGRATULATIONS ELLIOT AND VIRGO written in sequins around it.

"Not. One. Word," the blacksmith grumbled as he assumed his place at the wheel, slamming the door loudly enough to hide the eruption of laughter outside.

"Looking good, my friend," said Zeus as he helped Josie into the back of the limo. "To Brysmore! Let's bring our boy home."

The morning had flown by in such a blur that Elliot felt as though he'd barely arrived when the final assembly finished and school was over for another term. His heart was heavier than Mr. Boil's backside as he contemplated the loss of his home the very next day—although he did allow himself one moment of cheer as he passed his teacher in the corridor.

"Merry Christmas, sir," he grinned as Boil pushed passed him with a horrible grunt. "See you next term. Go easy on those mince pies."

"Get lost, Hooper," snarled Boil without stopping, furious at being stuck with this irksome boy and suddenly extremely hungry for a pack of mince pies.

Elliot and Virgo stepped out into the chilly afternoon.

"You did it," said Virgo, getting over the worst of her wounded pride at being beaten by Elliot in every single exam.

"Never thought I'd be pleased to come back to this place." Elliot smiled. "But it actually feels good. Not as good as leaving it, but pretty good."

"Yes, this Christmas break will be an excellent chance to get ahead for next term," said Virgo. "But I suppose we can take today off. After the surprise party—oh." She bit her lip as the words she'd been forbidden to say slipped out of her mouth. "Listen, look surprised when they all turn up. Urgh— I'm no good at this lying thing."

"You'll learn," said Elliot. "Trust me."

The pink limo sped into the Brysmore driveway, spilling the immortals and Josie out of the car. They cheered and pulled party poppers the size of champagne bottles over the triumphant children as the other pupils stared, bursting with jealousy.

"Remind me to teach you the word 'subtle.'" Elliot smiled as he ushered everyone back into the limo.

"Well done, baby," said Mom with a proud smile. "I love you so much."

"Love you too, Mom," said Elliot, giving her a great big hug. "Now let's party!"

The limo screeched around the circular driveway and raced back to Home Farm, leaving only a trail of party streamers, a waft of pink exhaust fumes—and one deeply suspicious history teacher, resolved to get to the bottom of the strange world of Elliot Hooper.

29

KNOCK KNOCK

Elliot, Josie, and the immortals partied with willful abandon all night long, pushing all thoughts of the next day as far from their minds as they could. But as Friday dawned, so too did the reality that this was their last day at Home Farm.

"The harpy-faced hag," huffed Aphrodite through her dark glasses. "Why, I've a good mind to scratch her evil eyes out—"

"Temper will get you nowhere," said Athene, reading through the paperwork for the millionth time. "But this is watertight. She has legally bought the farm."

"P'raps I should go and negotiate with her," said Hephaestus, sharpening his ax.

"We can't break mortal laws," said Zeus. "However unfair they are."

"Why can't Elliot just buy it back?" called Hermes beneath his sleep mask. "He only needs twenty quid. With the Earth Stone, he could buy King Croesus a condo."

"It's no good unless this stupid Horse's-Bum wants to sell it now," said Zeus.

"Chances of that are slimmer than a supermodel's sandwich," sighed Hermes. "There must be something we can do?"

"Maybe she'll have a change of heart," said Zeus, putting his arm around Elliot's dejected shoulders. "After all, the only person who can stop this sale now is Patricia herself."

"BOSH!" yelled Hermes as he shot blindly up in the air like a rocket, hitting his head on the ceiling. "That's it!"

"It is?" said Zeus, not at all sure what was what.

"Where are you going?" Athene yelled after the flying messenger as the discarded sleep mask hit her in the face.

"No time, babe," shouted Hermes, pulling on the invisibility helmet as he flew out of the gate. "Hold tight . . ."

"It's only a house, Elly," said Aphrodite as the clock ticked toward the midday deadline for Patricia's purchase. "We'll help you find a new one."

"I don't . . . what's happening . . . where are my things?" said an agitated Josie, trying to unpack one of the dozens of boxes that filled the farmhouse.

"It's our home," said Elliot, holding Josie's hand as he switched on the television to distract her. "It's the only place Mom knows. The only place that's familiar to her. We have nowhere else."

The Gods looked helplessly at each other as Elliot tightened his grip on his mother's hand and whispered reassurances in her ear.

At 11:55 a.m., Patricia Porshley-Plum tottered into the farm, still smarting from the smack on the butt that the open gate had administered on her way in.

"Hello, cutie-pudding!" shrieked Patricia, barging her way into the house.

"Can no one shut a bloody gate!" huffed Hephaestus, heading out to his fence.

"It's not midday," said Elliot angrily, looking at the grandfather clock. "It's not yours yet."

"Details, details, my pookie. Well, well, well—isn't this quite the party?" said Patricia, eyeing up the fuming immortals. "How nice to see you all again."

"Can't say the same," said Aphrodite tartly.

"Aw, that's lovely, dear, just lovely," said Patricia absently, looking around the house she couldn't wait to tear down. "It's so important to make lovely memories. And this will be a lovely memory of your last day at Home Farm. In fact, Home Farm's last day too. The bulldozers are outside the fence."

"I don't . . . I can't . . . what . . . ?" started Josie again, as Aphrodite put a comforting hand on her shoulder.

"Please," said Elliot frantically to the Gods. "Do something . . . anything."

"We can't break mortal laws," said Zeus sadly.

"We can break their snotty noses, though," said Aphrodite, her beautiful face screwed up in hatred as she made for Patricia on the other side of the room. Athene held her back.

"Aphrodite—let me handle this," Athene said, calmly approaching Patricia. "Mrs. Porshley-Plum. Without question, you are the most MISERABLE, TWISTED, ODIOUS GORGON FART!" she screamed. "I SHOULD TAKE THIS CONTRACT AND—"

Zeus quickly clamped his hands over Elliot's ears to spare the boy from the torrent of filth that spewed out of Athene's mouth. But from the hand gestures alone, Elliot could gather that whatever Athene was suggesting was going to be extremely energetic, very uncomfortable, and Mrs. Porshley-Plum was going to be doing it rather a lot for a long, long time.

"UNTIL IT DROPS OFF!" puffed a red-faced Athene, taking her first breath for over a minute.

"Charming, my dear," said Patricia, unmoved. "But in three minutes, I will own this farm. And there's nothing you can do about it."

"You're a monster," boomed Zeus.

"You're a witch," hissed Aphrodite.

"You're on the TV," said Josie, as Patricia's pointy nose appeared on the screen.

"What the devil?" huffed Patricia as Athene turned up the volume on the local news report.

"And finally, a lovely Christmas miracle to roast your chestnuts as we cross live to Little Motbury for a special announcement from local businesswoman Patricia Porshley-Plum," said the news anchor as the screen switched to outside Patricia's house.

"Wait! That's not me!" cried Patricia as her identical twin started to speak.

"This special time of year has caused me to reconsider my selfish and greedy ways," the on-screen Patricia started. "I realize that by slavishly pursuing my own wealth, I have hurt this community. Not to mention my roots—this hair dye is appalling."

"Are those wings on your shoes?" Aphrodite smiled, squinting at Patricia's high-definition feet.

"But, but, but . . ." stammered the Patricia in the room, regretting the second sherry she'd had her butler pour at breakfast.

"And so I've decided to give back to the community from which I've taken so much," TV Patricia continued. "I've donated all of my vast wealth to charity."

"NOOOOOOOOOOOO!" screamed Patricia as her cell phone started to ring.

"And furthermore," TV Patricia continued, striking a pose for the cameras, "I'd like to open my house to the poorest members of our society, to become a hostel for those in need of shelter and a place to get back on their feet."

"WHAT—WHAT—WHAT DO YOU WANT?" she screamed down her cell phone as the grandfather clock struck midday. "Bankrupt? No—that's not possible. Of course there are sufficient funds in my account, it's only twenty pounds! What do you mean I forfeit the sale? I can't lose Home Farm! I WANT IT!"

Elliot looked more closely at the picture on the TV. Patricia's shoes definitely did have tiny wings on the side. And there were a couple tucked into her perm as well . . .

"Finally, I'd like to take this opportunity to apologize to those I've wronged," said Hermes, disguised as Patricia. "Never again will I be the avaricious idiot I've been my whole life. And I will definitely get my colors done—these autumn shades make my skin look flatter than a banana pancake. Now, please—come and enjoy my wine cellar—the first ten inside get a free bottle of Château Lafite! Boom!"

"No—not the Château Lafite!" screamed Patricia, running for the door as Athene joyfully ripped up the paperwork for the house sale. "Stop—all you disgusting poor people, get your impoverished fingers off my lovely things. Stop! Stop!"

"Wait a minute!" shouted Elliot. "You forgot something."

He rummaged around in his pocket and pulled out a twenty-pound note.

"Here," he said. "Now we're even."

"Aaaaaaaaaargh!" Patricia raced out of the door and immediately tripped on the path, leaving one of her shoes stuck in the paving stones.

"Allow me to 'elp you," said Hephaestus, dragging her toward the fence.

"Get your filthy hands off me!" roared Patricia, kicking the gate with her remaining shoe. "GET ME OUT OF HERE!"

"Suit yourself," said Hephaestus, lumbering toward a large lever by the fence. "Cheerio."

And as the immortal blacksmith yanked on the lever, Mrs. Horse's-Bum was catapulted high into the air with a shriek, her petticoats flapping in the breeze, straight over the fence, past the retreating bulldozers and as far away as the eye could see.

Christmas Day was a celebration like none Elliot had known. By late afternoon, Elliot and the immortals were flopping around the creaking dining-room table, piled with enough food to feed a continent.

"I'm stuffed. Seriously," groaned Hermes, downing his fourth piece of Yule log cake.

Elliot happily tucked into his third bowl of Christmas pudding, fighting off Virgo for the last of the brandy butter.

"Who wants to pull another cracker?" said Aphrodite to a chorus of groans from the group, who were tired of being squirted with water or having a custard pie thrown at them from her trick crackers. "Spoilsports," she pouted, pulling one by herself and being showered in rose-scented pink glitter.

Elliot looked over at Mom, who was happily chatting to Athene. Elliot's mind flashed back to the previous Christmas, when Grandad had been so ill he couldn't make it downstairs for Christmas dinner, so he and Mom had sat around his bed with their tiny portions of cold turkey. He wished his grandparents were here to see the cheer around the table, but he knew that they'd be happy just to know that he and Mom were safe and being so well looked after.

"Prezzie time! Boom!" shouted Hermes, flying over to the giant Christmas tree, which was not only surrounded by mountains of presents but also topped with a real fairy.

"HELLO!" yelled the fairy down her cell phone. "I CAN'T TALK! I'M ON THE TOP OF A CHRISTMAS TREE!"

Hermes sifted through the gifts, flying them around the room until everyone had a pile at least as tall as themselves.

Elliot set to work on his particularly huge stack. Athene had given him an encyclopedia that contained every single subject known to man—plus a few that weren't—and projected moving holograms of each entry. Aphrodite immediately looked up the rudest thing she could think of.

From the Goddess of Love herself, Elliot received a box of mischievous potions, for everything from growing excess body hair to making someone speak backward—as well as the confiscated wishing pearl she had hidden in the bottom of the box, winking as Elliot slipped it into his pocket.

The gifts went on and on—his own bottomless satchel from Hermes, a pen from Zeus that threw thunderbolts with a click of the top, and his own copy of *What's What* from Virgo.

But his favorite gift came from Hephaestus, who quietly dropped a knotted handkerchief in Elliot's lap on his way out.

"'Appy Christmas," the blacksmith mumbled as he left the busy farmhouse for the peace and quiet of his forge.

Elliot unknotted the handkerchief. Inside was his father's watch, restored to perfect working order and complete with a set of pencil-scrawled notes on the improvements Hephaestus had made. Elliot wasn't sure he'd ever need his watch to unlock a combination safe or trigger an explosion, but he was truly touched by Hephaestus's gesture.

Virgo leaned over and stole a piece of Christmas cake from Elliot's plate.

"Hey—that's mine!" objected Elliot.

"Your rules." Virgo smiled, swallowing it whole. "Not mine."

"Do you have a minute, Elliot?" asked Zeus. "I think I need to walk off that fourth plate of turkey."

Elliot and Zeus walked up into the fields, which were still thriving with Demeter's exotic fruits and vegetables. It was slightly odd seeing giant pineapple trees covered in a thin layer of snow, but they appeared to be in excellent health in the icy field.

"How are you, dear boy?" Zeus asked Elliot. "Really?"

"I'm fine," said Elliot honestly. "Everything's fine now."

"You're a hero," said Zeus. "I don't know many mortals—or immortals—who could have resisted Thanatos like that. You're an exceptional young man, Elliot Hooper."

"I haven't stopped him, though, have I?" said Elliot, voicing the doubt that had been nagging at him since his return from the Underworld.

"No," said Zeus softly. "Unfortunately Thanatos still has allies. It won't be long before someone comes to his aid—indeed, I suspect they already have. But don't underestimate what you did. If you hadn't, Thanatos would have taken the Earth Stone, and I dread to think what could have happened."

"I'm sorry I stole it," said Elliot, desperate to unburden himself from the guilt he'd been dragging around for weeks. "I didn't think I had any choice."

"But you did make a choice. The right one." Zeus smiled, producing the Earth Stone from his pocket. "I never thought I'd see this again."

"What are you going to do with it?" asked Elliot.

"I was going to ask you the same thing," said Zeus as he came to a halt, his blue eyes meeting Elliot's.

"What do you mean?" said Elliot as Zeus placed the Earth Stone in his palm. "Why are you—?"

"Thanatos can't touch you," said Zeus, wrapping Elliot's fingers around the glowing stone. "You're the only person who can keep it from him."

"Are you sure?" Elliot asked. Thanatos's oath in the cave

swirled around his mind. The Chaos Stones in return for his mom. Could Zeus really trust Elliot? Could Elliot really trust himself?

"Guarding the stones won't be easy," said Zeus. "They are a heavy burden to bear. One that I couldn't face."

Elliot remembered how powerful he felt when he used the Earth Stone. He could get used to that feeling. Too used to it, perhaps.

"They corrupted powerful Daemons like Erebus and Thanatos—you'll need every ounce of goodness in your heart to makes sure they don't consume you."

"So you're saying I could end up like Gollum?" gasped Elliot.

"What? Running your own successful chain of high-end jewelers?" said Zeus. "No, I meant you'd go mad."

"Right," said Elliot, holding his Earth Stone up to the light and casting rainbows all around.

"This is serious, Elliot," said Zeus, in a harsher tone than Elliot had heard him use before. "The stone will do its very best to conquer you—don't let it. Only ever use its powers if your life depends on it. Every time you use the stone, it will tighten its hold over you. Be wise, Elliot. And be careful."

It was good advice. Elliot pushed Thanatos's oath to the back of his mind. It was best left there.

"Where shall I keep it?" asked Elliot, feeling a large diamond was probably against Boil's "jewelry" rules.

"Hephaestus thought of that," said Zeus. "Such a clever guy. Open your watch."

Elliot opened it and saw that the lid had been divided into four equal parts.

"There you go," said Zeus.

Elliot held the Earth Stone to the watch, wondering how it was going to fit, being at least ten times larger than the space allowed for it. But, as if hearing his thoughts, as soon as the diamond touched the watch, it shrank into its place, gleaming brightly as it filled a perfect quarter of the lid.

"We've still got three more stones to find," said Elliot, tucking the watch back inside his pocket.

"Yes, we do," said Zeus. "And after Christmas, we'll start looking for the next one. And the one after that. We'll beat Thanatos in the end, don't you worry."

Elliot said nothing, but desperately wanted to share Zeus's optimism.

"We'd better get back," said Zeus. "Your mother wants to watch the Queen's speech and so do I. She's a fine-looking lady, that monarch of yours."

"Be careful," said Elliot. "She could ninja-kick you into the middle of next week."

Zeus chortled happily as they set off back to the farm, where everyone had gathered around the TV on the plush armchairs. Virgo signaled to Elliot to come and sit by her.

"Listen," she said nervously. "There's something I've been meaning to say to you. Something important."

Elliot shuddered and gritted his teeth. Christmas brought out the mushy in people, and girls were the worst. He waited to hear Virgo's heartfelt declaration of love and wondered how he was going to let her down gently.

She punched him in his right arm. Hard.

"You are such a gorgon fart," she said.

"Shut up," said Elliot.

"You shut up," said Virgo, the two of them jostling on the sofa, neither seeing the smile on the other's face.

"Shhh—it's starting," said Josie as the Queen took to the screen.

Elliot listened to Her Majesty's good wishes for the following year with mixed feelings. On the one hand, he had no idea what it would bring. The Gods were a huge help, but Mom's health wasn't getting any better. Thanatos wouldn't be happy until the Chaos Stones were his and Elliot was dead at his feet. The Gods could only protect him so far, and Elliot knew that he was going to have to keep his wits about him if he wanted to be here next Christmas.

But for the first time in a long time, Elliot felt traces of hope. He had spent so much of his life facing an uncertain future that he knew he could handle it. And now he had something he had never had before. Whatever life had in store, whatever the future held, Elliot Hooper knew that he would face it with his friends.

A knock at the door reverberated through the house.

"Whoever could that be?" said Zeus. "Did someone forget to shut the gate again? I'd better go."

Hauling his bulk off the sofa, he padded out of the room to the front door. The others listened intently, poised for action as he unlatched the lock and pulled the creaking door open.

"What are y—" he started, before the visitor on the other side of the door stunned him into silence.

"This cannot be!" he yelped in terror from the hallway.

The other Gods leapt to their feet.

"How in all the heavens did you find me here?" screamed Zeus. "SNORDLESNOT!"

THE END.

(*For now . . .*)

THE THANK-YOU BIT

This book has had more lives than a recycled cat and I am indebted to all the hands that it, and I, have passed through. I hope you washed them well afterward. Seriously.

I owe a huge debt of gratitude (and probably cash) to everyone who helped my first edition of *WLTGO*. Without your brilliance I'm sure this one would never have happened. To Lucy V. Hay for her expert editing; Becky Jeffries for her dedicated design; Debbie Collins for her super subbing; and Mark Beech for his illuminating illustrations—my sincerest thanks to you all. Check's in the post. Honest.

To Veronique and Nicky, my not-so-secret super agents, I owe you everything. Or technically, fifteen percent of it. Thank you, thank you, thank you for keeping the faith.

To the Chickens—working with you has been a thunderbolt of pure joy. My enormous love and thanks to Lady Elinor, Rachel Hachel, Jazz (hands), Luscious Laura (keep jujjing), Corking Kes, New York Nick, Super Steve, Resplendent Rob, Dilligent Daphne, and, of course, the wizard that is Big Bad Baz. You have made my dreams come true. Sorry about that.

Speaking of the stuff of nightmares, I owe particularly mahoosive thanks to my Super Ed, Rachel Leyshon. You are the waxing strip to my hairy legs: painful, but I'm so much better for you. Thank you for your brilliant mind, wonderful heart, and naughty laugh—I have loved every moment working with you and my book and its author have been hugely enriched for having you in our world. Ta, luv.

To Mum, Dad, Len, and Ricks—I love you. Almost all the time.

To my husband—my best mate, first mate, paper mate, and soul mate. You always said this would happen. Congratulations. That's twice you've been right now. Thank you for being my sanity, my happiness, my rock, and far too disorganized to find a divorce lawyer. You are my Elysium.

To my babies—thank you for making every day an adventure. Sometimes a comedy, often a farce, but always with a happy ending. There isn't enough time or space in an infinite universe to show you how much I love you, but I'll give it a go. Just keep it down before seven a.m., would you?

And to you, my fabulous reader. Thank you so much for choosing my book, and I hope you had a nice time in it. I'm going to write some more, so I hope you'll come and see us again. You rock.

Love, and other things that smell like pink marshmallow,

Maz

Xxx

Debut author Maz Evans is also a scriptwriter, playwright, lyricist, journalist, poet, lunch lady, and whatever else pays the gas bill. As a freelance TV journalist, Maz has written for many British publications, including the *Daily Telegraph*, the *Daily Mail*, the *Sun*, *TV Times*, and *TV Easy*, and she regularly broadcasts on BBC Radio 2 and BBC Radio 5 Live in the United Kingdom. Maz has puddle-water eyes and very disobedient hair. She likes sunflowers, things that rhyme, and eating dessert first. She doesn't like rude, getting up in the morning, or Wednesdays. You can visit her online at www.storystew.org and @MaryAliceEvans.